Days to Hide

STEPHANIE FLYNN

Small Fish Publishing
USA

First edition
Cover design by Stephanie Flynn

ISBN large print edition: 9781952372124

Special Note

Time travel is real.
For a few short hours, you will be transported to 1854
and back again.
Enjoy the ride.

Chapter 1
Present Day, Green Bay, Wisconsin

For a while, Becca Wagner thought being alone in her house would've brought her misery—bad memories and lonely silence. Instead, having Brad out of the house was like excising a weight around her neck.

Sweat rolled between her breasts, but Becca wouldn't have it any other way. Sure, it was the middle of July, already a humid seventy degrees outside, and the air conditioning wasn't working. The landlord claimed he'd fix it—a month ago. Big negative on that one, buddy, but Becca had more pressing issues than a minor luxury.

She slid the baking sheet with dollops of chocolate chip cookie dough into the oven, while 375 degrees of heat blasted her face. Homemade cookies were the only acceptable form of the scrumptious confection. Store-bought cookies were relegated to the blasphemous bin, on par with kicking puppies, skipping the tip jar, and mixing cheese with sprinkles.

Not remotely acceptable. Ever.

Sometimes blood, sweat, and tears were a necessity to enjoy the finer soul-soothing things in life, and in this case—two of the three. She hadn't cut herself in the kitchen yet, but the day was still young. The other two? Sweat, check. Tears… Becca glanced at the stack of papers on the counter as if willing them away, but that never worked. She sighed and set the timer.

She had to be at work in an hour, so why was she baking at four in the morning? Quality sleep wasn't a thing for her anymore, not since Brad had the local sheriff serve her divorce papers. The coward hadn't had the guts to deliver them himself, and as happy as she was to have him gone, those papers were a failure. Something she had to face to close the door on that last few years of her life.

Becca swiped her damp forehead with her arm and flung the oven mitts off. She dropped down in a chair at the kitchen table and blew red ringlets out of her face. Time to get this over with. Maybe this time, she could read without the tears clogging her vision. "Petition without minor children."

That didn't last long. Becca swiped away tears of what should've been, and quickly moved to the next line.

"Divorce, check. I am providing the following information about myself. That all looks right. I am providing the following information about the respondent. Date of birth, yep. Blah blah lived in the county, yeah. Lived in Wisconsin, yeah. Currently on active duty, no. Respondent is currently pregnant."

Becca sucked in a breath. The boxes for that line were left unchecked. Becca's throat tightened while phantom kicks in her belly unnecessarily reminded her of her loss. She picked up her pen, swiped tears again, and marked the 'no' box.

She sniffled and flipped the page. "I am providing the following information regarding children: No children were born to or adopted together by either party before or during our marriage. Jerk was confident enough to check 'no' here."

Page after page, she worked her way through the documents until the last page—the signature that made it all official.

The timer beeped its monotonous tone, and Becca set the pen down. A fresh baked tray of cookies emerged, and she scooped them onto the wire cooling rack. She stared at them, her eyes losing focus, and the moment the cookies stopped steaming, she gathered a handful and returned to the table.

The pen dangled above the final line. Brad had said many terrible things—things she would never forget—but grief did that to people. She scarfed down a cookie and immediately the tension in her body softened—just like the center of her favorite sweet gooeyness. She licked the chocolate off her lip.

A framed photograph across the room on the entryway table caught her eye. Becca's feet brought her over to it on their own accord. The house they'd shared was a small two-bedroom, one-bathroom, last updated in the 1980s, but Becca didn't mind. It was her home, their home, and big enough to start a family. Becca wanted at least five, but Brad agreed to one. Turned out, she couldn't have any. Her OB explained the stillbirth was a chromosomal abnormality, likely a male factor, but additional testing was needed to be certain.

Brad's reaction showed her a side of him she never knew. He blamed her, spouted terrible things—words that still haunted her—and for her own sake, Becca couldn't drag out the pain.

He left her because of it.

Becca lifted the photograph of her and Brad smiling with arms wrapped around each other. They'd worn trendy activewear, name-brand sneakers, and coordinating bandannas on their foreheads. That day they were hiking the East River Trail, which was hardly a feat worth mentioning, since it was paved and snaked through the city. Walking was a better descriptor, but it was outdoors, fresh air, and energizing. She'd take what she could get.

She met Brad while they were both in college. Searching the unfamiliar boy's dorms for her study buddy in Animal Anatomy & Physiology, she'd been knocked into a wall by Brad's roommate hastily opening a door. Apologizing profusely, Travis had brought her into his dorm for a drink of water, and when she'd laid eyes on Brad, there was instant attraction. She'd been impressed he was a mechanical engineering major. It wasn't the potential paycheck that interested her—no, it was the brains, or so she thought.

With his critical mind, she'd expected to have interesting conversations, or things they could build together and test on fun camping trips. That moment she'd met him, he was playing video games, and years later, she still struggled to drag him outside. Despite the matching outfits and beaming smiles, this was the only photo of them on the only adventure they'd had.

As she held the weight of the wood frame in her hands, she realized Brad hadn't packed the photograph. Her eyes moved along the others on the table, and the ones hanging on the wall.

He didn't want it.

He didn't want any of them.

Why would he? In a burst of anger, Becca flung the photograph across the room, and the glass shattered against the wall. And like the pieces of her heart, the fragments were irreparable, abandoned, and forgotten in a corner, collecting dust. Becca wasted her life. No devoted spouse, no children, no adventure. Brad was nothing more than a bad memory, and the sooner she finished those documents, the sooner she could begin to heal.

Becca stalked back over to the table, mashed a cookie in her mouth, and vigorously signed on the dotted line. But not too vigorously—she didn't want to tear up the documents and have to redo them all. Brad wasn't worth that much effort.

Her cell phone alarm chimed.

"Oh, shit," she said with a mouthful.

Becca rushed to the bedroom and threw on a scrub top and pink pants. Good thing most tops had busy patterns—super easy to look coordinated—which these days, the easier the better. Plus, they were so comfortable that Becca slept in them sometimes. She certainly wasn't trying to impress anyone. Becca ran a thick pick through her curls and shrugged. "Good enough for today."

She double checked the oven was off before grabbing her purse and book and rushing out the door. Moments later, she ran back inside and scooped up another handful of cookies for the road.

Becca's fingers drummed the steering wheel of her old Corolla. Several times Brad had promised her car was going to be upgraded. She would've believed him if he hadn't crashed the last three cars he drove. To be fair, one was a drunk driver, one was a deer, but the third was his fault for running a red light. So it was Becca and her trusty Corolla, alone.

Tears threatened, and Becca blinked them back, changing her thoughts. She parked alongside the converted log cabin, next to the only other vehicle in the lot—her boss's SUV. Birds chirped their happy summer songs, and a delicate breeze pleasantly cooled Becca's sweaty morning. There hadn't been time for a shower, and Becca hadn't thought to spritz a little scent. If she were lucky, enough smelly patients would mask her funk. And since many of them did, in fact, have personal problems in the scent department, Becca popped into the side door without embarrassment or hesitation.

The fresh cut wood of the cabin filled her nose while Becca crossed the back hallway and emerged alongside the large registration desk. It was too early for patients to arrive, so the waiting room's stiff chairs waited for duty like sentries. Verity was already at the registration desk, which meant Dr. McCall must've been in his office. The two of them always came and left together. Becca kept her enviousness close to her chest—not that she had a thing for her boss. No, Becca wasn't interested in Dr. McCall in the slightest, but she certainly was wistful, thinking of what he and Verity had—what Becca had lost.

That was stupid. She and Brad never had anything like what the doc and Verity had.

"Morning," Becca said.

"How do you do on this fine morning?" Verity asked.

Becca inhaled a deep breath and swung her purse under the desk. She dropped into the rolling office chair, and it squeaked under her weight. She wondered if it were trying to tell her something. "One day at a time."

"I heard about Brad. I'm so sorry." Verity placed a bejeweled hand on Becca's wrist, and Becca fought the screaming urge to pull her arm away. She was happy for her co-worker, really she was, but it was crushing to be pitied.

"I'm not sorry. He's an ass anyway." Time for a change of subject. "How was your honeymoon?"

Verity's cheeks pinked. Her unusually wild hair had been tamed with a curling iron, and the look was great on her. Her big doe-y green eyes turned to Becca with a sparkle of excitement.

"Amazing. I'm just flabbergasted at how incredible the California Gold Rush is—was—and I'm so glad I got to see it in modern times."

Verity was spunky and bold—cute in an innocent way, and she always said the strangest things. Becca remembered Verity's antique outfit when she'd first met her and since then wondered if Verity was Amish. Becca wasn't crude enough to ask.

"How was your time off?" Verity asked, giving Becca her full attention.

Horrible. Wretched. She'd spent two weeks by herself, stewing over the divorce papers, mustering up the courage to face the facts, while obsessively monitoring her phone for messages. Oh, and she checked her social media accounts every hour in case Brad posted something. Uh, just pathetic. But there was a silver lining; there was always a silver lining. Becca devoured romance novels while stuffing her face with sweets and baked goods. At least the men in her stories never let her down. She wished she could be in her own novel—a glorious escape of adventure and a handsome loyal and devoted man at her side. Dream on, loser, she thought. "It was fine. Nice to have a break."

She worked alongside Verity for the last several weeks, ever since April and Kiko left, and Becca liked her just fine. But Becca didn't know how she was going to handle Verity's expanding waistline. She tried hard not to think about it, especially since Verity was only at the I-ate-a-ginormous-burrito stage.

"If you need anything, let me know," Verity said.

Becca smiled at her kindness and returned the favor. "You, too."

Becca dug her cell phone out of her purse, as she did every day, and set it on top of her latest romance novel, featuring the likes of Fabio on the cover. Despite her own love life crashing down around her, she was still a sucker for a dream man that didn't exist. Becca had no shame about her choice of books and had no intention of switching to an e-reader. Whenever she was in the mood to see the hero with her own eyes, a quick flick of her wrist and there he was. Didn't matter that he was almost always Fabio in similar clothes and poses. A girl could dream of a strapping, dashing man to sweep her off her feet and give her a pile of babies…if she could even have any.

And there go those thoughts again. "Any surgeries today?" Becca asked, while logging into the system, hopeful for a distraction. She didn't smell any telltale antiseptic.

"Not so far," Verity said and answered the phone.

Becca pulled up the day's calendar of appointments, and the first name on the schedule made her stomach leap into her throat, right as the front door's bell jingled. Becca sucked in a breath and tried not to release a torrent of swears.

Chapter 2

1854, Navarino, Wisconsin

JULY SUN BEAT DOWN on Jonathan Arris's arms, while the horse underneath him lazily clomped along the dirt road through town, kicking up torrents of dust. Jonathan removed his straw hat and fanned his face for a moment before replacing it on his head. His shirt stuck to his sweaty body, and Jonathan wondered what the hell he was doing here. He tilted his face up to the clear sky, willing some clouds to provide relief. And…nothing happened. If the man in charge ordered the weather to change, Jonathan bet it would happen. Unfortunately, Jonathan wasn't looking to replace the boss, so he had to play the cards dealt to him.

Hidden in the shade, a man slept in a chair tilted back against the exterior wall of a beaten down shop. As beads of sweat rolled down Jonathan's back, a pang of wasted enviousness fluttered through him. If Jonathan weren't riding with the bandits, as they were colloquially known, he'd be working his own land. He was, after all, a respected multi-generational corn farmer, so either way, he was destined for blistering sun and exposure.

Riding a horse while stalking prey was physically easier than watering crops during a drought, but when he worked the farm, at least Jonathan could be shirtless, take a break when needed, and not worry about getting shot.

Despite all the rumors around the tri-village area, the bandits weren't anything official—more like a group of men collaborating with similar goals. The bandits took what they wanted when they wanted, in order to sustain their nomadic lifestyle—or that was what everyone assumed. No one knew where their main base of operations was or how often it changed. Jonathan wasn't like them in many ways, beginning with him owning land.

While visiting home, Jonathan suffered complaints from his immature brother. The rascal better be working the farm right now in his stead. Someone had to lead and mind the workers. Picturing the workers lounging and singing while Graham runs off to flirt with the ladies, Jonathan squeezed the reins. It would be just like Graham to shirk his responsibilities to spite Jonathan.

"We ain't seen no ripe target for pickins." That was Nash, the pockmarked bandit Jonathan suspected had been beaten one too many times by his own brother. Where he lacked in brains, he made up for in unflinching barbaric skill with an impressive variety of weapons—trigger finger, blade master, and quick with the ropes. He had other, less savory, appetites as well.

Several months ago, the bandits held up a general store. While the other bandits observed their duties, Nash skittered off and found himself a scared woman hiding between the flour barrels. After a deplorable fight, the woman ended up strangled, and Nash had his way with her afterward. That was the way he preferred it. The boss had punished him, naturally, but not for his treatment of the innocent woman. No, Butch had no respect for helpless women, but because Nash ditched his robbing duties and Ruddy lost a finger from it. Jonathan shuddered.

"Patience—" Ruddy began.

"Yeah, yeah. I knows. It's jus' the sun's hot, and we've been ridin' all day."

"Silence," Butch commanded. The waif-thin Eddie Butcher was in charge, and what he said went, no arguments. For as long as Jonathan knew, Butch was always feared. Sure, his size wasn't anything intimidating. It was his commanding presence, vicious speed with a blade, and keen eyes, but mostly his reputation. Rumors—because Jonathan wasn't dumb enough to ask straight up—when Butch was a child, another larger, older kid picked on him, teased him for his scrawny shape, made fun of his impoverished home. One day, Butch'd had enough. Stole his mama's butcher knife and carved that kid up real good. No one could verify. Supposedly the kid's family fled town after Sheriff Clint Nelson refused to do anything about it. Ever since, Butch had lived up to his name, and he was feared by the whole town.

And now he led the bandits south through the village of Navarino, toward the neighboring village, Astor—where Jonathan lived—hunting down their next victim. Fingers, the rotund second in command, rode next to Butch. He was the money man, always securing the scored treasure and the pilfered food. A quiet man. Jonathan never heard him say much.

Ruddy, the towheaded gentle soul with a reddish face to match his hair, was Nash's best friend—at least that was what Jonathan had figured. Even though Ruddy was kind—as far as ruthless bandits went—he was deadly quick with a dagger.

Finally, there was Brawley. He was unremarkable in appearance, but the one aspect Jonathan noted was Brawley spoke as if he'd had an education, but yet acted like a broken horse—taking orders was all he knew. Jonathan glanced at the animal under him. Its head bobbed with its steps, long mane tangled. He wondered if in fact the animal were of an intelligence more esteemed than Brawley.

Jonathan didn't fear any one of them, but as a whole, they were deadlier than anything and anyone else in the area, and he respected their power. He dared never to cross them. The bandits sought to take whatever they wanted, and if anyone betrayed them, the bandits were relentless in exacting vengeance.

A high-pitched whistle jerked Jonathan alert. Butch flicked his head, and everyone sat up straighter. A single man on a covered wagon rolled their way, pulled by four draft horses.

The bandits broke formation to surround the unsuspecting farmer, and within moments, the victim, mouth gaped and eyes wide, slowed his horses to a stop. "What is all this?" he asked, head craning around in alarm, hand reaching down by his hidden feet.

Ruddy took up position just to his side and said, "Not so fast there. Hands where we can see 'em."

A pair of trembling hands raised toward the clear sky. The farmer was wise in his surrender. In addition to Butch's lack of respect for weakness, he also lacked patience for human life. The bandits were swimming in money, so it only made sense they'd have the best weapons, which meant no flintlocks. Butch favored a pair of revolvers, and his second choice was a rifle for distance. Right now, Butch only gripped one pistol while keeping a sharp eye on everyone's movements.

Brawley and Nash climbed up the back of the wagon.

"Whoo-hoo! Boss, we're lucky today!" Brawley shouted.

Fingers maneuvered his horse next to the men and opened his saddle bags. Fruits and vegetables were tossed in the air. Some landed in Fingers's bags, some he caught, but many fell onto the ground.

Jonathan held his shotgun butted against his shoulder. His job—backup. Butch had never asked him to do any of the thieving directly, and this time was no exception. Likely the bandits didn't trust Jonathan yet, but he was content to be involved as little as possible. Jonathan wasn't the thieving type, and the irony wasn't lost on him.

Ruddy climbed up the front of the wagon and searched the farmer for more prime pickings.

"Hey, stop. What are you doing?" the farmer pleaded.

Nash poked his head out the back of the wagon. "Boss, catch." Nash threw a fruit to Butch. He inspected the pilfered offering and bit down. There was something about a man whose taste buds were so broken that a raw onion was more savory than an apple.

Ruddy lifted a sack near the farmer's feet and tossed it to Butch, whose quick eye caught it. He opened it, and a crooked smile lifted his lips.

"Nice haul, fellas. We've got five dollars a-piece here," Butch said.

"Aye, boss. That's sam-tooten good," Nash said.

Five dollars Jonathan would earn from this—a week's worth of wages had he maintained a paying job, rather than the farm. As he held a shotgun on the farmer, his parents would've rolled over in their graves if they could see him, and if they were alive, they would've beat him raw and turn him in to the sheriff for justice. Jonathan didn't mind inheriting the farming path; it was all he knew, and after six months of running with the bandits, he'd rather be back on the farm—hard labor or not.

With Jonathan's firearm trained on the farmer's chest, their victim shook in his trousers as Ruddy ransacked the poor man's person. Nash and Brawley cleared out more than they could carry from the farmer's stash, leaving food crushed on the ground.

"That's it for this mark," Ruddy said, pulling his hands out of the farmer's pockets with a big grin on his face. Ruddy jumped down and mounted his horse.

Nash and Brawley followed suit, and the two men laughed at their ill-gotten goods and slapped palms together.

A gunshot cracked in Jonathan's ears. He blinked. And blinked again. Mouths moved, but he heard nothing except for deafening rings screaming down his ear canals. The ringing faded and horses stomped and neighed with agitation. Bandits craned their necks in confusion.

The farmer slumped over, and a pistol fell from his hand with a clatter.

Frowning, Butch blew a thin trail of smoke from his Colt and holstered it. "Keep your eye on the mark, Johnny. Next time it'll be your head."

Jonathan nodded, a response caught in his throat. If Butch hadn't been paying attention, Jonathan could've had his head blown off. The leader's threat was loud and clear, but pointless. If Jonathan did miss the next threat, then it didn't matter if Butch shot him.

Distraction was deadly around the bandits.

"Money's up," Butch said. The four men formed a circle. Jonathan joined them.

The leader dished out their earnings. Jonathan pocketed his share, and Fingers tossed him an apple. Jonathan turned it over in his hand while he glanced back at the smashed food and corpse left behind. On the farm, whatever food was left over after the season ended was stored for winter consumption, and any excess that would spoil was sold to bolster operations in the spring. With the drought for the last several growing seasons, having enough to survive the winter was a constant worry. Seeing the waste pummeled on the ground turned Jonathan's stomach.

"It ain't been poisoned. What's the delay? Teeth fall out?" Nash teased.

"Just inspecting it for blood," Jonathan said, only half-serious.

"Well that don' make sense. Fingers's bags been filled before the farmer lost his head," Nash shot back.

Jonathan nodded at the slip over Nash and reluctantly bit off a hunk of red flesh. When he swallowed he asked, "Butch, mind if I call it a day?" Every time Jonathan asked, the answer was always more irritated and carried more suspicion. How much longer would he be able to keep it up? Jonathan added, "The farm needs tending to."

Butch narrowed his eyes and sucked through his teeth. "I warned you to fix your affairs. You got three days to join us all in or be out for good."

And by 'out for good', Butch meant feeding the daisies.

"Yes, sir." Jonathan kicked his horse into a trot southbound toward Astor.

Three days wasn't enough time to make Graham mature into the man who could handle the farm on his own. Every person who had ever tried escaping or selling them out had been hunted and killed, and still the bandits freely roamed the roads. Jonathan would have to abandon the farm to prove his loyalty, displacing workers, and destroying his family legacy.

Jonathan had no choice.

Chapter 3
Present Day, Green Bay, Wisconsin

For longer than she'd been married, Becca had worked at Dr. McCall's veterinary clinic. Even the most selfish husband suffering from selective hearing would've picked up on her place of employment. Knowing she represented the face of the clinic, Becca plastered a fake smile on her face while internally swearing enough to make a sailor blush.

Her soon-to-be ex-husband held open the glass door for a well-groomed Shih Tzu with pigtails. The smirk on Brad's face boiled her veins. This was no coincidence.

"Welcome to Animal Care of Wisconsin," she said with disgust in her tone. "You don't like animals, Brad, especially dogs."

Brad leaned against the counter. "Things change, and now I have a dog here for an appointment."

"And you just so happened to choose my vet clinic." Her customer service skills fell off a cliff the moment she opened her mouth. She'd apologize to the doc later.

"Is that how you greet customers?" Brad asked.

"Only certain special ones. I didn't peg you for a pigtails kind of guy. Did you wrap the elastic and ribbons on the tufts of hair by yourself?" Becca tried to picture that and just...couldn't. Brad—video game connoisseur, beer afficionado, TV sports nut, who happened to be allergic to fresh air and terrified of cats. He'd never liked pets of any kind. It was a miracle she'd talked him into having a child. Although grateful now to have no lifelong ties to him, she wouldn't wish their loss on anyone.

"Of course, I didn't," Brad said.

Becca pressed her lips together to stop herself from grilling him for information. Since she'd signed on the line this morning, he was no longer her business. "If you're here for the paperwork, I'm dropping it off today."

"It's about time," Brad said, face brightening. "Because not only did I get a dog, I got something else, too."

Becca's stomach sank.

Behind Brad's bulk, a dainty woman stepped forward—blonde, rail thin, and with eyelashes that looked like spider legs. The only thing missing was the doggy purse carrier—oh, wait. There it was, on her gangly limb hidden behind Brad.

"Bex, meet Chastity. Chastity, my ex-wife Bex."

"Soon-to-be," Becca said. "We're still married, or did you forget?"

"Must've slipped my mind. Chass, can you wait for me over there?" He tilted his head toward the waiting room chairs.

Chastity rolled her eyes and took the leash from Brad. When she sat, she lifted the tiny dog onto her lap and talked it through the appointment coming up. Of course it was her dog. Brad was willing to bend his comfort zone for Chastity, but not for Becca.

"I don't even want to ask how long you've been seeing her," Becca said, voice low, trying to maintain her composure.

Next to Becca, Verity hung up the phone, and her eyes widened. "I'm going to the bathroom. Be right back." Verity slipped through the door behind the reception desk while Brad's eyes followed her. Despite being in a veterinary clinic, there was only one dirty dog present.

"Oh, but you do, otherwise you wouldn't have said that." Brad leaned closer over the tall desk. "Six whole glorious months." Brad's face turned to Chastity for a moment. He smiled as if Cupid shot him in the ass, and Becca believed whatever was between them was real—not just some fling to shove in her face.

"So, I can add cheating to the list too? The judge is going to love it."

"All I need is the stamp on the papers."

His callousness shouldn't have been surprising. "When you line up to bat, you sure hit a home run."

"I always play to win."

Becca couldn't fathom how Brad cheated on her shortly after she'd become pregnant with their child. The rotten core inside her soon-to-be ex-husband shocked her. He wasn't the man she'd married.

"I couldn't get your face away from the TV. Wherever did you get the energy to woo a woman on the side? Did you meet her in one of your video game chat rooms?"

Brad's face flinched for a second. She didn't know whether to laugh, cry, or punch him in the nose. Becca glanced at the woman who was selected to be better than her. The upgrade. Chastity didn't look like the kind of girl who played games, but since Becca didn't, what did she know?

"While you had your nose stuck in a book, I found someone willing to give me time, but if it makes you feel better, we didn't meet in person until recently."

"I was carrying our child." Becca had been obsessed reading all the usual pregnancy and infant books, trying to do everything right for the baby, for the three of them. Becca thought of nothing but her growing family, while Brad chatted up another woman.

"And that made you more obsessive and neglectful."

Brad might never have lifted a hand against her, but he sure knew how to inflict pain.

"You're despicable. Get the hell out of here," Becca said, chin trembling.

Brad's face twisted in surprise, and he straightened. "I can't believe you just said that. What kind of service do you have here? Expect a nasty review, bitch."

Becca hadn't expected that...in public.

Verity returned from the bathroom and sat in her chair. Her gaze bounced from Brad to Chastity to Becca.

"Please let the door hit you on the way out," Becca said sweetly.

"Chass, let's go. Now," Brad demanded, his smug tone suddenly gone.

Chastity's lips twisted in confusion, but she stood and walked the teacup-sized dog out the door. Brad followed behind her, and he flipped a middle finger at Becca on his way out. What a goddamn prick.

The door closed, and Becca watched them through the glass doors as they climbed into his pickup truck and drove off. No longer able to keep herself together, tears flooded her eyes and within seconds, uncontrollable sobs wracked her body. A tissue box was tapped against her arm, and Becca pulled a few.

"Thanks." Becca's eyes dipped to Verity's belly. Becca's shoulders shook with a fresh wave of sobs, and she blew her nose. "I'll be right back."

"Take your time."

Becca stepped into the bathroom, lowered the lid on the toilet, and fell onto it with a clunk. She unrolled several feet of toilet paper and mopped her face, but more tears just kept coming. Within a couple months of pregnancy, her husband had cheated on her. All those times she'd taken him to bed, and he was thinking about that blond behind her back. Becca had assumed he wanted to end their marriage because of the loss. Now she wondered if it was guilt.

But Brad was no longer her concern.

Becca wanted chocolate—lots of it—and Fabio. Fabio was a real man—a man who loved his woman, treated her with respect, was fiercely loyal and protective, and he would never ever consider cheating.

Plus all the babies.

But he was imaginary. A man like that didn't exist in the real world.

Becca needed a new life, one without Brad and his cruel truths, and no more half-empty house filled with their memories. Although Brad wasn't coming back to the clinic—that embarrassing display was clearly for show, Becca still couldn't stay here with Verity's expanding belly. Becca was thrilled for the woman, but the pain was too much to bear.

Her boss, Dr. McCall, had already told her Verity could handle the desk by herself, so Becca was already forewarned that she was free to quit without guilt. Somehow her boss had heard of her plan to move. She and Brad were supposed to find a bigger house, but that all had changed right after the loss, when Brad decided to leave. Becca's life fell apart, and she needed to get away.

Dr. McCall could always hire Kiko again if and when Verity couldn't stomach the surgeries. Becca had to do this.

Becca snorted and wiped up her face. She flushed the toilet, washed her hands, and marched straight into the boss's office. Clutter was all over his desk, and his monitor shined bright in his face. Dr. McCall clicked on the mouse. He wore his signature outfit of dress shirt and slacks with a white lab coat.

Becca rapped her knuckles on the door frame.

"Hey Becca, what's up?"

"Can we chat for a minute?"

"Sure." Dr. McCall was simply glowing, and it wasn't just his screen. He laced his fingers together on the desk, giving Becca his full attention. Ever since he met the strange Verity, he'd been beaming with excitement, happier than he'd ever been. Becca understood. He had a successful career, a beautiful pregnant wife, a cute dog, and a new house. He'd just returned from their honeymoon—an across-country adventure. He had everything.

Tears threatened again, and Becca blinked and exhaled a deep breath. Unable to move closer, she leaned against the door frame. "I quit."

"Oh." Dr. McCall's smile fell. "Okay. Did something happen?"

Becca shook her head. "It's just too many memories. I can't do it anymore. Brad was just here. I'm done."

"I understand. I'll mail out your last check."

"You aren't going to fight me on it?"

Dr. McCall smiled. "I had a feeling you were going to move on. I hope you find peace wherever you go. Oh, if you see Kiko, say 'Hi' for me." The corner of his lips lifted.

That was a weird thing to say. Why would she see Kiko? And he just dismissed her with little thought about what she was going to do, where she was going to go, or offering to give a good reference for new employment. Dr. McCall had fought Becca for weeks just to take a leave, and he was mad when she'd brought the work release form.

Oh…

He wanted her to quit all this time, like Kiko had, which was why he'd wanted her to say hi to Kiko. Becca's chin trembled, and she fought back fresh tears. She couldn't handle the idea of her boss wanting her out of his life, too. She nodded. Her throat was too tight to say anything. Becca closed the door behind her and collected her things at the reception desk.

"Everything okay?" Verity asked.

Becca shook her head. She swallowed a thick lump in her throat and composed herself enough to speak. "I'm leaving. I quit."

"Because of Brad?"

A sobbing gasp escaped her lips, and she shook her head. "A factor, but not the only reason. I need to go."

"Keep in touch. I'll miss you." Verity's hand touched her forearm, and another sob slipped out.

Becca clutched her things to her chest and dashed out the door. Inside her Corolla, she unleashed all the pain she'd been holding for weeks.

Chapter 4
1854, Astor, Wisconsin

Jonathan released his mount at the stables and crossed to the back door. The screen slapped shut behind him, and the emptiness left by his sister still haunted him. When he'd last seen Verity, she'd been wearing a dress that appeared royal and had claimed it cost more than Jonathan made in a year. Verity would've never afforded fabric as fine as that, even with her less than agreeable activities, so when she'd explained in detail where she'd gotten it from, he had no choice but to believe—his sister had no imagination. Verity had brought a man into his house, who at first glance seemed like a spineless city boy.

Jonathan was half right. That city boy, Mathew McCall, was sporting brass balls when he'd rushed the Grignon estate unarmed to rescue Verity. The massacre made headlines. The fallout still lingered.

No matter how much he wished his sister would adhere to acceptable societal standards, he was still grateful the city boy had rescued her. And even more grateful the man vowed to make an honest woman of her. Jonathan wished to see her again, but as long as she was happy in the future, he would have to be content with an empty house.

"Where've you been?" Graham asked, hands perched on his hips.

Almost empty.

"Answer me."

"It's none of your business what I'm doing during the day." Jonathan barreled passed Graham to his bedroom, stripping off his shirt. It was damp with sweat but felt far dirtier.

"It is my business when you abandon this farm. I don't own it. It's not mine. I don't want it dumped on me."

"When I'm gone, you are responsible for this property, whether you like it or not." Frustration made his reply come out harsher than he'd planned. "Mom and Dad are gone. Verity is gone. We are short-handed, so unless you want to find yourself a wife to help out around here and make a bunch of kids to work the fields, I'm doing what I have to. And so do you."

"I'm doing what has to be done to keep this place afloat. You run off during the day to rob people like a common criminal."

"I don't rob anyone." Jonathan removed his suspenders and unfastened his trousers. As they fell to the floor, traitorous coins jingled.

"Like hell you don't. What's that noise then?" Graham demanded.

"Payment for services rendered."

"Services? Yeah, robbing people for money."

Jonathan growled and shoved his legs into fresh trousers. "You don't know what you're talking about."

"I'm not stupid, Johnny. For six months you've been running with the bandits, ever since Butch knocked on our door. The only reason you joined was because getting paid was better than getting killed on the spot."

"And with those terms, you still blame me." Anger surged through his body, tensing his muscles. Fastening the buttons on his shirt was proving difficult. "You want to help fix the situation, Graham? I'll find a willing family and draft a contract for you to marry. Is that what you want?"

If he could find one. Guilty by association.

"Don't try to blame me for the farm's problems. This isn't my issue to fix. And just because Sarah Hartley didn't pan out, doesn't mean you can't get a new contract for yourself. Oh, wait! None of the local girls will go near you since you're a bandit now. All their fathers consider you black-listed."

Jonathan stalked out of his room, and Graham followed. His younger brother was right, though. Of all the women who had been interested in Jonathan—and truthfully, there had been many—none would even look him in the eye since he'd become associated with Butch's crew. Finding himself a new bride was the last thing on his mind.

"When are you going to quit and help out around here?" Graham pressed.

Jonathan spun on his little brother. "We need money to pay workers, or we need a big enough family to work the farm ourselves. Until one of those things is met, I have to do what I have to do. Adulthood isn't all it's cracked up to be. Enjoy your remaining time as a child and get to work, or I'll have to hire another hand and be gone longer."

"How is any of that supposed to help if you're in jail?" Without waiting for an answer, Graham marched out of the house, the screen door slapping behind him.

Jonathan sighed and ran his hand through his sweaty hair. He frowned at the oily mess and washed up in a basin of who-knows-how-old water. He'd told Graham he'd quit with conditions. He failed to elaborate that anyone who'd previously tried to leave the bandits was murdered. Jonathan didn't like to lie, but sometimes it was necessary.

A quick tapping at the front door turned his head. Mrs. Cottlewood walked inside as if she lived here. If she did, his life would be much easier.

"Good afternoon, Johnny. I hope you had a safe day with the bandits."

Jonathan groaned. "I don't work for the bandits."

"Sure, dear." Mrs. Cottlewood dismissed his denial and crossed the kitchen, carrying a full wicker basket in the crook of her arm. Jonathan helped her lift the heavy load onto the cedar table, grateful she made a late appearance after all.

"Oh, thank ya." She swiped her forehead, ruffling the lacy bonnet strapped around her head. "I couldn't make it this morning. Ol' Barry just had to work the fields again, and I had to send for Dr. Frank. Ever since he retired from the newspaper, he hasn't been able to sit his patootie in a chair for a day. Barry's going to work himself into a grave too soon."

Jonathan helped the sweet old lady transfer her basket of fresh fruits and vegetables, and when he fisted an apple, the nameless farmer's blank face flashed before his eyes, shortly after he was slain in cold blood. Jonathan set the apple in the countertop basket and wiped his hand on his trousers as if ridding himself of the imagery.

"I'm grateful for your continued help. Since Verity is gone, we need you now more than ever."

"Oh, don't be silly. One of these days you can send Graham."

Jonathan's head tilted in confusion. "Why do you say that?"

"Dear, I've been meaning to tell ya. I'm not getting any younger. It's enough for me to keep up with Barry's troubles. I won't be able to continue running errands for the Arris household much longer, I'm afraid."

The wind was knocked from Jonathan's lungs. The old woman had been helping the household for two years, and never missed a day—except once, the day Verity had a run in with Jaime Perez. Good thing Mrs. Cottlewood hadn't been around, or it might've ended poorly for her. And good thing that city boy was here to help Verity. Jonathan didn't want to picture how things could've been.

"I understand. I appreciate every day you come, and when your last day arrives, let me know ahead of time."

"Sure thing." Mrs. Cottlewood replaced her empty basket in the crook of her arm. "I'll see you tomorrow, if you're around."

"Thank you, Mrs. C."

She adjusted her damp bonnet and saw herself out.

Jonathan slumped into a kitchen chair and bit down on a crisp carrot. He missed the old days when Mom had run the household, and Dad had run the farm. Graham had been in diapers, and Verity was already a spitfire then, making a fuss with her chores. In the evenings, he and Dad played cribbage while sharing a pint of beer. Dad would've figured out a solution to the finances without having to sell his soul to the bandits—or winding up dead trying to decline the offer.

With Jonathan in charge, the finances were getting worse—he was going to have to hire yet another worker to replace Mrs. Cottlewood. She had been free. At this pace, he'd never be able to quit the bandits—not that they'd let him anyway. And he only had three days to abandon the property to prove his loyalty to the bandits.

Graham wasn't ready.

Jonathan didn't think he'd ever be ready. He propped his elbow on the table and rested his forehead in his hand while he finished off his carrot, stewing on how shit just kept rolling downhill.

Chapter 5
Present Day, Green Bay, Wisconsin

Becca unlocked the front door to her house and her eyes glazed over her things. A hollowness filled her. This was supposed to be her family's home. Now it was a painful shell reminding her of what should've been. She wanted to call her mom to tell her what Brad had done today and unleash her messy combination of anger and hurt. But she didn't feel like talking, and Mom wasn't great at listening ever since she'd started peddling for a multi-level marketing company.

'Oh, no, honey. It's direct sales. All I have to do is sell 100 point value products a month to keep my qualified distributor's status. Can you support my small business and buy from me? Your lipstick never was right for you. I have just the right shade to make your complexion pop.'

No, Mom.

'How would you like to work from home? You could earn full-time income from part-time work. All from your phone!'

I have a job, Mom, Becca would tell her.

'But your job won't make you rich! For just fifty-five dollars a year, you can become a distributor too. Then you order a kit for inventory. The basic one is only $345—a savings of over $485! I bought business cards, and I booked a table at the craft fair.'

That's not a craft, Mom, Becca would argue.

'Stop changing the subject. If you join under me, you'll get a discount! And the bigger your downline, the more money you get. Soon we'll both be rich.'

I'll think about it, Mom, Becca had said only once. Click.

Every time Becca called her mom, the conversation repeated the same pushy information as if she'd transformed into a corporate parrot. Mom rebuffed every rejection with the quickness of a script, so Becca decided to let Mom figure it out on her own. In the meantime, Becca only suffered through social gatherings and smiled and nodded when she had to.

Dad wasn't an option to lean on either. Her parents divorced when she was eight years old. Mom had been awarded full custody, but Dad never made an effort. When Becca had gotten engaged, he'd had no interest in walking her down the aisle. It was for the best now.

Becca wished she had a sister. She'd even take a brother, but there was nothing she could do about that. Her closest friend was April McCall, or so she thought. April disappeared, but according to her brother, she was happy as could be. But Becca's friendship didn't warrant a single text or call.

Becca dropped her armful of flattened boxes to the floor, cut the zip tie holding the bundle, and opened them up one at a time. The first box she left by the door with the top open, ready to receive all things garbage. Becca collected the frames off the walls, off the tables, and off her desk, and dumped them into the box. Her lips pulled into a genuine smile with promises of a new slate awaiting her.

In the closet, Becca found a random shirt Brad left behind, along with knickknacks and formal wear, a robe he never wore, some old CDs, faded college T-shirts, and...she held up his old Hawaiian-print button up short sleeve shirt. She loved the shirt—wanted her wedding to feel tropical even though it was at a park in Green Bay. But Brad balked. Whined. Fussed. Then he wore it for those four hours and afterward, Brad buried it somewhere. Becca never found it until now. She still liked the shirt, even if the man who wore it was a prick. What was she going to do with it now? Into the garbage box it went, along with an armful of his other junk.

By the end of the day, she had every trace of Brad in a box at the curb, and half of her own stuff packed up. Only necessities remained. Becca sat at her barren kitchen table and opened her laptop. She posted on her local buy-sell-trade page announcing free stuff and listed the address.

Becca collected the signed divorce papers, folded them into the pre-addressed envelope and licked that sucker shut.

With a breath of relief, she jumped into her Corolla and made a special trip to the closest blue collection box. She set it inside, closed the squeaky lid, and then opened it again, just to make sure it fell safely down. Becca needed to be sure some weirdo couldn't find the papers stuck on the hinged lid and destroy them for kicks. Farfetched, sure, but stranger things had happened.

Six months ago, she was happily married—as far as she knew—pregnant with her first, and excited for her expanding family. In the few short months, she'd lost everything. All the shrinks would tell her to live for herself. Find herself. Enjoy loving herself. Becca had spent many years without a boyfriend back in high school and early college. She knew herself well enough, but finding a new man was very, very low on her list of priorities. In fact, she didn't know why she was even thinking it. Finding a new man? Erased from the radar.

Without Brad and without a pesky nine-to-five, she could have Fabio all day long. At this very moment he waited for her on her nightstand. Suddenly the idea of curling up with a good book and a box of chocolates sounded better than anything else. She debated turning around and raiding the grocery store's candy aisle. Ultimately, it was getting late.

Becca drove back home, foot softer on the pedal than usual. She wasn't in a hurry, but she wasn't delaying her return either. Something about having sent off the papers made her feel lighter, less anchored down.

There was still a problem. Her house was a constant reminder of the two hundred pounds she'd just shed. Becca dropped her purse on the coffee table and resumed her seat at her laptop. She typed up a thirty-day notice to vacate for her landlord. All she needed now was a new place to live...oh, and a job.

This time of the night, nothing was going to happen. Becca crashed in bed with Fabio and drifted off to sleep with him resting on her chest.

EARLY THE NEXT MORNING—NOT four A.M. early, but still earlier than she would've preferred, Becca stretched, and Fabio fell on the floor.

"Sorry, baby. I'll be more careful next time."

She set the book back on the nightstand and pulled out her dresser drawers. She owned scrubs and pajamas. One could argue the difference. She also had winter clothing—not useful in July—and short shorts, which she didn't feel like wearing. Out of habit and comfort, Becca pulled on pink scrub bottoms and a fun patterned top. Now she felt like herself. It was just another normal morning.

Becca slipped a breakfast sandwich out of the box in the freezer and unwrapped the clear plastic. She dropped it onto a plate and zapped it in the microwave for—she checked the box—three minutes. Store-bought cookies were blasphemy, but prepackaged everything else was fair game.

She filled a glass of water and brought the hot meal to the table. Today was a new day. Becca opened her laptop and found the online listings for local apartments. She typed in the digits on her cell phone to call the first listing, but a knock at the front door interrupted her from pressing the send button.

Who would visit at this hour?

If Brad had a change of heart, all Becca wanted was his baseball bat, which was in the box at the curb. Brad was over and done with, even if he begged to return. With squared shoulders ready to face his bullshit, she opened the door. Her brows lifted. "Hi, Kiko. What can I do for you?" Becca didn't realize Kiko knew where she lived.

"I know this might seem weird, but I have a request, if you have a moment."

Kiko's long midnight hair streamed down the shoulders of her petite frame. Becca had worked with her for several weeks while April was missing. Kiko was a quiet woman who mostly kept to herself. Becca didn't know much about her except she was a college student at night and quit the clinic shortly after Verity arrived.

Becca could use a little company who wouldn't ask too many tough questions or push an agenda. She stepped aside. "Come on in; I just need to grab something quick." Becca rushed to the curb, dug through the box, and collected the bat, just in case. She brought it back inside with her and left it leaning against the wall by the door.

"Moving?" Kiko turned in place, noticing all the boxes.

"As soon as I can. I only need a pile of bricks to move my stuff into."

"I'm sorry about Brad," Kiko said.

Becca didn't want sympathy. Her throat closed with surging emotion.

"He was a dick anyway," Kiko finished.

Becca barked a laugh. She never heard Kiko speak like that before. "Yeah, turns out he was. Have a seat. Water? OJ? I might have a can of soda stuffed in the back of the fridge that the dick left behind."

Kiko chuckled. "I'm fine, thank you."

"What's the special request?" Becca didn't have any unique talents or connections, so she was baffled about what Kiko needed.

"I have a final project for my master's degree—" Kiko started.

"Psychology, right?"

"It's a study on dreams. I give you a mission and you have to complete it. Then I ask questions for my report."

Becca didn't like the sound of that. She pictured a stark white room, an operating table, and beeping machines and electrodes. A grimace formed on her face.

"It's only one night, and I promise you it'll be worth it," Kiko said.

Becca tilted her head. "In what way?"

Kiko smiled gently and touched Becca's arm. "I know this sounds crazy, but it can heal you from all this pain."

Becca blinked back tears. That sounded great, but... "How can a single dream erase the pain of cheating asshole Brad and our loss?" The words barely came out in a fluid string.

"It'll resemble being inside one of your Fabio books."

Becca cocked a brow. "Because I read them so much my brain will manifest a scenario just like one?"

"Something like that. And I promise there are no electrodes involved. Not a single one," Kiko said, smiling.

"How did you know...?" Becca shifted away. Now it was creepy.

"Matt worried about electrodes. Your face gave it away."

"Okay..." Kiko had said it would be crazy, and so far, she was right. If she needed help, Becca was willing to try out a little Fabio for herself. "When can we start?"

Kiko stood to give Becca space. "Now, if you want. Lay down on the couch and get comfortable."

Becca stretched out on the soft cushions. "But I'm not tired."

"You'll be just fine." Kiko stared at her hand and flipped it front to back several times as if something was wrong.

"What is it?" Becca asked.

"I'm just making sure I don't have a glitch again. It was weird once. Almost had to scrap the whole study." Kiko chuckled.

"So how are you going to monitor my progress or whatever?"

"Just do your best and report back when you're done."

"Simple enough," Becca said.

"I do have a mission for you, like I said."

"I can imagine what kind of mission I'll conjure with Fabio." Becca wagged her brows suggestively.

"This is serious." Kiko suppressed her own chuckle, but it was there, dancing on her lips. "There's a man named Jonathan Arris. I need you to find him and convince him to take the sheriff's deal. If he doesn't, he will be murdered."

"That's heavy. Do you have any lighter missions? I could find a book or something. Or give a message to a person? Dig into my subconscious and dissect my daddy issues?"

"The Arris mission stands. It's a quantitative measurement."

And with that, Becca checked out of the conversation. Stats was not her thing in college. Still wasn't. Becca closed her eyes and folded her hands over her chest in a sort of clinical comfort. "All right. Send me to Fabio."

A tugging at her pink scrub pants pocket snapped her eyes open. "What's that?"

"It's an emergency responder. What you're about to experience will feel very real. If you need to escape, you'll be able to press the button."

Becca closed her eyes and the corner of her lips lifted. "Not sure how I'll touch my pocket while asleep, but let's do this."

Silence followed, and then Becca's stomach churned. "Wait, do I take a pill or...?" Becca trailed off, nausea gripping her. She leaned over the couch for fresh air and opened her eyes. Becca's living room rippled before her. She squeezed her eyes shut and fought the urge to heave.

When the horrific sensation passed, Becca opened her eyes, burped, and pinched herself. What the hell kind of dream was this?

Chapter 6
1854, Navarino, Wisconsin

INSIDE THE FISH MARKET, a filthy stench of raw seafood filled Jonathan's nose while perspiration beaded on his forehead. Best friends Nash and Ruddy were smashing the owner's cash register with a rhythmic ping of metal. Fat Fingers trawled for extra treasures to confiscate, while Brawley sifted through the owner's personal belongings for anything of value. Jonathan, with Butch's steady barrel of a Colt revolver aimed precariously near his head, held the shop owner in place with the threat of a few unwanted holes. Butch watched everyone with his keen eye. Jonathan wasn't going to screw up today, or he'd be deaf from the gunshot.

And then dead.

Tim Van Cook stood on trembling knees. Since everyone knew the bandits had been wreaking havoc all over the village, the fool could've armed his store, but Timmy here thought with his stink he was exempt. Jonathan should've pitied the man who had done no wrong, but the man failed to protect what was his.

And now there were consequences.

Jonathan was not projecting at all. Nope, no way.

"Please leave. I don't have much. I only sell a few fish a day. There isn't much in there, I swear."

"Shut your pie hole," Nash warned.

Tim Van Cook whimpered and mumbled to himself. Nash and Ruddy continued smashing at the metal register, swiping sweaty brows, but so far, they hadn't gotten through.

"Butch, this of any use?" Brawley lifted a hand, and a pocket watch dangled from his fingers.

"Of course it is, you halfwit."

"Right, boss." Brawley scampered over, and Butch idly inspected the loot before slipping it into his trouser pocket. Something useful, but not impressive nor satisfactory.

Metal pinged one last time and shattered gears jingled along the hardwood floor. Nash and Ruddy hooted and scooped up their plunder.

Jonathan and Butch didn't move.

"Bu...bu...Please don't. That's all I have." Tim's lower lip trembled. At any moment he'd be whining and blubbering—completely pathetic, and then Butch's trigger finger would rid the world of one more weak man.

Jonathan couldn't watch and say nothing. "It'll be over in a minute. Don't move," Jonathan said. He held the shotgun snug against his shoulder, but in this small shop, it felt like overkill. Once again, he was backup—stop anyone from coming inside or cover anyone if there was an injury. Jonathan wasn't pleased to be an insurance policy, but as he preferred to keep his hands clean, he didn't argue.

With every coin secured in a burlap sack, Nash and Ruddy passed over the goods and left the store.

"That's enough, Brawley. Let's go," Butch ordered.

"Awe shucks, boss. I wasn't done yet." Brawley dropped a cloth garment of some sort and walked past the terrified owner with his head hung like a disappointed child.

Butch turned and followed his cohorts while Fingers covered his back and retreated with them.

Jonathan lowered the shotgun. "Tim."

"You already took everything. What more do you want?" Weakness spilled over, and Timmy wiped his eyes clear.

Jonathan steeled himself to check the disgust from his voice. "A piece of advice for you, the bandits aren't going anywhere anytime soon. Prepare yourself."

"You're one of them! Why are you telling me this? Are you saying you're coming back?"

Anger tensed his body, and Jonathan realized he didn't much like weakness either. "Look around. You have to protect what's yours or it will be taken."

Tim nodded and snorted.

Outside, the bandits had distributed their earnings and mounted up.

"Your share," Butch said, tossing a bag at him.

Jonathan caught it and opened the top. Two bucks and some change. He stuffed it the best he could into his small vest pocket.

"What caused your delay?" Butch asked.

"Oh, just making sure nothing was missed." Jonathan fibbed. He trusted them as much as he trusted a leaky row boat in rapids—not a chance.

Butch narrowed his shrewd eyes and nodded in acknowledgment. "Coming with us this time?" The question sounded genuine, without a tone of annoyance—an unusual change. Jonathan didn't like when the bandits acted differently.

"I'm set for today."

"I'll send Ruddy to you at high noon for tomorrow's hit," Butch said, and reminded him, "Two days."

Jonathan tipped his hat and guided his mount back toward home. The road south was long, dusty, sweltering and dull. Horse manure wafted from the roads and cow manure drifted from the fields. Jonathan kept an eye out for trouble while pleasantly nodding at passersby. None looked like ripe pickings for Butch—just dirty people traveling to and from work. The bandits had little interest in day laborers from the farms and lumber mills. He much preferred farmers and business owners. Occasionally, he'd find someone who was judged to be worthy of robbing—with their fine cut clothes and noses pinched at the smell, they were easy to pick out. Typically bankers and elite members of society just settling into the expanding area. Soon all three villages would become one city—he would bet on it.

So much change so quickly. How different would the villages become over the next decade? Society was shifting toward a foreign future, and that didn't settle well with him.

Another laborer passed, who opted to not return the pleasant nod. Jonathan shrugged. Most of them ignored him, despite his best attempts to be friendly.

But the man approaching him next didn't—Smith, previously a lumber camp worker, now the town drunk. No one took him seriously since his fall from grace, and people spoke freely when they thought the ears were too muddled with booze. So when Smith wanted to talk, Jonathan listened.

"Johnny, you better watch your back."

He bristled at the unexpected threat. "What are you talking about?"

Smith closed the distance to Jonathan's horse and whispered. "You aren't one of us anymore. You're scaring the ladies and vexing the gents."

"Vexing them how?" Jonathan attempted pleasantries with any sweet lady he passed, but he never received much more than a silent nod in return. Why would that anger the men?

"Being out and about. Trying to be friendly and all. You're labeled as bad news—dangerous, ill tempered"—Jonathan pressed his lips together, but Smith prattled on—"and your loyalty is to the worst scum in the village. Everybody knows what Nash does to women, and now you're associated with that."

"I'm nothing like Nash."

"Don't matter none."

Just great. His sister had a destroyed reputation, too. Guess it ran in the family. Jonathan wasn't looking for a bride; he knew his chances were zero anyhow. He definitely didn't want to be associated with Nash's unusual and grotesque ways, but he already had too many problems on his plate to give Smith's warning any head space.

Sheriff Clint Nelson appeared on a horse with its head bobbing, and Smith left with his head down.

Jonathan nodded in greeting as he approached. "Morning, Sheriff."

"Johnny, I've been looking for you."

A shiver skimmed along Jonathan's spine. That couldn't be good news. "You found me."

"Listen, kid. I've been around for a long while, and I know things," the sheriff said.

That wasn't the way to begin a pleasant exchange. "Oh?"

"For instance, I know that your parents were fine, hardworking, honest fellows. Rest their souls. And it's out of respect for the Arris's that I'm going to make you a deal."

Sheriff Clint Nelson's hand moved out of sight at the same time Jonathan's went for the butt of his shotgun. Getting arrested would throw a wrench into his day, and Jonathan had to do whatever necessary to prevent that, even if it meant turning full bandit.

Sheriff brought forward a pair of shackles, and Jonathan's breathing hitched while his heartbeat thumped in his ears. He had two days to settle his affairs for the bandits. If he found himself locked up, what would the bandits do to Graham? Would they shoot Jonathan for getting caught? The bandits didn't exactly lay out their terms in a contractual agreement, but Jonathan believed the worst he could imagine would come true.

"I'm going to arrest you right now for banditry, unless…" Sheriff trailed off.

Jonathan moved his hand back to the reins, intrigued by whatever the sheriff wanted. "Unless what?"

"In exchange for your freedom, I want your cooperation to help me take down the bandits."

"They kill anyone who betrays them," Jonathan said, muscles tensing. "You know that. You're asking me to die, so you can be praised as the hero sheriff who ended the bandits' terror on our villages. Is that it?"

Sheriff held out his hands. "It ain't gonna work any if everyone hears, kid. All I need to know is the location of their home base."

"That's all? You'll let me go free if I hand over the location where they rest their heads at night."

"That's all," Sheriff repeated with a smarmy grin.

The sheriff was one crooked man, who'd been in Jaime Perez's pockets, and turning his eye or taking a cut of the extortion. Even if Jonathan knew the location—he didn't—one sheriff wasn't going to take down all the bandits at once. And that meant Jonathan's head on a plate. The bandits were more fearsome than this one old sheriff. "You can't guarantee my safety if I betray them."

Sheriff glowered. "Think about what you're saying, Johnny. Help me or I'm arresting you."

"What for? I didn't do anything but stand there."

"Accessory to banditry, first degree."

The ridiculousness made Jonathan chuckle. "Now you're just making that up."

"This isn't a laughing matter, kid. Now, you agree or I'm taking you in, and the last thing you'll see is the crowd watching your toes hanging in the air. I'd wager many townsfolk will be thrilled about me cleaning up the streets, bandit."

"I'm not a bandit," Jonathan declared for the umpteenth time.

"Then what are you doing here?"

"Just traveling." Jonathan wanted to smack himself for a terrible fib.

"And that pouch there?" Sheriff pointed toward the loot still poking from his vest pocket. "Looks like the color of Timmy's sacks, and I don't see no fish."

Jonathan pressed his lips together.

"I'll give you one last chance. Me or them."

Jonathan considered the grim deal more carefully. The sheriff intended to hang him, and knowing how the sheriff worked, there would be no trial. Jonathan's only possibility would be escaping the jail cell and fleeing the area—abandoning Graham and the farm. And since Jonathan hadn't spent time in a cell before, a big cloud of doubt lingered.

His horse's tail flipped and slapped at the flies bothering it. Jonathan removed his straw hat and fanned his face when the corner of his eye caught an unfamiliar sight. A woman stood down the bank of the road, wearing trousers that were...pink? His eyes must've been playing tricks. Her bodice didn't lace or hug her form in a feminine way, and the adorned pattern was impossible. The woman's hair, long rusty ringlets, was stunning. And her shoes! They didn't have heels and their shape was so different, and whiter than possible.

Her head turned side to side as if she expected someone to meet her there. Between farm fields was a mighty strange place for a meeting. She lifted her hand to shield her eyes against the vicious sun while stepping up the incline to the road. The woman tripped, catching a knee full of dirt. Perhaps he could help a lady out. She seemed confused and lost, after all.

"Just a second there, Sheriff." Jonathan trotted over to the woman before Sheriff Clint could protest.

"Howdy there, miss." Jonathan tipped his hat in respect and stopped his mount next to her.

"Hi," she answered with a glance before continuing to wait for her missing party. Then her head whipped back up to him. "Oh... Hi, there."

Jonathan gave her a friendly smile. "Need a hand?"

"Um, I'm looking for someone, and I don't even know where to begin."

"And who might that be?"

Her eyes tracked the approaching sheriff. "Jonathan Arris. Is that the sheriff?" She pointed.

"I am and he is. Who are you?" Jonathan didn't recognize the strange sight, and being named troubled him.

"This is your last warning, kid," Sheriff said, and the clank of metal shackles turned Jonathan's head from the intriguing woman.

"I can't, Sheriff. I've got my brother to look after and the farm, too. If Butch thinks I've turned against him, he'll slaughter everyone on my property and ransack it. He's ruthless."

"Wait!" the strange woman yelled, interrupting them. She faced Jonathan. "You have to take the deal. You have to."

Jonathan's hackles rose. "Who are you to tell me what to do?"

"I... I was sent here to tell you that you have to take the sheriff's deal, otherwise..." she trailed off.

"Otherwise what?" he pressed.

"Now who is this here woman?" Sheriff interrupted.

"Otherwise what?" Jonathan repeated.

"You'll be...murdered," she finished softly.

"Well, now, how is it you know so much about a deal that's only just been discussed?" Jonathan asked. "Are you working for the Sheriff?" Jonathan turned to Clint Nelson. "Is she yours?"

"Most certainly not," the sheriff said, taking in her bizarre appearance.

"I don't know the sheriff," the woman said. "Look, I can't exactly explain where I came from. Only that I know you have to take the sheriff's deal and avoid arrest."

Jonathan's voice rose, irritated some stranger inserted herself into his dangerous business. "I am not taking orders from some woman." And with that, all plans to help her flew right out the window. Jonathan tugged the reins to leave, but his horse didn't move.

Sheriff's hand was fastened on the reins, and from his other hand dangled the shackles. "Best you listen to the lady."

"Please," she begged. "You have to take it."

Jonathan had had enough. "Excuse me, I have a farm to run. Miss." He tipped his hat in dismissal and cold metal clamped on his wrist. Fury roared through Jonathan's chest.

"That's a shame, kid. I really liked your folks, too."

"No!" the woman shouted.

When Jonathan turned his head, she was gone. North and south, he checked, but she vanished.

"You're coming to the station with me, and I'll have you booked. Either you cooperate and get your chance at a trial, or I'll put a round in your head here, saving me the trouble. I don't like paperwork none."

Jonathan complied while the sheriff cuffed him and secured his mount for the ride to the jailhouse. His only hope was to escape the cell, for Graham's sake.

Chapter 7

Present Day, Green Bay, Wisconsin

Becca wrapped an arm around her middle while she lurched for purchase against the horse. Her hand landed on her couch, and she rolled to her side. Becca sat up straight. "What the hell?"

Kiko stood next to her, sipping a bottle of water, as if nothing happened. A red journal Becca hadn't seen before was sitting on her coffee table.

"That was the most intense dream project I've ever participated in. In fairness, I've never done one before, but you weren't kidding about the realism." Becca scanned the living room for equipment. "Was I sleep walking? I don't see how you projected the simulation into my head." Electricity coursed through her, and Becca's lips pulled into a smile all on their own. Maybe this was some space-age new therapy program. Sign her up for a double dose. She wouldn't mind another eyeful of that cowboy, Jonathan Arris.

Kiko set the bottle on the coffee table and sat next to it, pinching her hands between her knees. "Remember when I said the mission was serious?"

"Yeah." Becca blew a ringlet out of her face. Her cheeks were hurting from the smile she couldn't shake.

"Well, I meant serious...and real," Kiko said carefully.

Becca stared at her. "Real how? Like 'made with real cheese' or a block of cheese straight into the pot?"

Kiko squinted. "I think the second one. It was fully real—tangible, history-altering real."

Now Becca believed she was dreaming. "Are you telling me that hot cowboy on a horse—?"

"Farmer," Kiko interrupted.

"Whatever. He was real?"

"As real as you and me."

Becca woke her phone screen.

"What are you doing?" Kiko asked.

Becca typed the words into the search bar, and she clicked the first legitimate-looking link. "Jonathan Eugene Arris. Eugene?" Becca shrugged. It worked on him. "Born in 1822 and died in 1854." The further she read, the slower the words. "Death by...hanging...after conviction of...banditry. Is that a real thing?"

Kiko nodded.

"Oh." Becca stared at the name on her screen, and as the gears turned, her smile waned. "That wasn't some fun romp through small-town Texas, was it?"

Kiko shook her head.

"Where did I go?" She feared the answer she already knew.

"It's not where. It's when."

"Eighteen-fifty-four." Becca's heart thundered in her chest, and she dropped the phone. Standing up, she paced around the boxes in her cramped living room. Her shaking hands couldn't relax. "That was real."

Kiko nodded.

"You sent me back in time to save that guy."

Kiko nodded.

Becca inhaled a long deep breath to calm herself. It didn't help much. Images of Jonathan flickered through her mind—a ruggedly handsome cowboy—okay, farmer—on a horse, armed and dangerous, and quick-witted. Stubborn too. She dismissed the attitude and suspicion because of the situation, but she had been fooled by handsome before—the outsides didn't always match the insides. Becca needed to check herself. "But you never said he was worth saving."

Kiko's brows rose, and she flipped her hand back and forth again, as if inspecting it for something. "It's a rare thing for me to be surprised. To answer your question, yes, he's worth saving."

This whole thing was just...ludicrous. "Time travel isn't real. How...?" Becca trailed off, trying to connect the right synapses to form thoughts that didn't lead to her mind exploding. "How was that whole thing possible?"

"It's my job," Kiko said simply.

Becca frowned and confusion pushed its way front and center "You worked with me at Animal Care of Wisconsin. We shared lunch sometimes, for Pete's sake."

"For a few weeks. It helps to gain a client's trust, and Matt needed help in the clinic." Kiko moved closer, but Becca took a step back. The smaller woman held out her palms in a pacifying gesture. "Don't be afraid. I'm not here to hurt you, on the contrary. I was recruited to help people meet who cannot meet for themselves. For a century, I've been time hopping and matching people. You were next on my list, which suddenly seems quite short, but never mind that," Kiko said. She had a bit of confusion rolling off her too.

"What are you?" Becca whispered. The Kiko she briefly knew wasn't this person.

"I'm just like you. I survived losing a love, but unlike me, you get a second chance." There was a sadness in her small smile.

Becca didn't know what she meant by 'second chance', but Becca focused on the glaring error in her statement. "Like me? Humans can't time travel. That's science fiction, not reality. And a century? C'mon do you really expect me to believe you're over a hundred years old?"

Kiko pointed at Becca's knees. A bright dirt stain on her pink pants showed the proof her brain couldn't accept. Becca placed a hand on her forehead and quickly dropped onto a kitchen chair before she cracked her foggy brain on the floor. Kiko set a glass of water in front of her. Every inch of her body screamed at her to run away, but Becca feared she wouldn't get a step without fainting.

April had trusted her as a roommate.

Dr. McCall had trusted her as an employee.

Something told Becca she could trust her, too, but she couldn't wrap her brain around the whole thing. "I...I believe you, I think."

Kiko smiled and sat across from her at the table. "I'm glad to hear it. When you're up for it, can we talk about what's next?"

"What's next?" Becca repeated. She couldn't string one thought to the next at the moment.

"You read on your phone Jonathan was arrested and hung. So, I'll need you to try again. Convince him to take the sheriff's deal."

"You want me to do that again?" It was just too unbelievable. But Becca's inability to convince the man led directly to his death. She was the reason his name was in this article. She'd failed him. His death at the age of 32 was her fault. "You said he was worth saving, but I didn't."

Kiko nodded.

"What if I screw up again?"

"You'll have one more chance."

That was not the answer she'd expected. Anger rumbled through her body. "Is this some sort of game?"

"I assure you it's not. Three trips there and back again. You've used one."

Becca remembered all the information Kiko had given her before the trip, and something was just not clicking, but she grasped at the strings. "You mentioned Dr. McCall worrying about electrodes. Why?"

The corner of Kiko's lips lifted, and she shrugged. "He seemed to be afraid of them."

Why else would Dr. McCall tell Kiko of his fear of electrodes, when Becca had the same thought just before... "Are you saying that my boss—my old boss—did this same time traveling thing too?"

Kiko nodded again, as if afraid to answer and wanting Becca to figure it out for herself.

"Verity!" Becca jumped to her feet, and the chair fell back behind her with a dull thud on the linoleum. When Verity had walked through the clinic doors with Dr. McCall, she wore a head-turning theatrical dress, complete with the butt bump, corset, and lacy trim. The pattern was very retro curtains. And the way she looked at everything and had no idea what a computer was—or a toilet—made her seem like a sheltered child from another world—curious to no end. "Verity was from the past! And Dr. McCall brought her here. Holy shit."

Kiko smiled. "That's right."

"You matched Verity and Matt." Dr. McCall had found his true love in the past.

"It was to be," Kiko said.

Becca placed a hand on her head to stop the spinning of the floor. "Are you saying that my match is back there—back then?"

"Yes," Kiko answered with a breathy sigh. "I don't normally let the matches know, so it doesn't interfere with the falling-in-love part, but you needed a little extra convincing, and you're sharper than most."

The small woman had told her Becca was going to a Fabio like in her books. Jonathan didn't look like Fabio, but he was still quite the handsome man with his tanned and glistening skin under the harsh summer rays, piercing green eyes, five o'clock shadow, and dark wavy hair. Could he be her match? She remembered the sharp tongue, the weapons, and the sheriff's words. If he was such a worthy man... "Why is he a convicted felon?"

Kiko smiled. "I don't read minds. You'll have to ask him."

The shackles had clanked on his wrist in a flash. Jonathan was stubborn, but so was Becca. "Send me back, but can I have more time, you know, to convince him? I didn't have enough before."

"I should've given you more time. That was my error. I can send you whenever you need to be. Realize though, that if you use that emergency responder, it returns you to the equivalent time. The past and the present have differing timelines."

Whatever that meant, sure. "Okay."

Becca switched out of her scrubs. She didn't have an appropriate dress for the year, but she had a cream blouse—clearly not a corset, but more formfitting than a baggy printed scrub top, which nicely concealed her stretch marks—and a pair of black skirt pants. The legs were so loose-fitting, when standing still, the pants could pass as a long skirt. She returned to her living room and Kiko slipped the transponder gizmo back into her pocket. "Do I need to take anything?"

"It's up to you, but the less you take, the better."

She thought of Verity and her layers of dress. What would Becca need to fit in? A bonnet, an apron? She wasn't a History Channel buff. Becca could only do so much with the time and materials available in the present. "I'm ready." Becca braced herself.

Kiko inspected her hand and frowned—a twisted face Becca had never seen on Kiko before, and now she'd seen it three times in as many hours. It was unsettling. "Everything okay?"

"I'm just checking that something doesn't go wrong."

"You said that last time. What exactly could go wrong?" Becca spoke slowly, caution flashing in her head.

"I had a glitch once before. Something is just a little off, so I'm double checking everything lately. But it's nothing to worry about." Kiko rubbed her head and flinched.

"Headache?"

"Yeah."

"I've got some pain relievers in the bathroom. Want one?" Becca asked.

"No. It's minor. Hold on to your horses, 'cause the future is about to blow you away."

Becca's eyes widened. "Next time, don't lead with that."

Kiko laughed, and Becca's vision blurred away while her stomach trembled. At that surreal moment, Becca wondered if she hadn't made a mistake.

Chapter 8
1854, Navarino, Wisconsin

BECCA RIPPLED BACK TO the ditch alongside the dirt road again. She scanned the area and shook her head. Alive in history. There was no way this was possible, because that meant people capable of time travel allowed the atrocities of history to stand. Someone turned their cheek while Hitler, Stalin, Pol Pot, Hussein, Genghis Khan, and Mussolini committed their atrocities. None of it should've been in the history books because none of it should've happened. Becca crouched down and scooped a handful of dirt and let it slide through her fingers. She was one unarmed woman with no experience in the chess game of war and genocide. What change could she really enact?

Was that the same thought the other time travelers had?

She was by no means blaming others for not preventing horrific acts in history; she was just frustrated she couldn't change it.

But she could change one man's destiny.

Last time Becca arrived, she found Jonathan speaking with the sheriff just a short distance away. They weren't there this time, which meant this wasn't the same moment as last time, and Becca didn't think to ask Kiko how to find him.

Becca climbed up the ditch and shaded her eyes against the blinding high sun. She wasn't an expert in sundials, but the tiny shadows made her believe no time had passed since her last visit. This had to be a different day altogether.

A wood wagon pulled by a pair of draft horses creaked and rumbled as it rolled down the road. The man wore a straw hat and coveralls with no shirt. Becca stared. This was all real, and she had to be careful.

Down the way was a building, and Becca started off, feet sinking into the dry dirt. Sweat rolled down her back, and she wished for a hat or trees to shade her from the harsh sun. She reached a store with wooden siding and painted lettering reading Tim's Fish Market. Becca went inside to see if anyone knew where she could find Jonathan Arris, happy for a break from the sun.

Pungent seafood entered her nose, and a wet slapping came from the wood counter. A pair of customers waited, watching a man wearing what was once a white apron. The stains made her appreciate clean restaurant workers' uniforms. A long fish—smallmouth bass, perhaps—fluttered with its mouth moving under the clerk's long fingers. He raised a butcher knife to chop off…

Becca turned around and exhaled a slow breath. She preferred her food already in neat containers.

The flopping on the butcher block was almost unbearable, and then the sudden thump and silence followed. Paper rustled before Becca turned back around.

"Have a great day, ladies," the clerk said with a friendly smile.

Two women in dresses similar to Verity's gave Becca puzzled looks before leaving. That was something to get used to.

"Can I get you anything, miss?" the clerk asked her.

It felt good to be called miss instead of ma'am. She'd been coloring her hair so long she didn't know how gray she was under the red dye, but lately, every stranger always called her ma'am. She'd like this guy if he wasn't holding a meat cleaver.

"I'm looking for Jonathan Arris. Do you know him?"

The pleasant features of the clerk vanished. "You don't want anything to do with him. Stay away."

Becca's hand moved to her chest. "Why do you say that?"

"Anyone who's anyone around these parts knows, but you look like someone new in town." The clerk leaned forward as if telling a secret. "He's a bandit. Don't get mixed up with them. It never ends well."

Becca's eyes popped. "Them?" The online newspaper article stated he'd been convicted of banditry, and Kiko had said the felon was worth saving, but she didn't mention the plural form. If Jonathan was a 'good' bandit, what about the rest of them? Oh, shit. What had she agreed to?

"Six that we know of." The clerk's knife glinted with intricate slices along a fish. "Do yourself a favor, and go back to wherever you came from."

Becca had the transponder gizmo from Kiko, but she only had two trips left to prevent Jonathan's murder. As her stacks of finished romance novels proved, Becca didn't give up when she set her mind to something. "I can't return, so how about you tell me where to find him."

The clerk paused, brows lifting in his own surprise. He shook his head. "Don't come back and say I didn't warn you."

That was unnecessary gloom. Becca tilted her chin up in challenge. She wouldn't leave without help.

The clerk uttered a noncommittal noise. "He's in Astor. Take Broadway south until you reach Lombardi Ave. Head west, and you'll see the old farmhouse on the left. Weathered brown. Can't miss it."

"Thank you—" Becca held the word to prompt a name.

"Tim. The name's Tim Van Cook. Don't tell him I sent you."

"Thank you, Tim." Becca turned to leave.

"Oh, miss?"

"Yes?"

"I didn't hear any horse hooves. If you're planning on walking all the way to Astor, it'll take you a while, especially in this heat."

Becca hadn't thought of how she'd travel. Good thing she wore sneakers—comfortable for anyone on their feet all day. "Thanks for the heads-up."

Tim Van Cook tilted his head and shrugged.

Becca wasn't worried—frustrated at the wasted time—but kind of bouncy in the toes about getting fresh air and some exercise without her life's issues interrupting. She found a safe walking path parallel to the road. The farther she moved, the busier the area became. Townspeople were shopping, visiting, conducting business, and heavy wagons carried produce for the market. It was so weird to see everything so fresh—and some, like the fish at the market and the horses' feces on the road, were too fresh.

She wondered if the food tasted different. Well, of course, it did. They didn't have MSG, seasoning blends, or hydrogenated vegetable oils. Hmmm. Was the food better or worse?

Becca wished for a hat and sunglasses. The bright afternoon rays made her squint until her cheeks hurt. She rapidly tugged at the front of her blouse to cool off her chest, but it didn't help much. Sweat rolled down her back and ribs anyway. Pebbles crunched under her sneakers, and she smiled and nodded to passing riders. Most of them stared at her and continued about their business without a greeting. That was fine with her—she was on a mission.

A man on a horse trotted up behind her and slowed to keep her pace. A redheaded man with a flushed face smiled at her with deplorable teeth. "Not every day I see a woman walkin' all by her lonesome, and even less to see one lookin' like you."

"You need a new pick-up line," Becca answered politely with a fake smile. Her heart roared in her chest from the heat, the exercise, and from the filthy creeper.

"I'm only asking if you need a ride anywhere." His tone was gentle, and Becca reconsidered. It wasn't like he could lock her in a trunk and kidnap her. She could jump off a horse.

She hadn't ridden since she was a girl on her grandparent's ranch, but it was just like a bicycle, right?

The offer was appealing. "Do you know Jonathan Arris?"

The rider smiled, and Becca shivered at the sight. "I sure do. Say, I've got a message for him, if that's who you're seein'."

"I can deliver it."

"Tell him Butch picked Tim's Fish Market for today's collection, and he can meet us there at the usual time."

Becca's heart dropped. The kind Tim, whom she'd just met, was next to be terrorized by the six bandits? And this red-haired creeper was one of them?

"The name's Ruddy. I'll give you a ride. Come on up." His grimy hand lowered in invitation.

"I...I think I'll pass. Exercise is what the doctor ordered. Thanks for the offer," Becca said sweetly.

"Are you sure?" Ruddy's face fell.

"I am. I'll put in a good word for you." Becca didn't know if that would help, but she hoped it deflected any possible anger.

"Well, I gotta get back to the house anyway. So, be safe, and don't forget the message."

Ruddy surprised her. Maybe his social skills—and hygiene—were lacking, but not his character. She waved him off and continued her journey, watching her steps so she didn't twist an ankle in the ruts.

Alongside the road and through a thin row of pine trees, farms were tended by horse-drawn plows. Field workers carried buckets of water by hand. Others were on rickety ladders hand picking cherries. The primitiveness was fascinating—nothing like modern commercial farms and orchards, but what made her smile was the singing. Beautiful notes of ethnic songs drifted to her ears and Becca walked and listened to their melodies. It wasn't a dream, but it felt like she'd stepped inside a history textbook—one of the rare, pleasant ones.

Eventually she reached an intersection, if she could call it that. Two dirt paths met, and a painted sign informed her the Arris farm was located down that road.

Out of habit, she checked both ways before crossing, knowing horses couldn't stop quickly. With the coast clear, she jay-walked through the intersection. Her feet were hot and swollen, and her shoes felt uncomfortably tight, but another mile down the road, she finally reached a house. Since it was the only one, and it was indeed unpainted brown, this must be the place.

The farmhouse was two stories tall and in obvious disrepair. She pictured a fresh coat of paint and new shutters, a neat trim of the bushes, and new boards filling the gaps of the broken decking. Nothing some love and elbow grease couldn't fix. Becca climbed up the wooden porch, watching where she stepped, and knocked.

No answer.

She knocked again and waited.

Still nothing. Becca cupped her hands around her eyes to see inside a front window, and there was no movement. She spotted things she recognized: a couch, a coffee table, and a threadbare rug. And that was where the familiarities ended. The kitchen was rudimentary with cast iron pots and pans hanging on the wall, open shelving for cabinets, and...no sink. Becca hadn't thought of that. No plumbing.

Yikes.

Even campgrounds had outhouses with toilet paper. When was toilet paper invented? A lump of dread settled in her gut.

With no one inside, Becca took it upon herself to check around back. Maybe Jonathan had workers like the ones she passed, and they could help her.

Unruly bushes rimmed the side of the house too, and from there she could see a rickety tool shed, a pigpen with its corresponding oinks, and rows upon rows of endless corn as tall as her knees.

"Knee high by July," Becca recited the adage to measure the crop's growth trajectory.

At the back of the house, Becca stopped in her tracks and her breath caught. A shirtless man with suspenders sagging by his knees walked by with a pole across his shoulders bearing pails of what she believed to be water. His skin glistened with sweat under the sweltering sun while his defined muscles controlled the weight. His dark hair flopped over his face with sweat—or maybe water. But Jonathan Arris was a sight to behold.

He stopped and turned while she ogled him, and he stared as if he recognized her.

She flicked her wrist in a friendly wave hello, and he bent to rest the pails by his feet. Jonathan swiped the floppy hair from his face and strolled over. Becca's pulse kicked up.

Chapter 9

JONATHAN PROWLED TOWARD THE empty-handed trespasser in his yard. Ever since Jaime Perez's men harassed him last year, Jonathan had a short fuse for encroachers. But since this woman was simply stunning in her unusual clothing, gorgeous head of red curls, and lovely eyes that drank in his half-naked form, he'd give her a chance to explain herself. Who was this woman brave enough to step foot on his land?

"Hello, are you Jonathan Arris?" The gentle cream of her top hugged her curves in an inviting way. But stranger yet was the shiny black material of her skirt and the white of her shoes, as soft and brilliant as fresh snow.

While another bead of sweat rolled down his chest, Jonathan would welcome a sprinkle of snow right now. He crossed his sweaty arms over his chest to both intimidate her and flaunt his strength. Her eyes rounded with owl intelligence, and Jonathan had to peel his gaze from her intriguing mouth to her flushed face. "Do I know you?"

"Not exactly, but I've been walking a long way, and I could really use a drink."

She appeared harmless, and he knew all the ladies in town—and they knew him. A complete stranger wouldn't be working for the bandits or the sheriff, and Jaime's crew was disbanded a year ago. There was no harm in offering this woman a quench of her thirst, and he was far too curious about her to deny the request. "Come inside."

Jonathan led her up the stairs and held the door open for her. It slapped shut behind him and she yelped. That screen door had been tricky for ages, but Jonathan never fixed it. He preferred the moment's warning of an intruder, and with his neck deep in bandit affairs, he had no intention of ever repairing it.

With a quick swipe of a mug from the shelf, Jonathan scooped up fresh water from the basin. The rusty-haired stranger stared at his photos along the mantle.

"You know Verity?" she asked, turning to him.

"Depends on who's asking." Jonathan held out the mug, and she swallowed twice and grimaced. Maybe she was one of Verity's friends. If she couldn't handle water from the well, definitely a city girl. Verity sure got around.

Her fingers played with the mug, tracing the lines in the pottery, as if avoiding another swallow.

"What's wrong with it?" he asked, fighting a lift of his lips in amusement. A city girl on the farm, both entertaining and frustrating.

The stranger swallowed down a few more gulps with a grimace, and she handed him the mug back. "I'm not used to the taste, but thank you."

He was right. A stunningly unusual city girl. He allowed the smallest hint of satisfaction to break through. If guessing her distaste for a beverage entertained him this much, his threshold for stimulation was terribly pathetic. In his defense, besides a shrewd Butch, the bandits were lacking in intelligent life, the workers didn't engage by trade, and the pigs and chickens weren't forthcoming with adequate discussions.

Graham was more frustrating than anything. Verity used to give him a run for his money, but she was gone. He missed her spitfire presence. The house was empty without her.

"Are you Verity's brother?" she asked slowly, as if trying not to misstep.

Jonathan crashed on the couch with a long groaning sigh, relaxing the aching muscles from head to toe. The crops didn't water themselves, so the longer he enjoyed a reprieve, the longer he'd be out working tonight—since he couldn't cancel the next meeting with the bandits. That reminded him. Ruddy should've been by to tell him the mark and time.

"Jonathan?" The stranger asked.

He pulled himself from the heavy worries. "Johnny, if you will."

She smiled and displayed a straight set of inhumanly white teeth. "It's nice to meet you, Johnny. I'm Becca Wagner, and I was saying that I know Verity. That is Verity in the photos, right?" She pointed toward his mantle.

"How are the two of you acquainted?" His sister always found trouble, but he couldn't say he'd met any friend of Verity's who was so unusual or as beautiful as this Becca. Meeting a friend of Verity's was the highlight of his day—or year, more precisely.

"We only met a few weeks ago."

Jonathan stilled. His sister left last December...for the future. Perhaps he knew exactly who Becca was...in a way, and boy was he intrigued. He scratched the scruff of his beard. "Is that so?"

Becca sat on the other end of his couch. "Yeah. She's great. She's sweet and wicked smart."

Jonathan chuckled. "My sister is as sweet as the leftovers in the pig pen, in the best way."

Becca laughed, and a warmth curled inside him. "Forgive me for laughing; that wasn't very nice."

"Then you don't truly know my sister."

"I guess not. She never mentioned a brother."

Verity, who was indeed wicked smart, was sharp enough to keep quiet on anything that might jeopardize her safety. Since she traveled to the future, society would doom her if they knew the truth. Unless…time traveling was normal in the future. Jonathan never wanted to live in a world where people freely traveled through time. He had enough troubles as it was.

"She didn't? That's a shame." Jonathan tilted his head with a smirk and spread his bare arms wide across the backrest of the couch, purposely displaying himself. Becca watched, but she didn't move away. "When Verity lived here, I couldn't get her to close that smart mouth of hers."

"That's not what I meant by smart." Her lips puckered with annoyance.

Jonathan suppressed a chuckle. Now that he thought about it, he missed bickering with his hot-headed sister. "How's she fairing these days?"

"Married, and they have a baby on the way," Becca said wistfully.

Jonathan's brows lifted. Mathew had asked for permission for her hand, but Jonathan never expected his sister to agree to children. "Are you certain this is the same Verity? My sister wasn't the domestic type."

"I'm sure. Dr. McCall even took her to California for their honeymoon before the doctor cut her off from flying." Her hand covered her lips, and her cheeks pinked. "Oops."

Jonathan smiled. "If I got you chatting long enough, I wagered you'd slip. So what year are you from?"

The woman's eyes widened. "What? How…? How did you know? Are you supposed to know?"

His chest puffed with his deduction skills. "Verity's rollers can't create your hairstyle. Trust me, Mom tried every which way to make a new hairstyle, and those curls can't happen, but after Verity visited from the future—same curls as yours. And your clothes stick out terribly. Finally, you said you met my sister three weeks ago. She left with Matt seven months ago."

"Verity visited you with fancy hair and clothes?"

"She showed me proof she traveled to the future. I didn't really believe her until you appeared at my back door. I know all the women here, and you...stand out."

"Well, I guess that makes my job easier," Becca said.

He was afraid she'd arrived for a reason. Jonathan remembered the trouble Verity was in before her rescuer appeared. Jonathan frowned. He didn't need a rescuer. He had everything in control, but he caught himself checking the front door.

"Is something wrong?" she asked. "You seem distracted."

"I'm expecting someone."

Ruddy had never missed coming over to announce the mark. What if something finally happened to the bandits? He didn't want to stay with them, and his gut told him he'd be relieved if they were all arrested. But what if the sheriff came for him next? And how would he keep the farm afloat? If the bandits were through, he didn't know what he would do.

"Oh, I think I met him along my way," Becca said.

Jonathan's brows rose. "A red-haired man?"

The woman cringed. "Yeah, with less-than-desirable teeth."

"Ruddy." So he wasn't arrested. Then what was taking so long?

"That was the name," Becca said.

"Did he say anything to you?"

"He had a message for you, but…" She trailed off, and frustration flickered beneath his skin.

"But what?" That came out harsher than he'd planned, but it was too late now.

Becca flinched. "But…I…need you to do me a favor first." She hesitated as if hatching the plan as the words fell out.

Jonathan's eyes roamed her body, and he thought she might have a nice shape under that outfit. If she was offering, he wouldn't say no after all this time and all those rejections. But withholding information was dangerous. "Interfering with Ruddy's affairs is not wise." And Jonathan's patience was torn to shreds by the time Verity was twelve years old. "What's this favor?"

"The sheriff is going to ask you something, and I need you to agree."

Jonathan scoffed and stood. Because Becca was from the future, what she told him to do was important, just like when Mathew saved Verity, because the city boy knew what was going to happen. The problem was Sheriff Clint Nelson was almost as crooked as the bandits, but no match for their strength and cunning. Jonathan stole a glance out the front window, as if expecting his untimely arrival. "What does that two-faced bastard want with me?"

"He's going to ask you to do something you don't want to do, but trust me when I tell you, it's imperative that you accept his deal."

Jonathan wiped a hand down his face, pausing at his chin. "Do you know what he's going to ask?"

Becca stood. Her eyes glistened with tears threatening to spill. "All I know is, if you don't take the deal…" she trailed off and glanced at the floor.

Oh, hell. He hated to see a lady cry. Instinctually, Jonathan embraced her. Her warm body pressed against his bare chest, and a once dormant feeling woke low in his groin. He hadn't held a woman for so long, he'd almost forgotten the sensation. But a new one occurred: gushing heat filled his chest with a protective need. She was the harbinger of his future. She alone held the answer to fixing his mess and getting out alive. He would do anything to keep her safe.

Becca's hair was softer than he could've ever imagined, and it brought floral scents to his nose he couldn't pinpoint. But there was something else.

Chocolate?

Cinnamon?

Whatever it was told Jonathan she lived a life of luxury, far beyond the manual labor of a farm. A small corner of his heart was disappointed. After every available woman in town rejected him, he never expected to get this close to someone, but she was still so far away.

Becca's arms wrapped around his middle, and she pressed her open palms against his back.

Jonathan closed his eyes, memorizing the feel and smell of her. "You can tell me the rest. I can handle it."

Becca inhaled a ragged deep breath, and her breasts pressed against his chest. Jonathan smothered his desire.

"If you don't take the deal, you'll be publicly hung for banditry," she finished.

That sounded...unfortunate. "That's not a thing."

"It is. I asked."

He didn't know what to do with that information. "Is there anything else you can tell me?"

She sniffled. "That's all I was told."

Jonathan chuckled at the lack of usefulness in her dire warning.

Becca pulled out of his arms. "It's not funny."

"That's not a fearsome threat, and ultimately not enough information to guide me. No one's been hung since, well, Gabriel Grignon almost two years ago."

Her chin trembled with a fresh wave of tears.

Jonathan pressed her against his chest, and she sagged against him. He wanted to reassure her that unlikely vision was even more unlikely to come to pass. "Have you taken a look out back? There are many ways to die on the farm at any given moment."

"I'm trying to save your life. Why would you say something like that?"

Jonathan was curious why she was so upset about it. Nothing happened yet, and she was a complete stranger, but questioning her emotions wouldn't end well. That much he was familiar with.

"I'm trying to ease your fears." Jonathan rubbed her back, and after every so many circles, he tugged her shirt back down. At once she dropped as if her knees gave out, and he caught her and maneuvered her to the couch where they sat together. She continued to cry, now with her face buried in her hands. Something else was upsetting her.

Becca lifted the hem of her shirt and cleaned her face. "I'm so sorry about this."

Stretch marks similar to his mother's covered her belly, but Jonathan daren't ask. "People in the future are built differently than we are. No need to apologize. I'm sure it's normal."

"Normal? I would hope not. Oh, this isn't helping." Becca sniffled and scrubbed her face. Gray tint streaked from her eyes down her cheeks.

Curious, his finger touched and wiped at it. It didn't come off.

"Oh, no. I must look like a raccoon!" She buried her face back into her shirt and scrubbed really hard.

"It's not that bad." His hands persuaded her to stop and she did. Jonathan glanced at his clean fingertip. "What is it?"

A small smile lifted her lips. "Mascara."

And...he was blank on that one. "Is that good or bad?"

She chuckled, and he was relieved to have coaxed her away from her troubles. "Neither."

Jonathan frowned.

"It's just makeup. Waterproof, yeah, right. So, you'll take the deal?"

"Uh…"

"Please. You must! I beg you."

He didn't want her to spiral out of control again. If Jonathan refused the deal, he'd be hung for it, so what choice did he really have? "I'll take the sheriff's mysterious deal."

She faced him with her gray streaks, red nose, and puffy eyes. She was a kind soul, but suffering from bouts of hysteria, though, unfortunately.

"You will?" Minty breath puffed against his face.

"I promise."

"Ruddy's message was 'Tim's Fish Market at the usual time'," she said.

Jonathan crossed the room and read the small mantle clock. He was late. "I have to go."

Becca stood. "I'm going with you."

"No."

"What do you mean 'no'? I have to make sure everything works out all right."

The harbinger of his future needed to stay safe. "I can handle this myself. You can wait here."

"Wait here? I'm not a child."

"If you were a child, you'd be out there working."

Becca's mouth dropped open. "That sounds like illegal child labor where I come from."

"Well, around here, children are the labor. Where do you think many of the farm workers come from? Mom and Dad."

His eyes moved down to her marked belly, but he didn't mean for it to happen. She stepped back, and her face burned red. Now it matched her nose.

Jonathan stalked into his bedroom, and at a shadow, he turned around with trousers around his ankles to find Becca in the door frame. "If you wanted to watch, you could've just asked." He flung the trousers off.

Her eyes followed him as he picked them up, folded them, and placed them on the bed. She said nothing.

"I'm not a prude, but do you mind?" He stood in front of her wearing nothing but his drawers and socks, and an ankle holster.

"I don't mind at all." Her breaths were soft gasps, and she peeled her eyes off his body. "We aren't done discussing this."

"I distinctly remember we are." Jonathan slipped into clean trousers—he wasn't about to change out of his drawers with her watching—and shoved his feet into boots. He stuffed his head into a shirt, grabbed a vest, and flung it over his shoulders while marching outside. His hands worked the buttons as he crossed the yard to the stable. The stubborn woman followed him.

"Wait. You can't leave me here."

"Too late."

"I am going with you."

"Can you ride?" Jonathan asked while mounting up.

She bit her lower lip. "Probably."

"That's not good enough, City."

She'd get herself killed, and he couldn't let that happen. She was too far out of her league here.

Chapter 10

Jonathan trotted his horse, leaving Becca behind in a cloud of dust, and she grunted in frustration, fists straining at her sides. A deep desire curled through her to prove the stubborn man wrong. She was capable, and she didn't trust his promise. How could she? She didn't know him. If Becca screwed up again, she had only one chance left to save his life. Since she already carried the crushing guilt of a life she couldn't save, Becca couldn't handle having two losses on her hands.

Becca needed to be there to make sure everything went to plan.

She chose the first saddled horse and climbed up, only stumbling once. Just like riding a bike, right? With the animal between her legs, she kicked it with her sneakers to give chase. It didn't move. She growled and squeezed the reins. She shook them, but it still didn't move. Left and right was easy. Stopping was simply a tug. How did she get this moron horse to move forward without spurs? Last she rode, she was a little girl with her grandmother guiding the horse, and

Nana never took her hands off the reins. Becca kicked at the horse's flanks with her sneakers repeatedly, and finally, it lazily walked forward.

Becca guided the horse to the front yard where she found the sheriff talking to Jonathan. Both were mounted, and their horses shook their tails, swatting at flies. She stopped her horse by the men. Jonathan's shoulders were tense, and the sheriff wore a frown under his hat. She didn't see any weapons or shackles. Yet.

She wasn't too late, but this was cutting it far too close for her comfort.

"...your parents were fine, hardworking, honest fellows. Rest their souls. And it's out of respect for the Arris's that I'm going to—" Sheriff paused and stared at her. "Hello there, miss. Can I help you?" His eyes roamed her body, and it made her twitch. She was in no mood for that shit.

Becca lifted her chin and said, "I'm here to help Johnny."

The sheriff's brows rose. "Is that so?"

"No, she's not," Jonathan cut in. "She's not involved. Becca was visiting and now she's leaving." He darted her a look that said to stay quiet. The harder he pushed, the more fire burned inside her.

"He's wrong," Becca said to the sheriff. Like hell she would be cast aside. At the bare minimum she had to confirm he would agree to the deal—or beg him to agree all over again. "I'm here for Johnny's business."

Jonathan made a noise, but the Sheriff eyed him with warning.

"And how exactly are you a part in all this?" Sheriff asked slowly, raking his eyes over her body again. "A woman...is unusual."

Becca released the tension in her jaw. "I delivered Ruddy's message for the meeting place today."

Jonathan groaned and dragged a hand over his face.

"Is that so?" The sheriff perked up. That couldn't be good. "I don't have criminals admittin' their association often, but in that case, I have a deal for both of you."

Oops.

"Sheriff, she doesn't know what she's saying," Jonathan said through gritted teeth. He cast her a squinted glare as if commanding her to butt out. Not a chance.

The sheriff eyed Jonathan with suspicion, and the old man's gaze shifted to her. Becca shivered even as the summer heat dripped down her chest.

"Sounds like the lady knows English well enough, so I need you both to deliver the bandits' home base location to me. If you're willin' to tell me now, you can save me some trouble."

"I don't know where it is," Jonathan said.

"I figured as much. In exchange for your cooperation, I won't arrest either of you for banditry. Do we have a deal?"

Before Jonathan could open his stubborn mouth, Becca answered, "Yes! It's a deal. We'll do it, Sheriff."

Jonathan glared at her with burning rage. Since he'd promised to agree anyway, he had no right to be angry, but Becca was satisfied. Her objective in this wild mission was completed.

After a beat, Jonathan shook his head, and his tone was much softer than she expected. Resigned, perhaps? "We'll do it."

"You got two days. After that, I'm coming with the shackles, 'cause I don't like turn tails. You hear?"

Jonathan cast her a warning glare. Becca was satisfied, so she kept quiet. "Understood."

Sheriff nodded and turned his horse around. Becca waited, not knowing what to do next, and Jonathan waited with her.

His jaw clenched and thick cords of muscle twitched with strain. When Sheriff was reasonably out of earshot, Jonathan said, "You don't know what you just did."

"Yes, I do. I made sure you couldn't renege our deal to accept his deal."

"When I give my word, I mean it. Now if I can't—"

"We," she cut in, feistiness curling her lips.

His jaw clenched harder. "If I fail to discover the bandits' base in two days' time, we'll both be arrested. I could break out of the sheriff's cell, but I can't guarantee I could get us both out."

"No, you wouldn't have," Becca said, remembering the article she'd read.

"Wouldn't have what?" His tone was sharp.

Becca flinched. Her mood tumbled from feisty to despair. She inhaled an uneven breath and slowly released it, fighting a repeat of her earlier meltdown. At least they were coming less often now. "You wouldn't have escaped," she said carefully. "Like I already explained, if the sheriff arrests you, you'll be hung. I read the article with my own eyes. It happened, and that's what I'm here to prevent. You have to take this seriously."

Jonathan ran a hand through his dark wavy hair, the anger draining from him too. "You believe all this?"

"I do."

Jonathan sighed. "Is there any way I can convince you to stay here?"

Jonathan had accepted the deal, but if he didn't find and deliver the information the sheriff wanted in two days, he'd still be arrested. She couldn't go home yet, but the idea of being alone in a stranger's house in a foreign century, while depending on Jonathan to go undercover in a pack of savage bandits was not happening. Trust was earned. "Zero chance."

He gestured with his head to move out to the road, and Becca suppressed a victory smile. "Let's go. I'm—we're already late. I wouldn't be surprised if we meet Ruddy on the way. Butch isn't a patient man."

"What would happen if you don't show up?"

Jonathan cast her a look that said the idea was unthinkable.

"I mean hypothetically," she added. "Of course we need the location."

"No one has ever left the bandits and lived."

"Anyone trying to turn honest is killed for it?" A breeze cooled the sweat on her back, and a shiver slithered down her spine. With the unbelievable trip Kiko had sent her on, the seriousness of the situation hadn't sunk in. Becca sought the transponder gizmo in her pocket for reassurance. If things became too intense, she could always pop back home, and try again. The next time, better prepared.

"If we canter the horses, we can be at the location in half an hour." Jonathan smirked for a second before vanishing down the road.

Oh, if that was his trick, no way was he getting away with it. Becca knew where Tim's was. She only needed to get her horse to move faster. Becca kicked it with her sneakers, and it walked. Becca groaned in frustration. She kicked it harder. "Let's go. Catch up to him, you lazy—"

A laugh stopped the less-than-pleasant stream about to pour from her mouth. A teenage boy dismounted, walked over to her, and grasped control of her horse. "Having trouble with the mare?"

"I can't get her to canter. I need to catch up to Johnny."

The boy looked her up and down, assessing her, and Becca resigned herself to all men doing it here. She should be flattered, but she was annoyed. Her clothes weren't that strange. The boy—upper teens—was a spitting image of Jonathan, but thinner and less lined with youth. A dark mop of unruly hair was longer than Jonathan's, but they shared the same piercing green eyes—the same as Verity's, too. "I'm Graham, Johnny's brother. Who are you?"

"Becca Wagner. I'm, uh, a friend of Johnny's."

"And yet, he left you." Graham shook his head with a friendly smile. "Sounds like Johnny. He can be an asshole."

Heat rose in Becca's cheeks. "I led on that I could ride better than I can." Why was she defending Jonathan's actions? Graham was right—Jonathan ditched her.

"Here. Angle your foot like... Those are weird shoes. No wonder she won't move for you. Here, one second." Graham rummaged in the saddlebags of his horse and returned with horrifically medieval spurs, unlike the modern nubs she was used to seeing. "You need a pair of these."

"Thanks." Becca had to be careful with them.

He slipped the straps over her shoes and tightened them secure. "Now give her a gentle jab. If the horse gets spooked though, it will be uncontrollable for a short while. Just hang on and try to steer. Best if you avoid spooking her."

A lump settled in her gut. "Uh, thanks."

"Give her a practice jab, and I'll watch until you're out of sight." Graham mounted up behind her.

"Thank you for your help, really."

"If you've got a sister, send her my way." He wagged his brows and clicked his tongue in a playful manner.

She rolled her eyes. "I'll keep you in mind."

Becca braced herself firmly on the saddle, gripped the reins securely, and gave a careful tap to the horse's underbelly with her shiny spur. The horse moved. That was a start.

"Little harder, and she'll go nice for you," Graham called.

Becca nodded and followed instructions. The horse bolted into a gallop, and Becca used all her lower body strength to stay in the saddle. Her heart thundered in her chest while the hooves pounded the ground. The wind blew her hair away from her face and plastered her shirt firmly to her chest. Paralyzed with fear, Becca couldn't turn her head to see if Graham was going to save her. Instead, she watched the road and awaited the intersection with dread.

As the crisscrossed dirt roads appeared, Becca pulled on the reins to slow down, but the mare didn't. Becca pulled harder and used coaxing words. Finally, the horse slowed enough to make the turn. She tugged the reins to the left and the horse complied.

This wasn't so hard. Not like riding a bicycle, though.

Chest puffed with pride, she kicked the mare back up to speed while heading north on Broadway. She had a long way to go to catch up to Jonathan.

Graham was a cute kid, sweet, too—just like Verity, so why was Jonathan so difficult?

Becca weaved through traffic—slower moving trailers pulled by oxen and some by draft horses, leisure riders, and some men that appeared to be going to or from work. No one paid her any unusual attention, but she was only focused on the path ahead.

Soon enough, she reached Tim's Fish Market, and unfortunately, she found a pile of waiting horses. She couldn't tell one from another, so she only assumed Jonathan was already inside with the others. Becca dismounted, thankful to be on solid ground again, and cautiously walked up to the door frame and peeked inside.

Well, shit.

Chapter 11

After the ear-piercing metal clanging of hammers breaking into the cash register, and the bandits having raided every cent they could find, Jonathan was grateful he'd left Becca behind. She didn't need to see this—the relentless pursuit of riches, and the utter terror of the shop owner. At any moment, one wrong move by Timmy, and he'd earn himself a new hole. Becca, the woman from the future, didn't belong among these cretins. And despite the sheriff's warning hanging over both their heads, Jonathan was going to take care of his mess, and leave Becca far from it.

With Tim Van Cook emptied of his valuables, Butch gave the orders to vacate the premises. Nash and Ruddy, sweaty with the effort, moved to the exit.

"That's enough, Brawley. Let's go," Butch said.

"Awe shucks, boss. I wasn't—hey, there, pretty lady." Brawley dropped a cloth garment of some sort and fixed his gaze at the entrance.

Jonathan turned to find Becca standing in the doorway, shaking like a leaf in an envious summer breeze. How did she know Tim's location? Without hesitation, Jonathan intercepted Brawley's approach and said the only thing that came to mind. "She's with me."

Brawley's features darkened. "Says who?"

Timmy blubbered behind the counter, but Jonathan ignored him, muscles tensing with Brawley's challenge. Jonathan looked down his nose and puffed his chest a little further. "Says me."

Brawley wasn't nearly the size of Jonathan, but the man was still quick and deadly—especially because the wheels in Brawley's head were more lopsided than round, leaving him with a lack of compassion for human life. The diminutive challenger stood sure-footed.

"I said let's go," Butch ordered on his way out. "I won't tell you again."

Obedient Fingers followed him.

Brawley relaxed his stance, and tipped his head toward Becca on his way out, leaving Jonathan and Becca alone with Tim.

"How...How did you stand up to him like that?" Tim sniffled and stood on gangly legs.

Timid Tim had everything—a family, a successful business, and a warm home, while Jonathan had nothing but a failing farm and a disrespectful little brother. Even still, Jonathan would fight for it with every fiber of his being. He tried to hide his disgust when he said, "You have to protect what's yours or it will be taken. The bandits aren't going anywhere anytime soon. Prepare yourself."

Tim nodded.

Jonathan led Becca outside by the arm. "Mount up," he said in her ear and caught a whiff of her cinnamon scent. A tremble rolled through him. As much as she should be far from these ruffians, he had to admit, her following him took courage.

"Your share," Butch said and tossed a bag at him. Jonathan caught it and stuffed it into his vest pocket without bothering to inspect the earnings. Becca had forced his hand to agree to the sheriff's precarious deal, and now he had to comply to keep her alive. After that, he'd figure out how to keep himself alive. His failing farm was a problem for another day.

"We'll see you tomorrow." Butch dismissed him.

The bandit leader had never done that before. Was Becca the reason?

Jonathan sent her a silent message to stay silent. He knew what he had to do, even if he didn't like it. "We're prepared to come with tonight."

Butch cocked a brow at him. "We?"

"Becca and I are a two-for-one deal now, if that's acceptable to you," Jonathan added.

The corner of Becca's lips lifted, and she turned her face away. He liked that shyness she had. It contrasted nicely with the bullheadedness. Toss in a sprinkle of hysteria, and she was an interesting mix.

"Less to go around. The woman gets a smaller cut."

Becca's mouth dropped open to protest, but Butch continued before she could rebuke, "The Astor House. Saddle up, boys."

Jonathan hoped for Becca's sake The Astor House was empty. That poor hostess Lizzy had to deal with the bandits at least three times a year, and fingers-crossed she hadn't wised up and armed herself. A bloody shootout flashed before his eyes, and Jonathan shook his head to clear the dreadful images. The trip to the neighboring village was going to take an hour.

He helped Becca into the mare's saddle and leaned in close by her thigh. "We'll be going back the way we came, almost an hour's ride."

Becca's face scrunched. "Where is The Astor House?"

"Near Mason Street, not far beyond the farmer's market. If you get hungry, we can find something there, assuming you can handle..." Jonathan trailed off, unable to tell her about the bandits' hijinks at night—half since he hadn't experienced them firsthand, and half because he didn't want to scare her. But dammit, she shouldn't be in direct danger.

"I can handle the ride," she said smugly.

It was best she didn't know. Jonathan tapped her thigh in acknowledgement. The contact surged heat through his body, and at once he'd rather be back at his farmhouse with his hands further exploring her thighs than in the midst of these animals. But for now, they were both trapped.

Jonathan mounted up. Fingers struggled into his saddle. Nash and Ruddy finished packing their confiscated goods and mounted up, too. Butch gestured for the group to move out.

Jonathan and Becca hung at the back of the pack for the lazy journey south. The hooves clomped with a dull rhythmic melody. Fat Finger's mount lifted a tail and defecated on the road in front of them, so Jonathan steered his mount closer to Becca to avoid his horse stepping in it, and to avoid the stench directly shooting him in the nose.

Becca scrunched her face at the sight, and Jonathan laughed. As quick as it started, he clamped his mouth shut. No one turned their heads back to see what the fuss was about. The less attention, the better.

"How long have you been working for these guys?" she asked him.

"I don't work for them."

"Seems like you do." Despite the circumstances, a playful tone danced through her statement.

"I work with them."

"Semantics. Why?"

"For the same reason why any of them work together." Jonathan had no intention of elaborating.

She added, "And that is?"

He paused, considering how much he wanted to say. He went with the obvious. "Money."

"I guess that makes sense."

Jonathan turned his head toward her. "How so?"

"Greed is what drives people to do terrible things. So, it makes sense that a group of men are robbing people solely for money."

Intrigued by the inferred point, he asked, "As opposed to what?"

"Oh, let's see, there's the whole Robin Hood concept—steal from the rich to give to the poor, sick, or injured. You know, to help others, like struggling widows, incapacitated men, people on the verge of homelessness, businesses on the verge of closing. That would be at least a little honorable."

He wouldn't admit he fell into her selfless categories—Jonathan wasn't a beggar—but he certainly didn't feel honorable.

"Hmmm," she added after a pause.

"What does that mean?"

"You didn't admit a greater purpose, so that leads me to conclude you are in the greedy group."

Not that he should care at all, but her words angered him. They were too similar to Graham's, and that kid didn't know anything about how the world worked. "I'm only getting paid for helping Butch and his crew. That's it. A wage for a job."

Becca scoffed. "You keep telling yourself that."

He didn't appreciate having his convictions questioned, so he gave her a piece of her own judgment. "How's the air up there? For someone so high on their horse, I'd expect you to have breathing problems."

"What does that mean?"

"Since you're so quick to judge, what is your job's noble cause?"

Becca's face pinched, and Jonathan felt a stab of satisfaction.

"Thought so," he said.

"Hey, now. I might not have a noble cause, but I do selfless work."

"And what's that?"

She bit her lip in an enticing way. Add saucy to her list of traits, and by the minute he was becoming more captivated with her, despite her unusual shortcomings.

"I'm a veterinary assistant. Well, I was...until I quit."

That profession sounded familiar, and Jonathan was going to impress her. "You check in patients and use something with credit cards?"

Becca's eyes widened. "How did you know?"

A smug smile tugged his lips. "Verity explained it to me when she visited. So why did you quit this noble cause?"

If steam were visible on a smoldering July afternoon, it would've risen from her head. "I help defenseless animals."

"I can't name any defenseless animals. Even deer will challenge you at the right time. Badgers are nasty fellows. The pigs—stay away from the pigs unless you want to be eaten. How's that noble again?"

"Once again, we have another case of male selective hearing. I said 'selfless'. You know, helping others. You should try it sometime. It might warm the cockles of your heart."

Jonathan hadn't heard that term before. Even though he didn't want to give her the satisfaction of explaining something to him, he also didn't want to be insulted without understanding. "Selective hearing?"

"Since I don't believe it's a clinical condition, in your case it refers to being selfish—only hearing what you want and ignoring the rest."

"I was listening. Perhaps your explanations need to be clearer," Jonathan said, an edge of irritation to his tone.

Becca grunted in exasperation, and Jonathan smiled at his perceived success. Was this a game? He didn't know, but it was fun to rile her up.

"I'm done talking to you," she declared.

"Good, because we're there."

All the bandits stopped and dismounted on the front lawn of The Astor House. There were only a couple horses tied up, unusually quiet, and with the sun kissing the horizon, only their reflection shone on the windows of the lobby.

"Nash and Ruddy, lookout," Butch ordered. "Fingers and Brawley, come with me. And you two"—he looked at him and Becca—"come in armed."

Becca stared at Jonathan with fear in her eyes.

Great, just great.

Chapter 12

Becca craned her neck at the glory of The Astor House. She'd heard of it, since the name was being used for a bed and breakfast in her present-day city, but not at the original location nor the original building. If she remembered correctly, this gorgeous estate would burn down in three years' time. Such a shame. It was a glistening white three-story building, a splendor to behold. The two upper floors had rows of identical windows bearing grass-green blinds. A pair of matching chimneys anchored the ends, and a cupola crowned the top center with a weather vane at its peak. The ground floor was nearly all glass, exposing the inside to the passing world—but with the evening's reflection, it only showed the bandits—filthy, armed, and pungent—and Becca, in a cream blouse and black skirt pants. One thing was not like the others.

Jonathan was armed and gritty like them, but that was where the similarities ended. He was distinguished, healthy, muscular and…ruggedly sexy. To her, he was a non-cowboy cowboy, and none of the bandits fit those descriptors.

She slipped off her borrowed mare and held the reins while the men dispersed around her, headed toward their assignments. What did Butch mean when he said to follow him 'armed'?

Becca didn't do guns.

She didn't have guns.

A baseball bat might've been nice, though.

Jonathan approached her quietly. The playful banter of their ride was now gone, and Jonathan's demeanor darkened. Was it disgust or anger? He clearly didn't want her to be here, but with Jonathan carrying a shotgun at her side, she could handle this, whatever 'this' was. Jonathan gave her a leather pouch with a handle sticking out—a knife. Or maybe not. "What do you want me to do with this?"

"Hopefully, nothing. If you feel the need to use it, then do so without hesitation. Pointy end is inside the pouch." He pointed. He actually pointed to the dangerous end. Ass.

His underestimation only gave her opportunities to impress him. She kind of liked that idea. "Thanks, Captain Obvious."

Jonathan's face twisted. "Who?"

"It's nothing." Becca cracked a smile.

Jonathan remained serious. "For the next several minutes, I am your captain. Do as I say, and we'll make it out of there in one piece."

"Wait. I was there for the end of Tim's armed robbery. No one got hurt. What do you mean 'in one piece'?"

His hand squeezed her shoulder, and he looked her dead in the eye. "I told you to stay at the farm. Since you're here, I need you to take this seriously."

Becca's brows furrowed at his using her words against her. She was taking this seriously; she just didn't realize how dire the circumstances were, but she couldn't back out now. Literally, if she took Jonathan's warning about leaving the bandits seriously, which she was. "You know why I'm here," she hissed.

"Hey, City" he said gently. "Let's get through this first. We can argue about it later."

"Let's move! Ain't got all day," Butch called to no one in particular, while he and Fingers entered the hotel. Nash and Ruddy took off in different directions on horseback.

Jonathan waved for her to follow him, and just like that, fear took over. Becca's trembling hands carried the leather pouch concealing a blade larger than a butcher knife.

Butcher...Butch. She wondered how the leader had gotten his name, and just as quickly she determined she never wanted to find out. What the hell had she gotten herself into? Okay, mental check. If things got ugly for her, she could whisk herself safely back home. But what about Jonathan? Could she see him hurt? Could she watch him die?

Could she leave him after he'd been wounded to save herself?

She didn't want to find that out either.

Crossing the threshold, Jonathan led the way like a human shield. Becca entered with squared shoulders. A whiff of dusty fabrics and vanilla entered her nose—reminding her of a funeral home. She shivered, her courage dissolving.

The hostess, wearing a plain green dress with an ivory bonnet, stood behind a lacquered reception desk, hands up in surrender. Fingers held her at gunpoint. Brawley attacked an old solid metal cash register. A hammer clanged with each strike. And Butch watched the robbery with a rifle casually resting at his side. There was no one else in the lobby besides her and Jonathan. No Ruddy, no Nash, and definitely no witnesses. Becca's stomach clenched.

Jonathan's advice for Tim came to mind. If everyone knew who the bandits were, why didn't they arm themselves?

"Johnny, you and the woman mind the doors," Butch ordered.

Jonathan nodded, keeping his attention split between the happenings in the lobby and the door behind them.

Brawley stilled the hammer and panted. He swiped an arm across his filthy forehead. "Boss, think we could get the woman to open it for us?"

The hostess lightly gasped and said, "I'm not opening it. If you want the money, you have to take it yourself."

Why wouldn't she open it? Didn't insurance exist yet? And where the hell was everyone else—a boss, an owner, or other employees? Becca couldn't imagine this woman owning and running this place by herself, but if that was the case, her admiration for the woman increased at the same rate as her fear for her.

"Well, that's a shame." Butch lifted the barrel of his rifle and fired into the wood wall behind the hostess. She startled.

Becca's hand went to Jonathan's shoulder, who stood partially blocking her view. She fought to keep her stomach contents contained.

Butch added, "Do you change your mind, Lizzy?"

Becca wanted to march up to Butch, sock him in the nose, and yell at everyone to leave, but she was no hero. Butch would shoot her for stepping out of line. The hostess, Lizzy, flicked her gaze to each person in the hotel lobby. The room was thick with the silence. Who was going to make the next move?

Becca squeezed the knife pouch and felt for the button to free the strap.

Lizzy nodded, agreeing with Butch's shotgun, and her hands moved to the register.

Brawley's lips pulled into a wide grin, bearing a few missing teeth, and he rubbed his hands together. Fingers and Butch didn't move. They kept their eyes on the hostess.

Becca checked behind her to see if anyone was coming through the front door, and the coast was clear. There was no sign of Nash or Ruddy yet. Was that a good thing?

Metal buttons clicked on the register, and Lizzy bent to finish whatever the process was. A quick metal sliding noise echoed in the open lobby, and before anyone could process what was happening, a loud bang shook the room.

Brawley stumbled back.

Lizzy stood up and a second loud bang shook Becca to the core. Lizzy dropped down out of sight, and not for cover.

Becca clapped a hand over her mouth to stop from screaming, and Jonathan pushed her further back from the danger, shielding her with his body. She had to see just what the bandits were capable of. Becca leaned for a better view.

Brawley hunched over with his hands clasping his middle. He shuffled toward Butch. Lizzy still hadn't reappeared.

"Where...where is she?" Becca whispered into Jonathan's ear. Sweat and leather entered her nose while he stood so close. She didn't allow herself a moment to enjoy it.

Jonathan gestured with his head toward the desk, but Becca wasn't brave enough to go investigate.

Brawley collapsed near Butch's feet. "Boss, this ain't good. I can't feel my feet." He lifted a hand, and it was smeared in blood. A sob escaped his lips. "Shit. Oh, shit. Butch. This ain't good at all."

"You've done a good job for me, so I'm gifting you mercy." Butch swung the muzzle of his rifle toward Brawley, and Becca sucked in a breath. They weren't going to try to save him? The next bang shook the walls.

Becca turned away. Her nostrils filled with gunpowder, and she fought tears and the need to break down and sob.

Butch's boots thumped against the hardwood as he left without another word. Fingers followed with creaking floorboards. A few minutes later, Nash and Ruddy came inside.

"Think we can crack this one?" Ruddy asked.

"Ain't no different than all the others. Give 'er a few swings, and she'll pop open like a whore's legs," Nash said.

Ruddy inspected the register. "I don't know. Somethin' about this plate here, don't look normal to me."

"Huh?" Nash leaned over and wrinkled his nose, inspecting the offending plate. He made a dismissive noise. "Gimme two minutes. Count 'em."

Ruddy smiled and shook his head. "I don't have a pocket watch."

"So count then, dummy."

"Hey, who you callin' dummy?" Ruddy said, genuinely offended.

"I'm lookin' at 'im."

The two men stared each other down.

A red pool flowed from under Brawley, and Becca gasped in disgust instinctually.

Nash and Ruddy turned to her.

Jonathan's shoulders tensed. "Need help getting the register open?" Jonathan asked, as if redirecting their attention.

Nash's face darkened. "Are you questionin' my ability to do my job?"

"No, not at all," Jonathan said.

"'Cause you need to watch this." Nash spit into his hands and rubbed them together. Palming a hammer, he smacked the register. It clanged with the metal on metal noise, and Becca cringed.

"I'm watching," Jonathan taunted. What was he doing?

Nash glared at Jonathan.

Ruddy lifted his hammer and said, "I'm gonna get it open before you do."

Nash's attention returned to his partner. "Put your money where your mouth is."

Ruddy nodded, grinning. Together they smacked the register a handful of times, until it finally belched its surrender. Coins jingled as the men emptied the machine.

"Showed you," Nash yelled with excitement. Pockets full, he went in search of something behind the desk and stopped, staring down at the floor.

Becca's fear swirled again. She grasped Jonathan's shirt, and his hand covered hers.

"Oh, lookie here, Ruddy. A fresh one." Nash rubbed his hands together, and a wicked smile crossed his lips.

Ruddy paused his collecting and stared at the floor too. "That's a damn shame. I've low standards myself, but even I wouldn't enjoy the pleasure of a woman after she's dead."

"Well, I don't know. I like it better when they don't fight any," Nash tipped his hat and scratched his head, letting gravity drop it back into place.

"Remember what happened last time? We got what we came for. Let's go," Ruddy said.

"I suppose you're right. We don't want Butch's wrath."

Satisfied, they dragged Brawley by the feet on their way outside. A bright red trail of blood followed the body, and Becca gagged.

Jonathan's hand rubbed her back. "Are you going to make it?"

After a few deep breaths and slow releases, Becca answered, "I think so."

Jonathan's bright green eyes were fixed on her, an unmistakable lusty glare. He shifted his body to hover over her, backing her against the wall and protecting her from the carnage. His thick arms caged her in. He leaned in and whispered, "You shouldn't have seen that. I'm sorry, but you understand when I said this was serious?"

She wasn't bantering now. Becca nodded.

Jonathan's eyes flicked from hers to her mouth. "I don't want to never have done this," he said.

"Done what?" she asked, now feeling a confusing surge of lust for the sexy man protecting her from a life-and-death situation. Her heart pummeled her ribcage. She couldn't think of anything but his lips and the touch and feel of him.

Becca's hands reached up and touched his jaw, and a quiet moan escaped his lips. Heat rushed through her body. The trimmed scruff was softer than she'd expected. "Done what?" she repeated on a whisper.

"This." And just like that, he closed the distance.

Jonathan captured her lips slowly, a single gentle press, and then he gazed into her eyes, seeking the response she was willing to give.

More, she silently pleaded.

After the pause, he moved in again, another gentle but stronger kiss. Becca's body lit with an electric current, sending delicious throbbing waves down below begging to be released. As he kissed her harder, learning her movements, her breathing became shallow. She wanted more, but Jonathan pulled away.

She opened her eyes and gazed into his sad features. Was the kiss because he wanted to taste her, or because...he worried they wouldn't survive the night? Neither of those possibilities was reassuring.

"We need to go," he said.

The hotel was silent and empty. Except... "What about Lizzy?"

Jonathan spoke gently, "There's nothing we can do. Let's go."

Becca nodded in understanding, and Jonathan helped her out the door.

Butch tossed a bag of coins to Jonathan, and he caught it with a quick strike. Blood money. Jonathan helped her mount up, and he pressed the coins into her hands.

"I don't want this." She held them out toward him.

"Take it. You might need it."

"A woman died for this money. I don't want it."

Jonathan's jaw clenched. "Listen, I don't like it any more than you do, but this is survival, and you might need the money."

"What for? You're with me."

"We have to find their home base. I don't know where it is or how it's outfitted. Or how long we have to continue with them until we get there. You might need money as a bargaining chip. Understand?"

Becca shivered and glanced at each of the filthy disgusting animals around them. Especially Nash. He was wretched in the worst way. Becca didn't like taking the money, but this was survival, like he said. How were the bandits getting away with murder and robbery? "What about the sheriff, a police department, or a mayor? Isn't there someone we can call?" Reluctantly she put the coins in her pocket. They felt cold and heavy—a dirty reminder of what happened.

"The mayor hasn't been around for a couple years. Heresay is he sailed to Chicago, but before he left on his voyage, he tasked the sheriff as judge, jury, and executioner. Since the sheriff was in bed with Jaime Perez, he's been unable to amass an effective force, and he can't take the bandits down alone, which is why we're here."

Becca exhaled a deep breath. "How do you people live like this?"

"Like what?" Jonathan asked softly, as if surprised or hurt by her revulsion.

Fingers spoke over everyone. "Brawley needs a burial before he gets ripe."

"Everyone back to base," Butch ordered.

The conjured image of the hostess returned. "What about Lizzy?" When the bandits faced her, Becca regretted saying anything, but for Lizzy's sake, she had to try.

Butch turned on her, a snarl on his face. "What about her?"

Becca's voice was much smaller this time. "Are you going to bury her, too?"

He waved toward the door. "You have my permission."

It was the right thing to do, and no matter how many injured animals she'd seen and helped, there was something different about a person. Becca didn't have anything to assist, and she couldn't save her. A woman killed in cold blood. The guilt was too much to bear. Becca didn't move. She glanced at the ground in shame.

"Then let's go," Butch added and directed his horse north.

Fingers rode up next to the leader, while Nash and Ruddy formed a row behind them. Brawley's corpse was tied to the back of Nash's horse.

Becca used her borrowed spur from Graham and nudged her horse into a walk alongside Jonathan, avoiding the bobbing corpse in front of her. All they needed was the location. Then they could escape and be done with this craziness, and she could go home where it was safe.

Chapter 13

From what Jonathan had heard, a life-and-death experience could alter a person's perception of what was important. After Butch slaughtered an innocent woman in front of him and Becca, Jonathan couldn't face down death by her side without knowing the feel of her lips. Jonathan was not disappointed. That was the best kiss he'd had in...as long as he could remember. The sensual softness and that lusty groan she made hardened his cock. But now wasn't the time for such steamy thoughts. He needed to focus.

The horse under him swayed with its lazy steps, following the ruffians north on Broadway, and Jonathan pictured himself putting a bullet in the back of each of their skulls right now. What was stopping him? He only had a dagger—useful for one, maybe two if he was lucky, and his shotgun, which offered an additional shot. But he couldn't risk Becca getting struck by crossfire.

Despite her thinking he was greedy and uncivilized, Jonathan wasn't so cold to not care about her safety. He was no murderer either, and he wasn't that reckless. Last winter, after he'd given Rob Bertrand and Jaime Perez plenty of warnings, Jonathan was justified in eliminating the threat trespassing on his property.

And after Lizzy was shot in cold blood, Becca hardly kept herself together. He wouldn't subject her to that again, unless provoked and necessary. Good on Lizzy for standing up for herself, but that wasn't the way to best the bandits. She was so far outnumbered, it was suicide.

"You all right?" Jonathan asked after Becca had been quiet for a while.

She shook her head and sucked in her upper lip, as if fighting back another round of hysterics. He wanted to comfort her, hold her again and inhale her chocolate and cinnamon scent, but he couldn't. "Hold on. It's almost over."

She nodded, and the bandits turned east on Mather Street, a short road off the beaten path. Jonathan kept his eyes peeled for potential locations, but two blocks later the road ended, and the bandits turned north on a small lesser-traveled street. The falling light of dusk and the densely packed trees gave Jonathan's sweaty arms gooseflesh. Songbirds chirped angrily nearby as if fending off an intruder.

At the end of the street, they stopped very close to the mouth of the Fox River. A trading company was across the river with boats coming and going. But on this side of the river, the orange of the sky reflected eerily off the weathered and beaten building before them. He recognized this place. The American Fur Company had shut its doors a few years back in 1844 and without maintenance, weeds sprung up from the dirt and around the building's perimeter. It was exclusive and hidden, just as he'd expected their hideout to be.

Ready to give the command to flee, Jonathan maneuvered his horse next to Becca and darted her a look. She pressed her lips together as if readying herself for the flight of their lives.

"As soon as I say," he whispered. "We—"

"All right, boys…and girl, let's get ol' Brawley here taken care of, and then we head home for dinner," Butch said.

Well, shit. This wasn't the base. He placed a hand on her thigh, and Becca's trembling hand covered his.

The bandits dismounted, and Nash and Ruddy pulled Brawley's body off the horse like a sack of flour. Jonathan slipped off his horse and helped Becca down. They stood together with the privacy afforded by the flanks of her mare.

Becca's fingers gripped his shirt like a lifeline. "This isn't the place," she breathed into his ear.

"I heard," he said. "They're going to bury Brawley, and then we'll be on our way. You're doing great, City."

Her hand trembled, shaking his shirt. Jonathan embraced her. Arms of desperation wrapped around him, and he closed his eyes. She was so frightened, but yet so strong for making it this far. She was wise—strong when needed, quiet when necessary, and bold when appropriate. If his sister were here instead? He suppressed a chuckle. Verity and her mouth wouldn't have lasted five minutes before they shot her. Good thing they'd never met her.

"Come on. If we don't go with, they'll get suspicious," Jonathan said and grasped her hand to lead her.

But Becca pulled away.

"It's safer if you take my hand," he insisted. "Remember that conversation between Nash and Ruddy? It's best if they think you're mine."

Becca's throat worked at a thick lump, and she frowned.

Jonathan gripped her small sweaty palm, and they followed the bandits through the dusty yard. As Brawley was dragged, red drying on the front of his shirt, Butch's slug having made Swiss cheese of his face, Becca turned her head away. They didn't bother to wrap him with cloth first.

Jonathan squeezed her hand tighter. It was all he could do.

Brawley snagged on a rock, and Nash grunted with the effort to yank him free. "So, uh, what's the deal with the skirt, Johnny? She a lady of the line or is she taken?"

Being 'taken' never stopped Nash before.

"Is he insinuating what I think he's insinuating?" Becca whispered to Jonathan with an edge to her voice.

"Probably," he whispered back. He couldn't read her mind.

"Hey, Johnny! She on loan or is she yours?" Nash pressed.

Jonathan cast her an apologetic smile and said, "She's mine."

Heat swirled in her eyes—was it anger or something else? Jonathan moved his gaze away and stared at Brawley's body bouncing over the rough ground as he was dragged along.

"Well, damn," Nash said.

"I figured when the lady said she was lookin' for Johnny that they's no hope for me," Ruddy said to Nash, and then smiled at Becca. "So, I didn't even try."

"Well, you're a dummy," Nash said. "You shoulda tried. Always try."

"Look at me, Nash, and then take a deep drink of the lady-killer here." Ruddy waved his hand as if showcasing

Jonathan as a trophy. "You really think I stand a chance against the likes of him? As I said, they's no hope for me."

Jonathan didn't know what to think of that, but he was glad the men weren't going to make a pass at Becca.

"I happen to think you're dashing," Nash said to his friend. "And if the lady can't see that, well, that's her problem. That's why I prefer my ladies not to fight."

Becca cringed. Jonathan didn't blame her.

Nash and Ruddy released the body on the grass at the back of the building. Fingers carried a bowl of rocks from the riverbed. Ruddy and Nash lifted Brawley into a seated position, and Fingers stuffed rocks down his throat, into his pockets, into his boots, and anywhere else they might be useful.

Jonathan pinched his face.

"What are they doing?" Becca asked quietly.

"Giving the man more weight."

Becca's features twisted in confusion. She gripped his hand tighter and turned her face aside.

Finished with their preparations, Butch stepped forward. "Fingers, give the eulogy."

Fingers cleared his throat and removed his hat. Nash and Ruddy copied and tipped their heads down toward Brawley's mangled corpse.

Becca's face pressed against Jonathan's shoulder and her breathing was erratic.

"Brawley was a good man," Fingers said. "Listened well, lived well, and knew how to have a good time. He was loyal as a mutt and irreplaceable. I remember that flapper he had at The Wounded Soldier in Greenleaf—the one he so generously shared with me. That was a great night." Fingers chuckled, and others joined him. "Anyone else have a story of Brawley to share?"

"I ran out of money at the bar one night an' Brawley spotted me a fiver. Good man," Nash said.

"Remember that day a bunch of lumberjacks was climbin' all over us, Nash?" Ruddy asked and received a nod. "Brawley swooped in and helped us kill 'em all. He was the best kind of friend."

"Yeah, I remember that." Nash smiled, flashing the holes in his gumline.

Jonathan rubbed his thumb over her hand.

"Joseph Brawley," Butch announced. "A fellow missing teeth and many functions behest a man, and yet, he was a great soldier for our cause. True loyalty is hard to find." Butch made a point to glance his way, and Jonathan tensed.

"We'll miss you ol' friend," Fingers added.

The men replaced their hats, and Nash and Ruddy picked up Brawley by his arms and feet. They carried him down to the riverbank.

"They're not...They won't..." Becca whispered.

"They will," Jonathan finished.

"But they said they were going to bury him!" she hissed into his ear.

"Do you have a problem with our rituals, woman?" Butch asked, a scornful note in his tone that irritated Jonathan.

"No, no, I don't. I'm just confused about the terminology. Burying usually implies under the ground, not tossed like chum into the—"

Butch approached, and Becca choked off her words while sliding behind Jonathan. The leader stood nose to nose with him while speaking to her over Jonathan's shoulder.

"Don't question our practices, or you'll find yourself learning about them with more hands-on experience," he told her. "And you. What business do you have bringing a woman along on our raids?"

Jonathan didn't have a good excuse. He should've planned it before hand, but he was too distracted. With strong conviction in his voice, he said, "She's with me, because she can't be anywhere else."

Butch lifted a brow and tilted his head. "Is that so?"

She'd refused to stay at the farm, and Jonathan couldn't leave her anywhere else. "That's the truth."

Butch's sharp eyes swooped down and back up his body. While glaring at Jonathan, Butch said, "Woman."

"Becca," Jonathan corrected.

"I don't care what her name is, boy," Butch said to him. "Woman, I want you to answer me a question. Are we clear?"

She nodded.

"I didn't hear you." Butch growled his words.

"I get it. What do you want to know?"

"Why are you here?" The deplorable leader was finally suspicious of the spies, and Jonathan didn't like it.

"I'm here to make sure Johnny does his job and to entertain him when he isn't. Sometimes a woman's distraction can be very useful." Jonathan's mind flashed to her idea of entertainment, and he wished her answer was true.

"Indeed," Butch said darkly.

A deep splash came from the river, and their heads turned. Brawley's body sunk with minimal air bubbles breaking the surface. Nash and Ruddy dusted off their hands, and Ruddy swiped a tear from his eye.

"Time to eat," Butch announced and turned to mount.

Jonathan blew out a breath. That was too close. They all mounted up, and Becca stayed next to him at the rear of the now-smaller pack.

"Quick thinking back there," Jonathan said to her.

"He seemed like the type to get angrier over a non-answer than one he didn't like, so I went with something that I thought would make sense to him."

"I hope you understand I only told them I owned you so they'll keep their hands off you. If I didn't, I'd have to fight them all."

"I'm not angry."

If that heat in her eyes hadn't been anger, then was she lusting for him just as much as he wanted her? If only they could be anywhere else but here... "How are your legs handling the riding, City?"

She chuckled. "Rough. Horrible. I never want to ride a horse again. I don't think I'll be able to walk after this."

"The home base can't be much farther."

They backtracked out to Broadway and continued north. Jonathan had never been out this far from town—had no reason to. Trees thickened the area, making it appear uninhabited. A sharp turn at the end of Broadway turned into a dirt road that just ended. What were they doing out here? Mud and mossy decay filled his nose, mosquitoes buzzed around his ears, and a sinking feeling returned to Jonathan's gut.

The bandits dismounted and held the reins as they guided their horses into the swamp. Great. Just great. "We're not going to be able to flee without them noticing. I don't want to tax you further at this point, so we have to follow."

"I get it."

Jonathan hopped down, wondering if this location was close enough to satisfy the sheriff, but like Becca, Jonathan was dead tired and famished. And he didn't want to push Becca to ride hard after her long day. He grasped the reins of his horse and said, "I'll lead. Stay close behind me. I don't know what we're walking into."

Jonathan followed the men marching in silence through the swamp. The path was hardly visible. If he weren't traversing it, he never would've seen it. Low hanging branches were brushed aside, and picker plants snagged his trousers. He blew at insects invading his face. Jonathan glanced behind him, and Becca followed, swatting bugs. The corner of his lips lifted. Damn, she was one amazing woman.

So resilient, and not repulsed by his bandit reputation.

At the end of what felt like miles, a small clearing opened to a cottage—a surprisingly homey squat wooden building with smoke puffing from the single chimney. It appeared big enough for a single bedroom and kitchen only. Not something he expected a group of nomadic ruffians to settle in. Maybe they intended to commandeer this home. Had they staked it out ahead of time? Jonathan inhaled and released a deep breath.

He was going to find out, unfortunately.

Chapter 14

The buzzing insects around her head bothered her, but not as much as the entire lower half of her body. On loose and tired legs, her knees wobbled with each step, and Becca didn't know how much farther she could go on. Fear and exhaustion took turns beating at her bones, but exhaustion was winning now, and the idea of getting back in the saddle made her want to cry.

This morning she'd packed up her stuff to move away for a fresh start, but hours later she'd traveled through time over a hundred and sixty years, as if that was believable. Then she'd hunted down a handsome but stubborn man, met the most dangerous men in her city's history, and followed them through two robberies and a murder. No one would believe that tale either.

Tonight she was in an isolated swamp with them, staring at a small cottage fit for a fairy tale evil witch. Patches of the roof were missing shingles, and a couple shutters were crooked as if missing a top fastener. The stone chimney appeared to be crumbling with age. As if the dilapidated building sensed it was frightening her away, grilled meat flooded her nose. Becca's stomach rumbled, which surprised her. After all she'd seen today, she didn't expect to be able to eat for a week.

The bandits released their horses in the clearing and walked inside the cottage. Jonathan approached and took her hand. "I don't know what we're walking into, but I want you to know, anytime I give you a squeeze, it means I'm right here. Understand? You've been amazing so far, and we're almost out of here." Jonathan gave her a demonstrative squeeze.

Becca nodded. "Thank you."

They walked inside and stopped. Becca didn't know what she expected, but a rounded older woman, white-haired and wrinkled with age, flipping burgers over an open grill, wasn't it. Fingers, Nash, and Ruddy pulled out wooden chairs at a well-worn table, eagerly anticipating the meal.

Butch waved her and Jonathan closer, as if being a gentlemanly host outweighed any suspicion of their motivations. "Johnny and Becca, this is my mother, Viola Butcher. Ma, these are our newest recruits."

Viola turned from the grill and lifted her gray brows. "You let a woman join?" Her eyes swept up and down Becca, and then she addressed her, "Oh, honey, what life you must've led to run with these animals."

Nash and Ruddy laughed.

Viola moved closer, cleaning her hands on her apron. "As my son said, I'm Viola. I'm sure it's a pleasure." She held out her veiny hand.

Becca shook it, shock stiffening her movements. "Becca. Thanks."

Viola's eyes swept Jonathan as well, but for a different purpose. As Viola's hand rested on Jonathan's shoulder, his face burned red. "And you. Fine choice with this handsome fella here, Butch."

Not that Becca was in any competition over him, but a surprising hint of jealousy sprung up from somewhere she didn't realize still existed.

"Oh, yes. He's a nice one." Viola tapped him on the nose and returned to the smokey grill. "Food's ready in a minute."

Jonathan rubbed his nose, a good sport about the old lady's flirting, and Becca held back a smile. Seeing the opportunity, Becca said, "We don't want to burden you. There's no way you have enough to cover us. We can find dinner elsewhere."

Jonathan squeezed her hand, and she suppressed a prideful smile from his approval.

"Nonsense. I have plenty. Now sit."

"Come on." Jonathan brought her to the table and pulled out a chair for her and tucked it under. That was weird. No one had ever done that for her.

Jonathan sat next to her, and she was well aware of his knee touching hers.

"Where's Brawley?" Viola asked, glancing at everyone at her table.

"He didn't make it," Butch said.

"That's a shame." Viola returned to the grill. "It's dangerous work, but you knew that."

They considered their job to be armed robbery? Becca didn't know where to begin to justify that.

"So what's the plan for tomorra, boss?" Nash asked and drummed his fingers on the table edge.

"Stay home and do nothing," Viola piped in, but she was ignored.

"I heard ol' farmer Richard Jorgenson was planning on bringing a wagon of produce to the market. Perhaps we should lighten his load," Butch said.

"Jorgenson?" Ruddy tilted his head. "Ain't he the onion farmer?"

"Onions again!" Viola said while lifting the mouth-watering slabs of meat onto plates. "I never raised my boy to eat raw onions. Wherever did you acquire a taste like that?"

Butch shrugged and slunk in his chair like a scolded child. "I just like them."

"That's not right. Here"—she set a plate in front of him—"eat something real. You'll need to keep your energy up. Such a beanpole."

Becca got a close look at the meat as it was placed before her. That was no hamburger or steak. It looked like someone took a jagged knife and sliced a hunk off an animal...blindfolded. Yep, she was sure that was skin still attached to the grilled muscle. It smelled good, though.

The men around the table dug in like a bunch of starving men in front of a pizza buffet, never flinching at the offering.

Jonathan cut off hunks too and ate without reserve. "Aren't you hungry?" he asked.

"Not really." Pizza sounded good, though.

"Try it. It's not as bad as it looks."

"What is it?" she whispered, fearing the answer. At least with Brawley, she knew they dumped him in the river.

"Meat," Jonathan said simply.

A snort escaped her nose, and Butch shifted his gaze for a moment.

She kept her voice low. "I figured that. I mean what kind?"

"Does it matter?" Genuine confusion came from Jonathan's tone. All the men ate their nondescript meat without hesitation, a pack of starving lions. As long as it wasn't people meat, she could try it. Becca reluctantly cut off a nibble and brought it her lips.

"How do you like the flavor of him?" Viola asked the group.

Becca's hand froze. Him?

"I think he needs more salt." Butch said.

"I don't trust your judgment," Viola retorted.

"Mrs. B, I think he's tasty just the way you made 'im," Ruddy said.

"I woulda used more pepper myself, but I ain't complainin' over free food," Nash added. "Thank you kindly, Mrs. B."

"You did fine, Ma," Butch said.

"What about you two?" Viola asked, ignoring a silent Fingers.

"Delicious, Mrs. Butcher," Jonathan said with chipmunk cheeks.

Becca nodded and smiled, but Viola watched, waiting for her to eat the bite hovering before her mouth. Was this a person she was going to eat? One of their previous murders? Her stomach squeezed.

"It's a shame Abner finally died," Ruddy said, throwing a glance her way. "He was a great pig."

Becca exhaled.

"Yeah, until he wasn't no longer," Nash added.

She chewed her measly bite, and Viola turned around, satisfied. It looked disgusting, but it smelled great, and turned out, it tasted okay. Could use seasoning and tenderizing, but Becca was hungry enough not to care, assuming this was really pork. It was like none she'd ever had before. Candle flame flickered across the small cottage while the men ate in peace. When their plates were cleaned, the old lady collected and washed them. Butch cleaned his teeth with a small pick and studied them. Ruddy pulled out a deck of cards.

"That was great Mrs. B," Ruddy said and leaned back in his chair, shuffling with skill.

"Thank ya, Mrs. B," Nash added. "Excuse me while I water the bushes quick." Nash popped outside for a moment and returned, likely having pissed on the side of the house.

Speaking of bodily functions… Becca whispered, "Is there a bathroom around here?"

"I'm going to say no," Jonathan said. "Since only rich folk have one."

Ugh. She suppressed a groan. "Where do ladies, uh, relieve themselves?"

"I'll ask," Jonathan whispered and then projected his voice, "Viola, is there a latrine nearby?"

"Out back." Her hand waved absentmindedly while she dried the water from a plate.

"What's a latrine?" Becca whispered. She heard that word somewhere, a movie perhaps, and for some reason the word brought dread to her bones.

Jonathan smiled with a sly curve of his lips. What was he up to? Jonathan stood and offered his hand. "Lady needs assistance. We'll be back shortly."

Becca quickly accepted, realizing Jonathan was sneaky, and he gave her a squeeze. Fed and rested, now they could escape—after visiting whatever the latrine was.

"The lady don't need assistance in the latrine," Butch said with boredom on his tongue. He dropped his pick onto the table, while candlelight danced across his menacing features. Porcelain clattered in the kitchen.

Well, shit. Yeah, she did, Becca thought.

"She asked for help, so I'm giving it to her," Jonathan said.

"What kinda skirt needs help doin' her business?" Ruddy asked with a fan of playing cards in his hand.

"Unless"—Nash elbowed his friend—"the business requires a man's help." Nash and Ruddy laughed, and Nash played a card, turning Ruddy's laughter into anger.

"Dammit!" Ruddy slapped Nash upside the head.

"Hey, it's fair play."

"Don't mean I have to like it," Ruddy said.

"No one asked you."

Viola paused from clean up and turned to the men. "What's this here about needin' help? If the lady needs help, then she needs it. If you had any experience, you'd know that."

Her words turned everyone's eyes to Becca, and Viola winked at her. Becca didn't know if their judging gazes were worse than the laughter.

"Ma, stay out of this," Butch said, boredom still there. Must've been an after-dinner grogginess. Now was the perfect time to escape.

Viola waved him off, dried her hands on her apron, and left the room.

Becca stood, prepared to go alone, but Jonathan joined her, holding her hand.

Butch scowled and stood. To intimidate them or perhaps his suspicion had returned, Butch crossed his arms over his chest like a bouncer at a club, but his skinny frame wasn't what had her nerves skittering. A knife at his waistband glinted in the candlelight, and the darkness in his eyes chilled her. Butch had shot his injured friend without taking a moment to try to save him, as if he were disposable, replaceable.

He'd think even less of her and Jonathan.

"The lady can take care of her own business," Butch said and glared at Jonathan. "You stay here."

Jonathan was rigid in challenge next to her, waiting to strike if needed. And all too quick, he nodded, bowing to the leader's orders. He squeezed and released her hand. She felt like she was floating away from her safety line and into dangerous waters. Becca glanced out the windows, and it was full dark.

"Go around back. You'll find an outhouse. Watch your step." Jonathan winked at her.

Becca nodded and excused herself, dreading what awaited her with a thick lump in her throat. She stole a glance over her shoulder at Jonathan. She had to leave him exposed to these suspicious thieves and murderers, and she hoped nothing would happen to the man she needed to save.

Chapter 15

Jonathan nervously sat back at the table, wishing he'd been able to escape with Becca. He hoped the city woman could handle herself out there.

"Why's she really here, Johnny?" Butch asked.

Nash and Ruddy paused their game, eagerly anticipating his excuse.

Jonathan used a line he remembered from his sister's adventures. "She angered a man who wants her dead. I'm protecting her, so from now on, where I go, she goes."

Butch still held his arms across his narrow chest. "Who?"

Shit. The air rushed from Jonathan's lungs. He had to think fast, and he had a perfect scapegoat. "Pool."

"Ben Pool's dead, last I heard," Nash said and played a ten of spades.

"He means Joe. You mean Joe, right?" Ruddy leaned forward with interest.

Now the bandits would have an extra reason to dispatch the one that got away from Jaime's entourage. Since the man had been guilty of enough himself, Jonathan didn't feel the slightest drop of guilt. "Joe Pool."

Nash laughed and pounded the table with his fist. "Y'all remember? That varmint and the rest of Perez's gang killed my brother in cold blood. Oh, boss, can we help? Our brother-in-arms needs assistance, and I say it's time for payback."

"What say you, Fingers?" Butch asked and unfolded his arms.

Fingers was busy licking his...fingers. His face was smeared with grease, and when he smiled, hunks of meat were caught between his teeth. "I say it's far past time we send Joe Pool where he belongs—with the rest of his crew."

"Are you boys talkin' of murderin' someone?" Viola returned from the side room. Apparently, the conversation finally piqued her interest.

Jonathan didn't like where this was headed. He wanted to pin some extra guilt on the weasel, not cause a witch hunt.

"Awe, Ma. Just one bastard that got away last year," Butch said.

"Jaime's man, did you say?"

"That's the one," Butch said.

"Oh, in that case, please do. That rat shouldn't be breathing after what he did to your brother, Nash."

Nash nodded his agreement and grinned like he just struck gold.

Jonathan couldn't believe the tailspin from his little lie.

"So, what's the plan, boss?" Ruddy asked.

"In the morning we set out." Butch leaned forward and tented his fingers. "Nash and Ruddy—scope out the area. Find where Pool's been hiding. Fingers and I will raid Farmer Jorgenson. Johnny—"

Jonathan met Butch's gaze.

"Since your woman is the target, get any and all information on Pool from her. Then we're going to position her to lure Pool in."

"Uh—" They were going to use Becca as bait to kill a man based on a story Jonathan made up. Oh, hell.

"What's the matter?" Butch cocked a brow and his hand stilled the pick.

"Nothing. I...think it's a great plan. I'll go find her."

UNDER THE DIM MOONLIGHT, Becca marched through overgrown grasses, kept inadequately trimmed by the horses, and found what Jonathan meant. A weathered, unpainted shack stood at the edge of the yard. She'd been camping many times before, but those facilities had proper ventilation, an actual toilet seat, toilet paper, and a latching door. Even the more primitive ones still had a toilet seat and toilet paper. Becca swung the door open and muttered several curse words.

"This is so not like camping."

The moonbeam shined on a wood platform on the ground with a hole in it. The smell alone had her suppressing a gag reflex. No lights and no toilet paper. That wasn't going to do. Becca scouted the edge of the woods for a substitute, while trying to recall what poison ivy looked like. She thought she'd have better luck choosing from a tree. A dangling oak leaf was a safe bet. She plucked it off the branch and inspected it for an insect infestation. It looked clean in the not-so-trustworthy moonlight.

Becca brought it into the outhouse. She found the circular opening in the very dim interior without touching it with her hands and balanced while squatting. She used the leaf with a grimace, and when she finished, she ran out and gagged. Her eyes watered and her stomach convulsed. Deep breaths of fresh air helped soothe the involuntary reflexes. She counted to ten several times before regaining her senses.

Crickets chirped, frogs ribbited, and a bird's wings fluttered in the trees.

Becca stood alone in the shadowy moonlight. She was free, and she had the location to the bandits' hideout. What if...she just fled with her mare and tracked down the sheriff, freeing her and Jonathan from the deal?

If she disappeared, what would happen to Jonathan? What would the bandits assume? She couldn't risk leaving Jonathan undefended in the heart of the bandits' refuge. Who knew how many weapons and ammo they had packed in there? Maybe Viola would talk some sense into them, but how could Becca trust a woman who raised Butch to be the way he was?

On that thought, why had the bandits accepted Jonathan in the first place? What had Jonathan done to earn their trust? Well, she hadn't done anything before getting recruited herself, but she didn't believe that to be the case for Jonathan.

Or she could just zap herself away, having completed her mission. Jonathan accepted the deal, so she prevented his murder. Like her, Jonathan had the location for the bandits' hideout. Next time he found the sheriff, he just needed to hand over the information. Done deal. With a press of a button she could be back home with clean clothes, a working shower, air conditioning, a car, and easy access to a drive-thru.

It was tempting until she remembered waiting for her back home was no job, no husband, and her spare belongings packed in boxes. Back home, where she would be forced to expose her marriage's failures to the courtroom where dickhead Brad would flaunt his new happy life again, where she'd wallow in pity over her loss—the daughter she would never see smile.

Becca's eyes stung with tears. Not now, not now, pull yourself together, she pleaded with herself.

What did she honestly have to lose by staying? Besides her life, of course. But after losing everything that mattered to her, she didn't value that too highly. That was a low point. Right here and now was the lowest point she'd ever been.

She had to admit, besides the cringe-worthy leaf, questionable meat, and lack of hygiene in the company she'd kept, this time travel experience was the wildest, craziest adventure she could've ever asked for. Something she never thought possible. And maybe she hadn't lost everything.

Something about the way Jonathan looked at her made her feel warm and protected. The way he held her hand and squeezed it at just the right moments as if he knew what she was thinking. It sparked a sense of desire in her, as if she really mattered. She didn't owe anyone anything, but she wanted to keep going for him.

Becca circled around to the front of the creepy cottage. The door opened, spilling candlelight on the ground at her feet, interrupted by a shadow. Becca stilled while a figure closed the door behind him.

Jonathan left the cottage to give Becca the help she'd asked for, if he wasn't too late, and plot their escape. Because of his big mouth, she was in even more danger.

Becca stood before him, standing in the moonlit grass. Her eyes glistened in the light. He closed the distance and inspected her for cuts and bruises. He gave a discreet sniff, and she still smelled like cinnamon. "Latrines aren't in the future, are they?"

Becca smiled and shook her head. "It's not that."

"What is it then?" He kept his tone smooth and calm. He didn't want the bandits to overhear, but he also didn't want to upset her more.

"Just reminiscing about what I left behind."

His eyes darted to her ring finger. It had indents as if a ring used to be there but was missing. He hadn't thought about what she'd left behind to save his ass. That was probably the source of her breakdown before. He appreciated her help, but she clearly needed to get back home. "It'll be over soon. I promise."

She smiled and inhaled deeply a couple times as if preventing another fit of hysteria. "Do we have to go back inside, or can we just escape now?" She reached up and swiped a thick lock of curly hair aside. In the glow from the windows, he noticed a distinct line in the color of her hair. What nutritional deficiency would cause that?

"I have some bad news," Jonathan said carefully.

Her lips twisted in anticipation, and a small shaft of pain pierced through his chest, but he brushed it aside.

"The bandits want to use you to draw a man out."

"You mean bait?" Becca asked rhetorically. "Do I know him?"

"No."

"If it means we get away from here, what do I have to do?"

"I don't know yet, but they're expecting information from you. I told them you were running from a man who wants to kill you. The name I gave happens to be an enemy of theirs. Now they want to hunt him down—more so for their own revenge than your benefit—but I expect they'll want kudos for the effort."

She grimaced, and Jonathan feared what she thought of him now.

"What do you mean by kudos?" Becca asked cautiously.

"I can't say for sure, but remember those coins I gave you?"

"Yeah?" The quiet hesitation in her voice made him want to embrace her.

"Keep them on you. If you find any more money for any reason, take it and keep it."

"Why would you tell the bandits something like that?"

"They needed a believable reason for you to be here, and since I know what kind of people they are, they'd respect you if you've done something..." he trailed off, uncertain of how to finish without her being more disgusted with him.

"To anger a man to murder," Becca said dryly.

"That's exactly it." Jonathan rubbed the back of his hair and kicked at the dirt. "They have no use for weakness."

Becca turned, shook her head, and mumbled for a moment, and Jonathan waited for whatever she decided.

She scoffed. "I can't believe this. None of this can be reality. What would possess a man to…?" She inhaled deliberate deep breaths and let them out, calming herself. "None of that matters. We need to figure out a plan to get out of here. Do I have to make up a gruesome story about a man I never met?"

"I recommend you do." The fact that she was considering helping him with his cockamamie scheme made him respect her even more.

"What could I do to drive a man to murder in these times?"

That was easy, and Jonathan answered without a thought. "Make him fall in love with you and leave him."

She paused and looked at him pointedly.

He cleared his throat. "Or maim him where it counts. That's what my sister did."

Becca's eyes widened. "Verity had a murderer after her?"

"Yeah, the boss of the man we are now hunting."

"Yikes. Why did she maim him? She seems so nice."

Jonathan laughed. "If only you knew the real Verity. Maybe she didn't fully flex her arrogant chops in the strange world of the future, but believe me when I tell you she's bullheaded, smart-mouthed, and very spirited."

"I can see that."

"She hated housework. Never wanted to be a wife or mother. When our parents passed, she set out for California, her dream, but she never made it. When dancing for traveling money, she turned down a man who refused to accept no for an answer. She maimed him in the groin to escape, and he hunted her for over a year. Eventually he was killed at a massacre in his own estate—after she maimed him again on his deathbed. If there weren't witnesses backing up the story, I'd never believe half of it."

"That sounds insane. I can't go with the maiming story. There aren't any scars to back it up." Becca wrapped her arms around herself. She was afraid, and Jonathan wanted nothing more than to reassure her she'd be completely safe, but he couldn't.

"You might've publicly humiliated him."

"That's enough?"

"Doesn't take much for some people."

"But he could deny the story. If he acted confused, the jig would be up," Becca said.

"By then, the bandits will be so driven to kill their enemy, any truth would be lost."

She mulled this option over for a moment, biting her lower lip. He wanted to take her mouth, both for the temptation and out of desperation, but she wasn't his to take. "And where is this guy? Where would it have happened?"

"He might be in Bridgeport, at the old estate. You could borrow Verity's story. Say you humiliated Pool in Greenleaf at The Wounded Soldier."

"His name is Pool?"

"Joe Pool. One of Jaime Perez's followers. His loyalty changes to whoever is in charge at the moment. Somehow, he survived the massacre at the mansion."

Becca shivered.

Jonathan rubbed his hands on her upper arms to warm her. She appeared exhausted, and she was in no condition to flee. "Let's go inside, give our small tale, and the bandits can figure out their next steps for the morning."

"What about us? Are we going along with this?"

"We'll be sneaking out in the middle of the night. So rest quick."

Becca nodded and they headed inside, holding hands. An energy pulsed through him with the contact of her bare skin, and Jonathan didn't know how he was going to send her home to her life. He wanted her to be his life. What a mistake he made letting her in.

Chapter 16

Becca wasn't much of a liar, and now she had to convince a group of ruthless thugs a fake, deplorable story of a strong woman who survived a harrowing ordeal was true. Easy as pie—not. Inside the dilapidated cottage, Nash pounded his fist on the table in excitement, and a lit candle teetered, threatening to topple over. The bandits animatedly discussed ways of killing a man that would produce the most gore, and therefore, respect. Becca covered her mouth with her hand. She hadn't considered killing anyone before, but, picturing Brad's face, she could muster up something.

"Come sit," Butch said to her, surprisingly in a good mood. "We need to settle our plans and rest up for a fun day tomorrow."

Becca returned to her seat at the table, and Jonathan was right next to her. His sexy scent overrode the stench of the bandits, who clearly hadn't bathed in a while.

"What's the story with Pool?" Fingers asked.

Becca cleared her throat, remembering the concocted lie borrowed from Verity. "I met him at The Wounded Soldier."

"Oh, I know that place," Ruddy said, brows lifted. "Jaime's favorite hideout."

"Don't interrupt, Ruddy," Nash said. "Go ahead, Becca. We need all the details."

Becca needed conviction in her story, a believable woman scorned. That prick Brad might come in handy after all. She overlaid Verity's brief story with Becca's embarrassing interaction with Brad and his new Chastity. "He and I weren't on the same page. I thought he wanted one thing, but he wanted something else entirely." Nash chuckled. "When I confronted him about it, loudly, turning heads from everyone else in the room, Pool's face burned with anger and embarrassment, but I was safe for the time being. He wouldn't dare do anything with witnesses around. Recently, he saw me on the road. I ducked into Johnny's house for cover and explained the situation. Johnny's been protecting me from him since." Becca sent Jonathan an appreciative smile. There was more truth to her story than she'd realized.

"Such a familiar tale with Perez's men. Savages, the lot of 'em. Where's he been staying?" Butch asked.

"I imagine the Grignon estate would be a wise place to check," Becca repeated Jonathan's intel.

"Indeed," Butch said without conviction. "Just a shame we've scoured that mansion several times searchin' for that bastard and never found a trace. He must be around if you're still hidin' from him." Butch had suspicion in his voice.

Becca wiped her clammy hands on her skirt pants. Damned polyester wasn't helping. Becca remembered something Jonathan had told her—the bandits had no use for weakness. She could be strong and fierce, starting with a little snark in her lie. "When Pool found me on the road, I dodged him. He wasn't offering tea at his house."

"Oh, she's sassy, boss," Nash said, and his lips curled with amusement.

Becca swallowed a thick lump in her throat, and Jonathan's hand found hers under the table. His touch calmed her racing heartbeat, but only a little.

Butch leaned back in his chair and blew out a long breath through his nose. His fingers laced together over his middle. He wasn't convinced.

Digging deeper, Becca added, "And if we find the prick, I get first dibs."

Butch's lips twitched, and Nash and Ruddy laughed. Fingers even cracked a smile. Jonathan squeezed her hand.

"Nothing terribly useful. Stick to the original plan, fellas," Butch said. "Nash and Ruddy—pester everyone you find for information on Pool's whereabouts. Fingers and I are going to extract information on our way to Jorgenson's onions. And you two, stay public tomorrow. I want you ridin' in plain sight. If you see Pool, one of you distract him while the other finds us."

Great. She knew who was ordered to do the distracting.

"Solid plan, Butch," Jonathan said.

"Yeah, boss. How am I gonna sleep tonight with our excitin' plans for tomorra?" Nash asked with a broad grin on his pockmarked face.

"There's gin in the cabinet," Butch said, and then yelled, "Ma! Bring the gin!"

The cottage was way too small to justify that volume, but maybe Viola was hearing impaired. The sly lady didn't seem like it though.

Viola shuffled out of a side room. "Oh, finished planning your murder of that Pool man?"

Becca stifled a chuckle at her casual words. She still couldn't believe this was real.

"You betcha," Fingers said. "Pass around the gin so we can all rest well."

Viola poured small glasses full in a straight line like an experienced bartender. She carried them over, two at a time to the table, and Becca shifted uncomfortably. "Thank you," Becca said as a warm glass was set before her.

Jonathan tipped his head in thanks, and after Viola was finished dishing out the booze, she lit a couple extra candles.

"Bottom's up," Fingers said and dumped the whole glass down his throat. Viola shuffled over to him with a refill.

Butch, Ruddy, and Nash held their glasses up in a silent toast and slammed them back. The empty glasses thumped the wooden table with a quick rhythm, and Viola refilled theirs as well. Jonathan kicked back his glass, and Becca worried for a moment how well he could handle liquor and keep his wits about him to escape.

She looked at her glass, filled to the brim. She wasn't a drinker and had only heard of gin the card game. While she stared at it, Jonathan leaned in close, his hot breath tickling her ear, sending a sizzle of heat through her body. "Do you want it?"

If only that question referred to something else. She closed her eyes and pictured him having his way with her. That sounded like a much better time. Becca shook her head, both in answer and to remove the tempting images from her head.

While the other men emptied their next glasses, Jonathan took hers and swallowed it down. He set it back in front of her, so it looked like she drank it.

"Refill, my dear?" Viola asked.

"No. Thank you, though. I'm a lightweight."

"That's a strange thing to say, but all right. How about you, Johnny?"

"That's great gin, ma'am."

"Finest in the whole Midwest," Viola said proudly. "Brawley snagged this bottle from Grignon's personal stash. We've got plenty more."

"Thank you for the offer, but I'm going to pass," Jonathan said.

The other men had either seven or eight rounds; Becca lost count. And finally, their ability to sit upright faltered.

Nash hiccuped. "Hey boss, remember that time when ya said you wanted to marry Johnny's sister? And she turned ya down. That was a knee-slapper!" Nash laughed and slammed his palm on the table. Ruddy joined in on the laughter. Fingers only downed another glass.

Jonathan's hand tensed in hers, and Butch's glassy eyes locked on Jonathan's.

"I wouldn't say it was a knee-slapper," Butch said.

"How do you know Verity?" Jonathan asked, jaw tense.

Butch's lips pulled into a broad smile. "Me and her go way back. There's something special about that woman. Where is she, anyway?"

"She never mentioned you," Jonathan said, an edge to his voice.

"Oh? Maybe if you weren't fightin' her so much, you could've listened."

Jonathan's hand left Becca's and formed a fist over his lap. "How do you know her?" he repeated.

Amusement played on Butch's lips. "I escorted her through town when Jaime's men were fighting over her. She also fed me a couple times. And she bought rounds for the whole house at Stanton's Spirits. You don't suppose she's single again?"

Jonathan leaped to his feet, kicking back the chair. "Do not speak of my sister like that."

Butch stood in challenge, and Becca's heart thundered in her ears. She placed a hand on Jonathan's leg to remind him of where they were, but he ignored her touch.

"I'll talk about her however I please in my own house. If you don't like it, then get out," Butch said.

Jonathan's body was rigid as a board, and Becca hoped he heard the window Butch offered. Finally, he relaxed. "Yeah, fine. You want it like that? We're out of here."

"No," Butch cut in. "Just you go. The lady stays."

Becca's insides turned to liquid, and she didn't know which end was going to be affected first.

"I'm protecting the lady," Jonathan reminded him. "Where I go, she goes."

"We are perfectly capable of protectin' her from Pool, and it would be a great service to us if the bastard swung by, so you ain't needed."

Oh, no, no, no. This can't be happening, Becca thought.

Jonathan sat back down.

"Now you don't trust us?" Butch asked, remaining standing, and Becca watched his hands.

"You barged into my house," Jonathan said. "And tried to kill me. Why the hell would I trust you?"

Becca's eyes widened in the candlelight, but no one paid her any attention.

A curling sneer filled Butch's face. "The only reason I allowed you to come along is because I made a mistake and couldn't best you. I respected that strength, at the time, but seeing as I'm always prepared"—Butch slipped a long knife out of his belt—"I reckon that I could finish what I'd set out to do all them months ago."

What the hell was happening?

Jonathan remained seated but wound tight as a coil. "I'm not going to fight you."

Butch laughed. "Don't like your odds now?"

Jonathan's gaze flicked to all the faces around the table. "I'm not suicidal."

Fingers belched, and Nash and Ruddy laughed. Soon the whole room was barking with laughter.

Jonathan turned to Becca. "No matter what happens, I won't leave you." His arm curled around her shoulders, and she wished it was for more than just reassurance.

"I know." Becca leaned into his shoulder, and together they watched the men laugh and drink themselves into a stupor. After a while, Viola shuffled from the side room and blew out the candles.

"Good night, everyone. Sleep well," Viola said.

Becca swayed with exhaustion. Jonathan stood up and took her hand, leading her to the wall closest to the door. Nash and Ruddy folded over and rested their heads on the table. Butch and Fingers stretched out on the floor. Every one of them looked like they'd have cricks in their necks and sore backs in the morning.

Becca sat on the floor, leaning against the wall, and Jonathan joined her. They watched the men, but her eyelids drooped several times. She nestled her head against his shoulder and drifted off into a dreamless sleep.

Chapter 17

WHILE THE BANDITS SNOOZED, Jonathan forced himself to stay awake. Two shots of gin had warmed his insides, and the splendid woman from the future, resting her head against his shoulder, warmed something else. Jonathan wanted to explore every soft inch of her body and make her cry out his name, but he brushed that hopeless picture away. She needed—and wanted—to return home to the future, to a place Jonathan could never imagine. She was bold when needed, cautious when appropriate, and sweet just because. Becca was too good for him, and she was used to a life he could never give her.

Jonathan lifted his trouser leg and checked the holster. His eight-inch dagger waited against his calf just where he'd left it. Butch was a mean bastard, but he didn't have the strength and agility Jonathan had from hours laboring on the farm. If Becca weren't here, he would've taken Butch out with his knife and probably two others before taking any damage himself.

Two things stopped him. One, awaking the bandits and absorbing injuries would significantly decrease the odds of getting Becca to safety, and two, he didn't trust Viola not to appear with her own shotgun. By choosing to slip out quietly, they'd have the best chance of escape.

Jonathan rested his cheek against her head and wayward hairs tickled his face. She deserved so much better than this. What would his parents think of him right now? They'd probably be ashamed and make it clear just how disappointed they were. What was Graham up to right now? Jonathan hoped his little brother stepped up to the plate and managed the farm in Jonathan's absence, but with Graham's attitude, it was more likely he gave the workers the day off.

Or his house was emptied of everything of value.

Listening to the rhythmic snores of the men and watching the soft rise and fall of Becca's chest, Jonathan's eyelids became heavy. Her chest was a nice view—not too big, not too small, just something there for him to explore. Except he couldn't. His eyelids lowered, and when he opened them again, the men's snores were quieter. His head still leaned against hers, and Becca was still curled up against him. Moonlight filtered in through the windows, but Jonathan couldn't tell how long he'd been out for. He shook Becca awake.

With shock and confusion of their strange surroundings, she bolted upright.

He hushed her. "It's me. Time to leave."

They climbed to their feet, shifted to the door, and upon opening it, the hinges creaked, but the bandits didn't appear disturbed.

Outside, under the pale blue cast of light, Jonathan collected his horse and Becca's mare and passed her reins to her. He led the way down the narrow footpath very slowly. The dense underbrush and canopy shadowed their footing. A twig snapped, leaves rustled, and the horses' hooves sloshed through decaying leaf litter. At the dirt road, they mounted.

Becca grunted in pain.

They were so close to escaping. At any moment, one of the bandits could rouse and sound the alarm. "Everything all right?"

"Sore. Very, very sore."

"We don't have time to waste. Can you ride?"

"I think so, but can we go slow? I feel like my whole bottom end was paddled with a brick for hours on end."

"After all the gin they drowned themselves in, let's hope we have a few hours. We'll walk the horses." Jonathan headed down the road, and Becca followed.

"Where are we going?" Becca asked.

"The sheriff's office is on the way back to the Arris farm. We're heading straight to him."

"I'm glad he's along the way. Riding this much sucks."

Jonathan gave her a wry smile she probably couldn't see. "It'll get better. If not, it's almost over."

"What will happen after the bandits find out we're gone?"

Until someone dispatched the bandits for good, being caught was inevitable. "If they find us before the sheriff finds them, I planned on telling them you fell sick."

"Using me as a scapegoat?" A hint of playfulness told him she wasn't angry.

"They respect strength, but they believe women are weaker than men. If I tell them you were sick, they'd understand, but if I tell them we escaped to find the sheriff, then they'll hunt us down." Jonathan turned his horse onto Broadway, heading south back toward town. Becca stayed right at his side. Something about that just felt right.

"I wish someone would arrest them all. They shouldn't be allowed to hold everyone in fear and get away with murder. I mean, not you, of course. You're nothing like them." Becca yawned.

She didn't rope him in with the monsters. If she could see it, why couldn't Graham? Jonathan yawned too. "Don't do that."

"Sorry. I'm surprised to be functional after—what?—a few hours of sleep."

"Thereabouts."

"How are you doing?" she asked.

The question surprised him. No one had ever asked how he was handling things. It was always expected he could without complaint. "Why?"

"Like them, you had gin, too. Headache or dizziness or anything?"

Jonathan's smile was cloaked in darkness. "Two shots don't affect me."

"Oh." After a stretch of silence, Becca asked, "What happens if we run into that Pool guy? We're not really going back to alert them, are we?"

"You're talkative for being tired."

"Chatting is keeping me awake. I don't want to find out the hard way what it feels like to fall off a horse."

"It's something you'll never forget."

"You have?"

"Plenty of times." Jonathan laughed. "Most don't break easily."

"What do you mean by 'break'?"

For the moment, he had forgotten she came from the future. A small kick to the gut reminded him of how short their time together was. Verity had mentioned unusual terms for transportation and the speed at which people traveled. "Breaking in a horse means to tame it for riding."

"You should pick a nicer term. Break sounds brutal."

To him, the future sounded like a place where everyone was as nice as Becca. Perhaps it wasn't so terrifying.

A man on horseback with a small lantern raised above his head approached.

Jonathan hadn't answered her question. "City, whatever issues the bandits have with Pool is their business. If we come across him, exchange pleasantries only if necessary."

"Copy that."

The rider's face came into view, shadowed in yellow light, and he nodded as he passed without a word.

"Was that him?" she whispered.

"No."

Becca released a long deep breath.

"Are you going to make it?" he asked, worried for her.

"I'm not sure how I'm going to ever sleep again until this is all over."

He wished to sweep away her troubles, which were his fault, but he couldn't. "The sheriff's office is just around the corner. After we report the information, we only have to concern ourselves with the bandits until the sheriff takes them out." Somehow, he thought.

"You're pretty good at that," Becca said.

Jonathan didn't know what she was talking about, but the compliment puffed his chest anyway. "At what?"

"Making me feel better."

"You're welcome?" He didn't know what else to say.

Becca chuckled, and he closed his eyes, enjoying the melody of her voice and committing it to memory.

They reached the intersection of the main roads through Navarino. Houses were dark, and silence thick as bread smothered them. Not even an owl hooted.

"Take a left here. Sheriff Clint Nelson is just beyond the courthouse on the left side."

The sheriff's office was dark too, but someone was always here to watch the prisoners. Usually the sheriff, sometimes a kid who aspired to replace him someday. Once they learned what kind of man the sheriff actually was, they didn't last long.

Jonathan stopped his horse in front of the building and hooked the reins around a post. Becca copied and met him at the door. He found her hand in the dark, and together they went inside. A candle was lit on the desk and big boots were planted on top. Jonathan followed the boots to a man with a hat covering his face, leaning back in a chair. He didn't look like the sheriff—too thin, and he wasn't the current prospective kid—too big.

Jonathan cleared his throat to startle the sleeping man.

"What...what? Is it time to get up already, Sheriff?" The unidentified man shifted his feet off the desk and leaned forward. He lifted his hat off his face and blinked at the pair of them standing before him.

Jonathan stared dumbfounded, eyebrows half up his forehead, at the long narrow face of the elusive Joe Pool. Last he saw Pool, he and his accomplice Rob Bertrand threatened Jonathan for Jaime Perez's extortion ring. Rob Bertrand became pig feed on Jonathan's farm, and Pool never returned. Jonathan assumed the man fled town after the massacre at the estate, never to be seen again, which made him the perfect scapegoat for Becca's tale.

"You're on the wrong side of the law, Pool. How'd you manage that?" Jonathan asked.

Becca squeezed his hand, and he rubbed his thumb across her knuckles.

Pool scrutinized Jonathan and frowned. "Well, howdy ta you too, Johnny. Sheriff made me the new deputy, and I'd say I'm on the right side of the law for once. Now I can do what I want, and the sheriff'll back me up. The town praises me too. I like this side, Johnny. It's only because the sheriff told me about his deal with ya that I'm not arresting you right now."

Pool wouldn't stand half a chance against Jonathan, and he wasn't exaggerating. The small man might be good with a blade, but Jonathan had arm's reach and far more experience.

"Well, we appreciate that," Becca said.

"What are ya doing here in the middle of the night anyway?" Pool asked.

"We have the bandit's home base, and we were promised immunity for it."

"Then hand it over," Pool said.

"At the end of Broadway, the road turns into Prairie Ave."

"We've been down that way. There ain't nothin'."

"I would've thought so, too," Jonathan said. "There's a single foot path, hardly noticeable, and after about fifty yards, it opens to a small cottage. Butch's mother lives there, along with the remaining bandits."

"Remaining?" Pool repeated.

"Brawley was taken out by Lizzy during a stick-up." And finished off by Butch, but that wasn't relevant.

"Huh." Pool leaned back with satisfaction on his face. "That's a fine woman. Did Butch spare her? I suspect not."

Jonathan shook his head.

"That's a shame. I'll call on the sheriff, and we'll check it out. If we find the place, you're clear," Pool said.

"There was no 'if's' about the deal, Pool. We gave you the information."

"How do we know you ain't lying?"

Pool had a point, and until the sheriff and Pool found the bandits and subdued them, he and Becca remained in danger. He needed Pool and the sheriff to win this battle, which meant they needed to be as prepared as possible. "That's fair, but the bandits are gunning for you. They said they have been since the shootout at Grignon's last year."

Joe Pool chuckled. "I've been hidin' in plain sight, and they never so much as noticed me. Let them come."

"Good luck. Drop by the farm when this has blown over."

"Will do with pleasure," Pool said and tipped his hat to Becca. "Miss. I didn't get your name, but it was a pleasure to see ya."

"Becca," she said, holding out her hand. "I'm Becca Wagner, a friend of Johnny's."

Joe Pool made a show of looking at their entwined hands. "Some friend ya must be. Stay out of trouble, both of ya."

Jonathan tipped his head to the new deputy and brought Becca back outside. Daylight was just blooming on the horizon, turning the line between trees and skies a beautiful shade of rose. Jonathan and Becca unhooked their horses and mounted up.

A horse snorted nearby, and Jonathan craned his neck to find the source. It was still too dark to see any movement, and he heard nothing more. "Let's go home and get some real rest."

"Sounds like heaven," Becca said.

Jonathan pictured himself tangled in his sheets with Becca at his side. He was too dog-tired to act on his fantasy tonight, but picturing her naked in his bed helped him stay awake for the ride home.

Chapter 18

BECCA PROTESTED HER BRAIN's attempt to wake up. Her dream was so vivid, starting with Kiko showing up at her door—how weird was that?—to talk about time travel—uh, huh—and finishing with closing the deal at the sheriff's office, with the deputy who used to be one of the bad guys. How absurd! It was almost as if her subconscious was inspired by her latest book. Becca swung her arm out to grip her current read, donned by Fabio, of course.

She touched air, and a warm, heavy arm draped over her chest. Now that was something unusual. Brad wouldn't have crawled back into their marital home already. He had Chastity to warm his bed.

Had she picked up a stranger last night? Becca didn't remember anything besides packing Brad's stuff and dumping him at the curb. Then Kiko showed up. Had Kiko drugged her and dragged her out for a fun night?

Becca's eyelids fluttered open, and a buttery yellow popcorn ceiling stared back at her. That was not her ceiling. Hanging on the wall like decorations were a rifle and a long blade. Worried, Becca turned her head and found...Jonathan snuggled up next to her. Becca's neck and face heated. Her chest bloomed with...nerves? Excitement? Anticipation? Alarm. What had happened between them?

Becca investigated without disturbing him. Her clothes were on. That was a relief, she thought, maybe. Jonathan appeared to be missing his shirt, but she wasn't sure if he wore pants, and she wasn't brave enough to send a hand down to check.

Becca lifted her head, and the bookshelves lining a smaller wall and an end table with a gas lamp told her this must be Jonathan's bedroom. There was a closet door wide open and a small square panel outlined on the back wall of it.

The man was a sight to behold. Well-cut and tanned from strenuous labor. Rugged and brave, but still level-headed in the face of stressful situations. And the kindness! The unexpected kindness melted her in every direction. Why on earth was he still single?

"What?" Jonathan mumbled through his pillow.

"Nothing." Did she say that out loud? Awkward.

Jonathan sat up, indeed shirtless, and heat burned her face. She had seen him mostly naked before, but when she had been arguing with him, over who-knew-what now, she wasn't as aware of how truly attractive he was.

He rubbed his face, as if trying to wake up. He stretched his arms and toned back and sent her a lopsided grin. "Why on earth am I still single?"

A hot flash rushed through her body. It wasn't her business, but the more she absorbed of his incredible...everything...the more she truly wondered. "Uh, yeah. I didn't..."

"My parents, before they passed, negotiated a contract for me to wed a blacksmith's daughter in Bridgeport." A sadness on his face made Becca want to comfort him. With everything she'd experienced recently, she only imagined how they'd died, and it wouldn't have been pleasant.

"How did it happen?" she asked gently. Becca sat up and pulled the sheet higher. She still had her shirt on, so it was only a matter of reflex. Jonathan didn't see her scars.

His upper lip twisted in confusion. "They drafted a paper with agreeable terms to both parties—"

She chuckled. "No, I mean, how did they die?"

Jonathan blew out a deep breath. "Mom caught the fever, and Dr. Frank said it was likely Dad died of a broken heart. Dad was singing her favorite song as he drifted away."

Becca gasped and covered her mouth with her hand. "How awful but sweet. I'm so sorry."

Jonathan reached for her other hand and rubbed her knuckles with his thumb—a small affection that made her smile. "It was an adjustment. I think Graham struggled the most. He was closest to our parents, and as the youngest, I think they went easy on him all the time. Verity was probably relieved on some level. They disagreed about her future frequently. As for me, their passing meant I had to take over everything."

"That must've been hard, being handed the family business to run by yourself. Even your dad had your mom to help," Becca said.

Jonathan's expression softened, and his thumb rubbed her hand again. He said, "The girl I was supposed to wed was spirited—too much like Verity—and younger than I preferred. Still, I would've completed my duty as a husband should."

Clearly seeing no evidence of a wife in the home or a wedding band on his finger, Becca asked, "What happened?"

"She was in love with someone else."

"And since then?"

"What do you mean since then?" His smile was sly.

Okay, now he was fishing for compliments. Becca had no reason not to be honest. "You run this farm, which means you're intelligent. You're strong and brave, able to hold your own against the bandits, but kinder and more thoughtful than any man I've known. And seriously you're hot, so why hasn't another young lady scooped you up since?"

"I'm always hot at night." Jonathan bent over the edge of the bed and picked up his shirt off the floor. "Sorry about that."

Becca's cheeks heated. "That's not what I meant. 'Hot' in my time means attractive."

"Oh." He paused and turned. The sly smile returned, and Becca swore he flexed a bicep. "You think I'm attractive?"

Becca struggled to refrain from tugging her shirt to fan herself. "Yeah, okay, you know you are. So, why are you single?"

Jonathan slipped the shirt over his head, the playful levity gone. "I asked a couple of women I thought would be a fit for me, but they turned me down." Jonathan chuckled when he looked at the disbelief on her face. "Apparently their fathers didn't approve of my illicit activities."

"That makes sense. You are a regular scoundrel after all," Becca said sarcastically.

"Let's eat." Jonathan went out to the living room.

Becca checked that she was fully covered and finger-combed her hair. Her curls were likely sagging and half-squashed, and she dreaded what she had to ask. Becca followed him out to the living room.

Jonathan placed cast iron pans on the wood belly stove.

"Is there a bathroom around here?"

"A latrine out back. If you want somewhere to wash up, there's a basin in the closet there, and a hand pump outside."

Okay. More camping style. She could handle this. Becca found the basin and set it in the grass under the pump and filled it with fresh cool water. Then she found Jonathan's latrine, which was much nicer than Viola's. His had an actual seat. Becca brought the clean water into the kitchen.

"Mug?" she asked Jonathan, who was lighting a fire in the stove.

He pointed, and she found one herself, scooped it into the basin, and slammed the whole thing down. After the second mugful, the flavor registered on her tongue. Her face pinched involuntarily.

"Now you know why everyone drinks liquor," he said.

"I do. Wow. It's...not good." Still, Becca would rather choke down iron-flavored water than rely on gin every day. How was that sustainable?

Jonathan fried up eggs and bacon for their breakfast, and she didn't want to tell him, but she hoped Jonathan's food was better than the bandits' Abner.

Becca had no shame watching him do the work. Brad had never done any food prep. Weren't men supposed to be proud of grilling the best hunk of meat? She especially enjoyed Jonathan wearing an apron. How modern of him. "I didn't expect you to be the cook. Don't you have someone to do that?"

"I did. Verity left."

"Who does the shopping?"

"We had Mrs. Cottlewood run household errands for us, but her days are nearing retirement." He tipped a basket to inspect what was in it. "But she came this morning."

Becca checked the clock over the mantle. They had slept until noon, and the lady hadn't woken them up. They were both exhausted last night.

Jonathan placed a fresh fruit on each plate—three plates.

"Who's joining us?"

"It's a peace offering. Graham's going to be furious."

The back door slapped shut, and Becca startled.

"Oh, hi," Graham said to her, stopping short. He did, in fact, seem mighty pissed. "I see you found him. Good—someone needs to keep a leash on Johnny."

Becca kept her eyes wide and her mouth shut. She didn't want to get between the brothers' disagreement.

"Sit down and eat." Jonathan's baritone voice was commanding, authoritative, sexy.

"I'm only sitting because you're feeding me, not because you told me to," Graham said.

Becca suppressed a chuckle at the teenager's protest.

"Understood." Jonathan set the filled plates before them, removed his apron, and tossed it onto the countertop.

"Where were you?" Graham asked and stabbed his food with a fork.

Becca dug into her eggs and bacon, and each bite was amazing. It could use seasoning, but compared to what the bandits had fed them, Jonathan's cooking was delectable.

Jonathan leaned forward. "The sheriff planned to lock me up, but we made a deal."

Graham scowled. "Another deal? Don't you see how well the last one went?"

Jonathan sighed. "In exchange for locating the bandits' home base, I'll be pardoned."

"I don't know what to say to that," Graham said.

Jonathan pressed his lips together. "Would you just listen? Becca and I found their hideout last night. We went to tell the sheriff, but we found Joe Pool stationed as the deputy."

Graham laughed. "Since when did you get an imagination?"

"I'm not making this up. We told Pool the bandits' location, but until the sheriff and Pool arrest them all—if they can—the bandits might catch wind of our deal. Understand?"

"So you exchanged Perez's five enemies for Butch's countless enemies."

"Four."

Graham's brows popped. "Who died?"

"Lizzy shot Brawley at The Astor House."

"Good for her. Say, were you joking about finding me a contract, because that hostess, she'd be great," Graham said.

"She didn't make it."

Graham turned to Becca for confirmation, and she nodded. Graham's face fell, and Becca couldn't stay silent. "I'm sorry, Graham. There was nothing we could've done."

His eyes watered, and he allowed a tear to fall before swiping the rest away.

Becca swallowed her bite and said, "Butch shot her in retaliation."

Graham tensed, and his brows furrowed. "And now he's gunning for both of you?"

"Keep on your toes," Jonathan said and finished his last bite. "Want seconds, anyone?"

Becca shook her head.

"No." Graham stirred his eggs, resting his face in his hand with his elbow on the table.

Becca reached out and covered his with hers. "I really am sorry. She seemed like a smart girl who made a desperate move."

Graham caught her glance, and his eyes shimmered. The kid broke her heart. She crooked her fingers at him, and he leaned into her arms. His hands went up to his face to swipe away tears at her shoulder.

"If there was anything we could've done, we would've. It was senseless murder, but now the sheriff has the information he needs to stop them."

"He better, or I will." Graham pulled away. "That bastard is going to get what's coming to him."

"If all goes to plan, the bandits will be arrested soon, but if Sheriff Clint fails, they will be hunting me down for being a traitor."

"No one ever survived leaving the bandits," Graham said quietly.

"We'll figure out something," Jonathan said. "Oh, and Mrs. Cottlewood is retiring."

Becca wondered what the 'something' was.

"Retiring? When?" Graham asked, worry on his brow.

"She didn't give a date, but soon. Barry isn't doing well. So, is there anyone besides Lizzy who catches your eye?" Jonathan asked, and his intense gaze flicked to Becca for only a second.

Becca's face burned, but she wouldn't read anything into it.

Jonathan forked another bite. His second serving was half gone already.

"Not particularly," Graham said. "I feel like half the ladies reject me as guilty by association." He scooted back his chair and carried his plate to the counter. He clapped his hands as if shifting mental gears. "So, the farm needs tending. Stay out of trouble."

Jonathan saluted, and Graham left.

"He was really broken up about her," Becca said.

"I'm surprised myself. He never showed interest in anyone before." Jonathan stood, collected both their plates, and washed them in the basin in the kitchen.

Becca watched his muscles flicker with the movements. She remembered when his lips took hers in a moment of desperation at The Astor House. A flash of heat cumulated into a pleasant throbbing that demanded attention. She stood and walked over to his back. If she made a move, she'd have to face Jonathan's scrutiny. But she couldn't resist. With a feathery touch, she caressed his arm with her fingertip. "Need any help?"

Jonathan turned around and set the last plate on the counter. "Now that you mention it, I do." He gazed into her eyes and Becca tipped her face up, inviting him to kiss her.

Jonathan reached out and pressed her against his body. With a shaky breath, his mouth met hers. Soft presses increased the throbbing, and sensitive ripples danced through her lips. Becca's hands found his perky ass, and she grabbed him. Jonathan groaned, and taut muscles shifted under her fingers. Before she realized it, her hands lifted his shirt off and flung it away.

"That's better," she said, admiring the view.

Heat burned behind his eyes, and he lifted her up in the air and carried her to his bedroom. He set her down gently on the mattress and paused with his face near hers, eyes roaming her features. Becca tugged her shirt back down into place. Jonathan brushed the loose hair from her face, while Becca's heart thundered in her chest.

She'd never been with anyone since Brad...since she'd lost her child, and the marks left behind. Becca was no longer a dreamy-eyed twenty-something. She was in her thirties with baggage to prove it.

"What's—?" Jonathan started.

The screen door slapped shut, and Jonathan stilled, alarm on his fine features. His head craned back toward the bedroom door. Heavy boots thumped. His eyes widened and he whispered, "Get up. We have to go now."

The heavy boots snapped her alert. Graham wasn't that heavy. She jumped off the bed and rushed over to Jonathan, where he opened a secret hatch in the back of his closet.

"Inside here, now."

She crawled into the dark hole and scooched back for Jonathan to fit. For a moment, she worried he would close her inside alone.

A familiar voice grumbled from the kitchen. "Over here. I heard somethin'."

Nash.

Jonathan squeezed in with her and closed the hatch behind them. He held his finger to her lips in the blackness. "We have to get out of here and make a run for it," he whispered.

"Run? But we don't have anything. Food, water, weapons. You don't even have a shirt!"

"They're going to find us in here. The closet door is wide open, and the sun is shining right on this hatch."

"So how do we get out?"

"I added an escape door after Verity was found in here." Jonathan maneuvered around her and opened a similar hatch. A square of light shined by her knees.

Jonathan jumped out and held it open. Then the gentleman offered a hand and helped her out of the narrow passage.

A built farm worker paused his path toward the pig pen to watch the spectacle.

"Tony," Jonathan yelled with a whispered tone. "Bring us a horse—fast!"

The worker spun on his heels and ran across the yard.

Becca's stomach flip flopped with her pile of eggs, and her eyes darted to the front and back of the house. They had nothing to hide behind. The other side of the house at least had shrubs. "What if they find us before Tony comes back?"

Jonathan turned her to face him. He grasped her upper arms and looked her straight in the eye with total confidence and seriousness. "They won't get you."

His touch was comforting and soothing, but after all she'd seen in the presence of the bandits, she couldn't believe him. "How can you be so sure?"

"I'll explain later."

Becca trembled in his arms while her eyes darted, waiting for that moment when angry armed men charged.

"You're shaking. It's going to be all right. Remember, there're dozens of ways to die on a farm. We're not getting taken out by common thieves."

Just as the words left his playful lips, a man came around the back of the house, bringing a horse with him. Becca exhaled a shaky breath.

Jonathan met him and took the reins. "The bandits are in the house. Stay away from them."

"Will do, boss."

Jonathan helped Becca onto the horse's saddle. Her limbs were stiff and uncoordinated with the trembling, but when he hopped up behind her, she relaxed just a little. With a jab of his heel, the horse galloped through the corn stalks toward the woods, and Becca pushed aside her soreness.

A single gunshot echoed through the fields, and Becca's only thoughts were about staying on the horse and if Jonathan had been hit.

Chapter 19

JONATHAN HALTED THE HORSE where the cornfields met the woods and dismounted in a flash. He helped Becca down, and slapped the horse's flank to obscure their direction. He gripped Becca's hand and rushed her into the coverage of thick brush. Scrapes stung his bare flesh, but with bloodthirsty bandits hell-bent on vengeance chasing them, he ignored the stings.

"Where are we going?" she asked while staying by his side.

He was impressed with her stamina, but he couldn't focus on how amazing she was right now. "Far from here, but we have to cross Broadway first."

The brambles thickened, slowing Jonathan's progress to lead her to safety. Blood pounded through his veins while he held branches out of Becca's way and sliced through thicker stems with his dagger. He checked behind them to see if they'd been discovered.

Becca's head turned to check, too. "Are you sure they weren't coming to talk about Pool?"

Jonathan knew the bandits well enough. "If they wanted to converse, they would've announced their presence, not crept into the house." His slapping screen door literally saved his skin.

"I hope Graham is okay," Becca said.

Jonathan's stomach twisted. Hopefully, the kid heeded his warning, but worrying Becca further was of no benefit. "He's a bright boy. He can take care of himself. Don't tell him I said that."

Becca chuckled for a second.

Green vegetation crowded his view forward and now mostly blocked his view from behind.

"How much farther are we going? Ow!"

Jonathan stopped and inspected Becca's forearm, a red gash sliced across it—superficial, but he hated to see her wounded. "The bandits aren't hunter-trackers—just thieves and opportunists. I don't suppose they'll follow too long, but we can't be too careful."

"Murderers. You forgot that key part."

"Correct."

"Do you suppose they figured out the fake story about Pool or your traitorous deal with the sheriff?"

"If they saw us reporting to the sheriff's office, sure, but since they were inebriated and asleep when we escaped, I doubt it." Jonathan remembered the invisible snorting horse after they had left the sheriff's office and now wondered. Had that been one of the bandits?

Becca remained silent as if she were playing grim scenarios in her head. He didn't want her to worry. Jonathan firmly gripped her upper arms and leaned down to her face. "We're going to be all right. Butch has quantity, but he lacks quality." Jonathan flashed her a smug smile.

Becca laughed. "I'm glad you're confident."

That bright smile of hers was irresistible. If circumstances were different, he'd take her right here in the woods. Alas, he gestured and returned to their escape.

Laborious marching through dense vegetation during the peak of summer meant Jonathan couldn't avoid the sweat on his torso dripping to his waistband. He swiped a hand across his forehead to keep his eyes clear, and after far too long, the woods finally thinned out. Broadway was just ahead. Jonathan ducked down and waved for her to join him.

"Anyone coming?" she asked, breath heaving in a distracting way. He peeked up over the ditch and checked both ways. Not a single rider, but there was a loaded trailer headed away, so the driver wouldn't see them.

"It's clear. Let's move fast."

They dashed across the open dirt road. The sun beamed down on them as if exposing their location for the world to see. His legs pumped harder, eating up the distance, and he came to a sudden stop just inside the safety of the woods. Becca kept up, and Jonathan lifted his lips into an appreciative smile. What a fine woman.

Both of them panted. Working the farm didn't involve so much sprinting. "We've got about twice that distance to reach the river. Can you make it?"

Becca swiped her brow. Her once perfectly formed spirals framing her face were now half frizzy and half flat. He wanted to run his hands through her hair and feel the texture tickle his skin. Her eyes were drawn with worry, but there was something, some kind of spark there.

She smiled. "I'm an outdoor girl. I can handle it."

Jonathan's lips pulled into a grin. "Perfect. Let's go. Daylight's ticking."

Minutes turned to hours and exertion was on the verge of becoming exhaustion. They ducked, climbed over, and sliced as they made headway. Jonathan chopped at a nest of branches blocking their path, but he worried Becca hadn't told the truth. He craned his neck to see how she was doing. "Almost there," he said reassuringly.

She nodded, breathless. Was that how she sounded while making love? Jonathan glanced at the indent on her ring finger and realized something. Last year, he considered marrying Sarah Hartley a duty, a means to an end to help his family. But when the contract was terminated, he felt free, excited at the possibilities of doing what he wanted with his life.

He didn't expect the farm to struggle. He didn't expect Verity to leave for the future. He didn't expect to work with the bandits, and he didn't expect Mrs. Cottlewood to retire. One thing after another snowballed. And finally, something wonderful happened. Becca had bravely walked into his backyard. What he would give to wake up with her every morning! Jonathan reminded himself she needed to go home, but this time, the fact was disappointing. Crushing? Yeah, he could say that.

"We're here," he said sadly.

"Are you okay?" she asked.

"Of course."

"Your tone changed."

Oh. He hadn't meant to allow the disappointment to slip. So he didn't interfere with the life she was meant to live, he'd have to watch that. "No worries." Jonathan sent her a smile, but he didn't feel it in his heart.

She gazed at him, studying him, trying to decipher the truth. He smiled a little harder, and she turned away, satisfied. The smile fell from his face like a weight he could no longer hold.

"Wow," Becca said, approaching the river. "This is the Fox? It's so...clear."

"It's not in your time?"

Becca laughed. "No. Too many ships, manufacturing plants, and lots of waste runoff. The East River is worse—completely brown."

"The future sounds horrible," Jonathan said.

"It has its pluses and minuses." Becca stared at the water's surface. "Are those...logs?"

"There's a lumber camp upriver."

A smile of amazement tugged at her lips. "So now what?"

"I say we take a boat."

She laughed. "You have one hiding somewhere? 'Cause I don't see one."

Jonathan pointed across the river, just slightly downstream.

"And how are we going to get it?"

Jonathan removed his trousers and unlaced his boots, all too aware of her eyes watching him. "The only way."

BECCA DIDN'T HAVE LONG to admire Jonathan's muscular shape before he dove into the broad and swift Fox River wearing only his antique boxer briefs. His splash was eerily quiet. How was he going to avoid getting pummeled by logs while dragging a boat across by himself? How was he going to win against that current?

He hadn't surfaced yet. Becca searched for something she could use to help, but unless she mastered the art of braiding cattails for ropes, she was out of luck. She scanned the river's surface, but he was nowhere in sight. She shielded her eyes from the sun and searched the logs, hoping to find him taking a break and floating.

He was nowhere. This was a mistake. What was she going to do now?

Jonathan finally breached the surface, and Becca exhaled in relief, placing a fist over her heart. He paddled through the water, pausing and shifting position to avoid the logs, like a real-life version of Frogger, while the current pulled him straight downstream toward the beat-up wooden skiff.

Beached on the bank and half in the water, she wasn't convinced it would float. It was small, canoe-sized, with just enough room for a couple of people to fish. Becca slapped a mosquito and fanned herself with the front of her shirt. She considered jumping in to help, currently feeling like a sweaty hormonal high school student who'd just run a 10k race—she needed a bath.

Then she remembered the transponder gizmo Kiko had stuffed in her pocket. She couldn't risk getting it wet and damaging it. Then she'd be stuck here forever.

Jonathan was the strongest swimmer she'd seen. Stroke after stroke, he brought the beat-up boat closer, avoiding the hazards roaring downriver, and when Becca knew she could wade in and not damage her lifeline, she helped drag it on shore.

Jonathan stood, panting, and ran his hand down his face to clear river water from his eyes. His floppy hair hung in wild directions, dripping down his well-carved shoulders, rippled abs, and sculpted hips. His boxer briefs clung precariously, showing her a tease of what she wanted to see, and Becca's face heated. Yep, she could watch him walk out of water any time. Becca fanned her face with her hand while Jonathan wrung the water from his underwear. If only they hadn't been interrupted this morning...

Hot flashes raced through her body, and Becca tried to suppress the growing throbs between her legs with different thoughts.

Jonathan put his pants back on, and that helped. So did thinking of injured puppies, and that smell left behind after emptying anal glands on dogs and cats. Oh! The smell of pus after surgically removing infected tissue—before and after gangrene set in.

That was too far.

"Everything all right?" Jonathan asked. He was back in his pants and boots, but he still had no shirt.

Becca couldn't decide at the moment whether that was a good thing or not. "Yeah, good, fine." Becca diverted her attention. "Wait. There's water in the boat."

"As long as we don't hit a log, we'll be fine."

Becca watched with horror as log after log barreled downstream toward the sawmill.

Jonathan chuckled. "It's fine. Trust me." He held out his hand, assisting her inside. He pushed off and hopped in after. The boat rocked alarmingly with his weight, and water spurted up from a hole in the floorboards.

"Are you sure that's okay?" She pointed to the fountain.

"Can you swim?"

"Yeah," she answered, eyeing him suspiciously, but she couldn't let her gizmo get damaged. Becca didn't know how it worked, but anything with a button meant electricity, and mixing electricity and water meant bad things happened.

"Then it's fine."

She wasn't reassured.

A pair of oars rested in the boat, and Jonathan set them on their pivot points. Lazily he stroked the oars through the water leading them upstream. There was a path in the water near the other side of the river that appeared clear of logs. Becca leaned back against the bow of the skiff and made a point to admire the view.

Jonathan smiled, and Becca could swear he blushed.

"You aren't supposed to enjoy being chased by scorned bandits through the woods," Jonathan said.

"That's not the part I'm enjoying," she said, inspecting his bare chest for imperfections. So far she found none, but she wasn't willing to give up the search just yet. Becca wasn't a quitter.

"Then what is?" Jonathan's muscles bunched and released as he pulled the oars through the water.

"Oh, I can think of a few things. They're all right in front of me." Yeah, she was flirting, but she didn't care. Becca knew what she wanted...to take his mouth and ride that cock until it burst.

Jonathan exhaled and grinned. "We need to change this discussion before I end up stopping this boat and getting us caught."

Becca chuckled. "I can be quiet. Can't you?"

Jonathan groaned, and there was definite blushing going on. Becca relished in his sexy reaction.

"So what's your story, City?" Jonathan asked. "Who did you leave behind?"

Becca's eyes widened. "How did you know?"

He tipped his head toward her fingers. "You're missing a ring."

Becca stared at the traitorous dent and rubbed her fingers around it, smoothing away the reminder. That was a cold splash on her libido. "I was married to my college sweetheart."

"Was?"

Becca couldn't meet his eyes. She stared at the dent and remembered things she'd hoped to bury.

Bury.

Like the painful memory of her daughter. No, she didn't want to bury her memory. Becca only wished the loss wasn't so painfully debilitating. Her daughter never had a chance to experience anything. Becca wanted to show her everything good about the world and teach her about all Becca's favorite things—namely books and exploring nature. Becca was excited to be a mother, but some greater force decided she wasn't good enough.

Just like Brad decided she wasn't good enough.

And now all she had was a dent on her finger and scars on her belly and thighs.

Becca looked at the ripples and reflections in the water, trying to maintain her composure, and she sucked in a sharp breath. "Oh god, this is the river where they dumped

Brawley." She scanned the surface, searching for his remains, both curious to confirm her suspicions and terrified of finding his floating corpse. With all her tumultuous thoughts, Brawley's cold blooded murder—point-blank gunshot, body being dragged, stuffed full of rocks and tossed into the water—sent her over the edge. Tears streamed and sobs pushed free. Becca covered her mouth with her hand.

"Come here." Jonathan urged her closer, and what she really needed that moment was a hug.

On shaky limbs, Becca crossed over the bench and kneeled in front of him. His well-defined and bare arm curled around her and pulled her to his chest. With her palms on his pecs, she leaned against his shoulder. His touch was comforting.

Jonathan released the oars and held her snug. "We won't find him. If they didn't succeed in sinking him, he would've washed out to the bay by now. Either way, we're going upstream—the opposite direction."

"Such a horrible thought—what they did to him." Strong arms helped her feel steady and in control.

"That's how they operate. Now tell me about this failed marriage of yours." Jonathan released her to take up the oars, and Becca turned around, leaning her back against him.

"When I was in college, I was looking for my classmate's dorm when a door sprung open in front of me, hitting me square in the head. The guy, nervous about liability or litigation, brought me inside for a drink of water to make sure I was okay. Brad was there, a guy who appreciated machines and moving parts, whereas I was into animals and...well, their moving parts." Becca managed a chuckle. "Everything about him was such a stark contrast to me that I felt more complete being with him, like a yin and yang situation. And that sounds ridiculous."

"That's not ridiculous."

Her head shifted with each stroke of the oar. "Well, I thought we made a good team, but I now realize he wasn't home enough to even count as my teammate. He worked long hours, and when he came home, he was too tired to do anything. I tried to get him to take a vacation with me. Several times we ended up booking hotels in various big cities. He liked casinos."

"What did you want to do?" Jonathan stroked the oars harder, as if they'd lost momentum.

"I wanted to go camping. Bon fires, s'mores, and a tent where the neighbors can hear every sound you make. The soft splashing of waves against the shore. The star-speckled night sky. That was relaxing to me."

"That sounds splendid."

"We never went." Becca sighed. She had been so blind.

"Not once?"

"We went hiking on a trail through town, after convincing him to take a break from his video games. It was a paved trail for god's sake, but he hated every minute of it. Ultimately, I was busy myself working at Dr. McCall's clinic, and I thought that's just how life was. Some couples have equal compromise, and some don't. We happened to fall into the latter group. Then we decided to try for a family." She paused, and her eyes stung with tears.

Jonathan's arm wrapped around her in a comforting embrace, allowing her to speak. "We would've had a baby girl, but she didn't make it."

Becca sobbed and covered her face in her hands. She let herself unleash the pain she'd stuffed down deep, hidden from everyone who pretended to care but didn't want to see her weakness.

Jonathan's embrace was like the spirit of her daughter telling Becca everything was okay. That her daughter wasn't in pain, wasn't suffering, and wasn't missing out. That she could see everything and she was proud of her mother for doing her best to bring her into this world. Becca mumbled through wet tears, "I'm sorry, I'm sorry, I'm sorry."

Jonathan rocked her, and a melodic humming grew into words. Becca cleared away her sobs to listen.

> I see your tears, and wish they were mine.
> I see the weight of the world, pressing your fault line.
> Let me take it.

The ache in her chest softened. The words struck home, and the tears rolled down.

> Those memories so painful, an affliction endless.
> Those dreams suddenly vanish, but never hopeless.
> Let me show you.

Becca sniffled and cleaned her nose on her shirt, which was no longer cream.

> Tell me sweetheart, how can I ease your trouble?
> When the light of day fades away, there is only you and me.

Another sun shall rise, and I will find you smiling.
You'll see.

Jonathan reached his face to meet hers, and she tried to hide her smile. When he smiled back at her, a laugh broke free. "I'm sorry, it's just...that song is beautiful. But..."

"I can't sing," Jonathan politely finished for her.

"Not at all, but I loved every word of it. It felt like it was written for me." She twisted to face him, probably full raccoon again unless all the mascara had finally washed away.

"It always made Mom feel better, and I hoped it would help you. I would do anything to take your pain away."

Becca believed him.

Jonathan gestured for her to return to his chest. She nestled against him with a fat grin on her face. She continued her story a little easier now, body shifting with his oar strokes. "After our loss, we separated, and I found out after I signed the divorce papers he had an affair. A small part of me—okay, a big part—wondered if our failure was all my fault. That I wasn't yin enough for his yang, turning our round circle into a floppy oval."

"I happen to have one side of the story, but I'm certain your marriage's failure was not your fault. I've personally experienced what you call camping, and I've been to a casino. If Brad couldn't make you happy, that's entirely on him. He's an imbecile."

Becca snorted a laugh. "You're calling a mechanical engineer stupid?"

"Any man blind to how wonderful you are doesn't deserve you. No offense to your decision to marry him. Love can blind people."

Becca recalled how she and Jonathan worked so well together. Every plan was considered without insults or dismissal. No fights to make meals. No arguments for a quick jaunt outside for fresh air. Sure, she and Brad had never gone undercover with ruthless bandits and been chased by them, but that wasn't the point.

Jonathan respected her.

Brad didn't.

And Jonathan was right; it wasn't her fault. She was going to be okay, like a burden was lifted from her shoulders. The book slammed shut on the past. Had a new chapter already opened?

The woods thinned along the banks and men shouted nearby, followed by a heavy splash. Jonathan tensed behind her.

"What is this place?" she asked.

"Lumber camp. We don't want to be seen. The bandits will question them on their way back to town." Jonathan tipped one oar out of the water to turn the boat around. On the slow arc, a log banged into the skiff, listing it sharply to the water's surface.

Becca gasped, and she flailed for purchase.

The hole in the floorboards spurted up above the rail, and gallons of water poured in.

"Well, looks like we'll have to make camp here," Jonathan said and struck both oars back into the water to navigate toward shore before the boat capsized.

Becca had never felt more at home, but she still feared for the gizmo, because she knew in her heart she had to go home to her life, her parents, and to the modern amenities she knew.

Chapter 20

Jonathan had a problem, a big one, about a-hundred-and-fifty-pounds' worth—and not the sinking skiff. Becca scooped water out of the boat's hull while he struggled to row to shore. Her story made him want to grab her and comfort her, protect her from the evils of the world, and promise she'd never feel that kind of pain again.

He was grateful the ladies in town declined his affections, because now, they would never live up to what he dreamed of—Becca. The idea of this red-headed… Jonathan trailed off, frowning at the demarcation in her hair. "City?"

"Yeah?" she asked while grunting with the effort to keep the boat afloat.

"I have a question, and I don't want to upset you."

Becca tensed, pausing from the effort, chest heaving. "Okay," she said hesitantly and tugged her shirt back down. "Is this about my stretch marks? Because I thought my story implied—"

Jonathan smiled. "There's nothing wrong with any marks on your body, but I am concerned about the food in the future."

A sweet laugh burst through her lips. "It's a valid concern, but what brought this up?"

"Your hair has a stripe. The red changes to light brown with streaks."

Her hand went up to cover it, and she laughed. "You think this is a nutritional deficiency? I was cursed with grays at thirty, and I feel more like a redhead anyway. Don't women color their hair here?"

Jonathan shook his head. "Not that I know of."

She smiled gently. "The red strands are permanently changed, but the new hair growth is my natural color. The level of harm is debatable, but nothing to worry about."

Jonathan didn't understand most of that, but he did worry less. "Let's beach it here, a safe distance from where we entered the woods and from the lumber camp." Jonathan inhaled deeply and rowed with maximum power until the bow ran aground. When the small skiff stopped violently rocking, he helped Becca onto shore and dragged the bow farther up on land. He brushed his hands clear of dirt, and his stomach rumbled.

"Tell me more about the future." Jonathan led the way into the woods, dagger in hand, slashing at the brush to make a path toward better cover.

Becca followed. "Well, the future is fast. Everything is so fast. Work is a fixed schedule. If you're late more than a couple times, usually you're fired. Dr. McCall is different, though. Let's see—meals are rushed and mostly taken at restaurants or the drive thru. In general, only rich people have horses. Everyone else uses public transportation or they own a vehicle. You can fly around the world in a day or two. So many events, activities, and there's the Internet—anything you ever wanted to know with a few clicks of a button at any time. People eat poorly, sleep terribly, suffer from record stress and anxiety, but that's modern life."

"That sounds horrible." And similar to Verity's tale. Why would his sister choose that over life in Astor? Jonathan continued slashing at the brush, but it was thinning.

"It has its good points, too. Regulatory bodies to enforce safety in the workplace, everyone without a felony can vote—"

"Everyone?" He loved Becca's outrageous stories.

"Just about. Medical care is amazing, although the cost can bankrupt you. Other countries have that figured out better.

And there's leisure time. When you're not working, running errands, going to activities or events, there's leisure time to work on hobbies."

"I have time for hobbies, even with running a farm and the bandits' demands. Can't comment on healthcare though. Not sure what that's like. Dr. Frank arrives if you call upon him. That's about it."

"Well, life expectancy is in the upper seventies, so things that kill people now, would be nothing but a thirty-minute office visit and a trip to the pharmacy in the future."

"None of those things were all that convincing. Sorry."

Becca snorted. "I've never tried to convince anyone the time I live in is better than theirs. It's not usually an option, so it doesn't come up."

That surprised him. What made Jonathan so lucky to experience it twice—second-hand, of course. "Time travel isn't common in the future?"

Becca chuckled. "Still science fiction as far as the public knows. Hell, I still don't believe it, and I'm here!"

The brush thickened once again, and Jonathan was satisfied with its cover. "Let's find somewhere suitable for a few days to hide."

"You want us to hide for days? Here? What are we going to eat or drink? And we need shelter."

"Follow me." Jonathan led a fresh path through the ankle scratching brambles and found a small clearing for them to rest. "We'll stay here. We don't need shelter since it's the hottest point of the summer, and it's sufficiently shady here. Water is just where we came from. And food, leave that to me."

"Wait, what?" Her voice lifted in panic. "What are we going to do for days?"

Jonathan could think of a few things to pass the time, but those suggestions would be inappropriate at the moment, so he only hid his amusement. "I thought you liked camping?"

"This isn't what I had in mind."

"We only need to wait for the sheriff and Pool to do their job or for the bandits to lose interest."

"And then what?" Becca pressed her hands on her hips, a familiar stubbornness returning.

"We go back to the farm and prepare ourselves for their return."

Becca's anger retreated. Her eyes were drawn, and she wrapped her arms around herself. He hated to see her so afraid.

"Don't worry." Jonathan touched her upper arm. He didn't want to tell others why he did what he did, but he wanted Becca to know. "There's a reason why the bandits let me join in the first place."

"Because Butch couldn't kill you when he came to rob you?"

"Sit down."

Becca cleared a space in the pine needles.

Jonathan plopped down right where he stood. He folded his legs across himself and rested his elbows on his thighs. "You remember the story of my contract with Sarah Hartley?"

"She married someone else," Becca said.

"The contract termination clause was a hefty sum. With those funds I was able to hire workers on the farm to increase production. The plan was to have enough food to last us and the animals all winter with extra leftover to sell and continue to grow operations. But with the drought we've had this year and last, the savings dwindled. It wasn't long until Jaime Perez and his men came knocking, demanding a weekly payment for protection from the bandits." Jonathan chuckled at the irony. "Even if I thought they could help, I had nothing to give. They harassed me for months. After I put a bullet in one of them, Jaime left us to our own devices. The farm was on the verge of closing."

"So you looked for a job?"

The corner of Jonathan's lips lifted. "Not quite. Traditionally, I would've sought a new contract. A bride price would've sustained us long enough to create a family of our own to run the farm, but I wasn't interested in starting that circus all over, and Graham was too young. I was at the dining room table pouring over the dismal numbers when the bandits arrived. At that moment, I wasn't sure if I should've run for my weapons or laughed at the irony of them thinking I had anything of value. We had a pleasant discourse for a short while, and when I refused to hand over cash I didn't have, fat Fingers held me at gunpoint. Brawley, Nash, and Ruddy dug through my home for valuables."

Becca gasped.

"Butch went to supervise. He never was very hands-on. When Fingers turned his attention, I picked up the chair I was sitting on and threw it at him. With his excessive size, he was thrown off balance and struggled to regain his composure. I collected a kitchen knife and hunted Butch—who I found raiding Verity's personal effects. I got a few good swipes on his leathers before he alerted his boys to rescue him. Had he been alone, I would've taken him down with little trouble. His minions came swiftly, and I managed to fend off their guns and give each enough damage to call a truce. In the end, we were all panting, and their leader laughed." Jonathan shook his head at the moment his life went to hell. "It was the kind of laugh you'd expect after telling a joke at the bar. I'd heard the stories of the bandits, but never met them until then. Taking no chances, I gripped that knife and calculated my next move when Butch said, 'Boy, I never saw a fella as fearless and quick as a snake like you. Tell you what, rather than we all fight 'til we collapse, how about you ride along with us and you'll get an equal cut of the take. With the six of us, we can take on bigger targets. There's no limit to the wealth.' For our livelihood and that of my employees, I didn't hesitate."

"To save the farm you accepted his offer?" She condensed.

"That's it. Noble enough for you?"

Becca frowned. "And now they won't let you go."

"From the stories I heard at the bar, a man named Fitzgibbons ran with the bandits for a couple weeks—long before me. When Fitzgibbons was satisfied with his take and his wife wanted him to quit, the bandits took his head off. There were others before him."

"Jesus, Johnny, no one could blame you for doing what you had to."

Jonathan pressed his lips together and rubbed his hands down his face. "Graham does."

"Does Graham know the whole story?"

"He knows we have money troubles, but he has no idea about Jaime's attempted extortion. Graham thinks there's another way."

"And that is?"

"In all his youthful wisdom, he hadn't expressed any solution. I offered to get him a contract now that he's old enough, but he refused."

Becca traced a finger through the pile of pine needles. "Even knowing the background of the bandits, and their policy of killing those that quit, you still joined?"

Jonathan sighed. "When a man is desperate, he'll do anything for the ones he loves." He gave her a pointed expression, but she glanced aside as if working the details out herself. Hopefully she didn't hate him for his choices.

"I have a question, but don't take this the wrong way, okay?" Becca brushed debris from her hands. "If you were so much stronger than Butch that he needed all four of his men to stop you, why didn't you just take over—be the leader yourself? That would've solved your money problems, giving you a cut of the...take, as you call it, but as the leader, you could've quit without the death policy."

Jonathan would've been angry if anyone else had asked him that question. Instead, he felt slapped, insulted, degraded. "You think I'm that kind of person? One who would kill a man for money?"

"Well, I..." Becca trailed off, shifting uncomfortably.

"I'm not a murderer." Jonathan scowled. "The one man I killed trespassed and threatened my family."

"I know you're not. It's just for your situation, for survival, it was a more logical decision."

He didn't know whether to be angry with her or grateful she didn't hate him for joining. Giving her grace for being from the future, he decided on the latter. Besides, kissing her was more fun than holding a grudge. Jonathan leaned in close and said, "You are a very wise woman."

Becca's cheeks pinked, and he caressed her blush with his thumb. She leaped at him, tossing him back against the pine needles, and her lips found his in a demanding, desperate fury. Heat rushed through his empty stomach, and his limbs were taken over with a need to be inside her. His heart thumped wildly in his chest.

Becca's stomach growled too.

Jonathan suppressed his groan and reluctantly pulled her back.

"What is it?"

They hadn't eaten since breakfast. Jonathan stood up and brushed debris from his trousers, checking himself for obvious signs of pleasure. "I'll get dinner."

Becca exclaimed, "Wait! You're leaving me here?"

"It's better if you stay hidden. Where I'm going, women aren't allowed, and word would get back to Butch easily."

"Okay," Becca said with disappointment. She scooted her back up against a tree and brought her knees to her chest. "Are you going to bring cups too?"

Jonathan chuckled. "I'll try. Be safe, stay quiet, and I'll be right back."

She nodded, and he unsheathed his blade to make a path through the forest. He would bring her the best meal he could find, because she was worthy of nothing less.

Chapter 21

ALONE IN A FOREIGN century, hungry and filthy, an emptiness settled in Becca's heart, which was ridiculous, since she barely knew the guy. But for some reason, being around him just felt right, safe. At first, she'd judged Jonathan for being a bandit, but after all they'd survived, she knew he was a good man, and the story, in its entirety, only made her want him more. And right now, she only wanted him!

While waiting, Becca couldn't sit idle. What could she do to make this camping experience better? First, she needed a shower, but since that wasn't a thing around here, a dip in the river would have to suffice. Becca followed Jonathan's primitive trail back to the water's edge and checked for prying eyes. They hadn't seen anyone since Broadway hours ago. Becca stripped down naked and folded her skirt pants carefully, so her transponder gizmo didn't fall out or get wet, and she set the stack down neatly.

How much would it cost to replace that kind of technology? Becca didn't want to ask Kiko.

Having already scooped pouring water out of the skiff, Becca just swooshed into the water. A short yelp escaped her lips as the cold enveloped her whole body. She rubbed her skin to remove as much grime as possible without soap, and dunked her head, washing away the sweat on her scalp. When she surfaced, she flipped her soaking hair back, and once again, searched for prying eyes. Becca waded back toward shore fighting the current pulling at her legs.

She squeegeed the water from her skin with the edge of her hand and shook off like a wet dog. After drip-drying for a few minutes while wringing out her hair, she climbed back into her dirty clothes. The dried sweat on her clothes was gross, and the fabric clung to her while she yanked it into place. She verified the gizmo was safely in her pocket. Now this was roughing it.

What a story she'd get to tell...who? Her parents—no. They were practically ghosts. Her friends, Tess and Amanda, like they'd believe her. They'd probably block her and assume she was nuts. Verity was an idea. Maybe she could find herself a new friend in Jonathan's sister. They'd talk about the past, about Becca's experience. Verity would want to talk about her brother, and that would be painful. Not a great idea. But Dr. McCall—he'd understand, and then maybe he'd rehire her. She could resume a normal life after a chat with her boss.

Brad's face popped into her head. She never wanted to think of Brad again so long as she lived. The cheating prick Brad. He wasn't worth the brain power to fight the anger from bubbling under her skin. Instead, she pictured Jonathan. His smiling face, his amazing cooking, his selflessness ever since she met him. Oh, and when he first stepped out of the water in nothing but his underwear. That was an image to preserve. But that wasn't going to happen either. He'd already told her he 'wasn't interested in starting that circus all over'. Besides, she had to go home. Technically, since the sheriff had the bandits' location, Jonathan wasn't going to be arrested or murdered...by the sheriff. She could technically zap back home now, but with the bandits now hunting him, Becca couldn't go just yet.

Becca was tired to the bone in the way that a person who was used to a convenient routine and thrown into a survival situation would be. She watched birds overhead diving down for surface bugs. It was surprisingly tranquil without the hustle and bustle of the city, the ordinary noise that came from neighbors, or just noise from other campers. There was only her and nature. A peace settled over her, and she released a long sigh with a smile. Becca tilted her head up to the summer sun and relished the warmth drying her skin.

She wrung the last of the water from her straight limp hair and hiked back up the trail Jonathan had made, resolved to enjoy her time with him as long as it lasted, making sure he defeated the bandits and survived. That was what mattered to her. Then she'd meet with Dr. McCall and return to her pitiful life.

Along her hike, she picked up loose sticks and brush for a fire tonight. When she found the clearing she had made in the pine needles, she knew she found the right spot. Becca dropped the pile of sticks at one end and crouched down and scooped pine needles into a makeshift bed. Not exactly a Serta, but it would do.

There was nothing in the area to use for a tent or canopy in case of rain, but they could always relocate to the base of a dense pine tree. The boughs should be enough to keep them dry.

And now what?

If she were back home, Becca could be browsing social media on her phone, or mindlessly clicking through Internet sites, baking cookies, or reading a book. She wished she had her Fabio-wrapped books now. Even one to pass the time would be great. Who was she kidding? Although Jonathan didn't look like Fabio, or act like him, Jonathan was almost everything she'd hoped for. Joining the bandits and running for her life wasn't on the list, but how much closer to a wild adventure could she ask for?

When she went home, at least she had these memories to take with her. Becca wished she could have what she really wanted though—a family of her own. If Jonathan found out about her inability to give him what he wanted, he'd gladly send her packing. It was for the best he wasn't interested in a relationship anyway.

Becca parked her rear underneath a tree and leaned against its trunk. She split her hair in half and braided each side, hoping to salvage some curl when it dried. Chipmunks scurried in the fallen leaves. Birds fluttered along the branches overhead. She heard a splash, but she couldn't see anything. Probably another bird diving for dinner in the river.

How exactly was Jonathan bringing dinner? He wasn't planning on hunting a deer with his bare hands, was he? She didn't know whether to be impressed or horrified.

Heavier steps than squirrels and chipmunks approached, and Becca stood with a smile. He hadn't been gone as long as she really expected, but she was hungry enough to eat whatever it was he brought, as long as it wasn't still alive. How was she going to make a fire? Did rubbing two sticks together really work? When she'd camped, she went prepared with supplies and equipment. This was a whole other level.

Boughs were pushed aside, and Becca turned with a grin on her face, only for her stomach to leap into her throat and for her breath to be stolen right from her lungs. A face she didn't want to see approached. Becca backed up a step, forcing her expression to remain neutral.

Nash stepped forward with a smug smirk and a pistol pointed at her chest. Becca glanced around him for signs of the other bandits, but no one else was around that she could tell. She needed to play dumb, and she kept her hands casually at her sides.

"Found ya," Nash said.

"Hi, Nash." She made an obvious motion to look around him as if expecting the bandits to show up with their mark. "Did the others find Joe Pool yet?"

Stay calm, stay calm. Johnny will be right back, she thought.

"Oh, we found him all right." His dark tone made her stomach flip. "We got 'im right where we want 'im."

"Great! So, what's with the gun?" Her insides swirled, and her body trembled, but she kept her voice even while pretending their fleeing the farm didn't happen. The delay card was all she had to work with. Like a mouse cornered by a cat, her pulse roared through her veins. And with Nash's snarl, the only thing she could think of was him wanting to have sex with a dead woman's body. Becca wanted to hurl.

"Since Johnny took off, he owes us an explanation."

"Oh, that's all?" Becca kept her tone light, so he wasn't triggered into more deplorable behavior, but her trembling was getting worse. She wasn't going to be able to keep up the façade for much longer. "I can give you the explanation. We were asking around for Pool, just as Butch ordered. But when Joe Pool saw me, he flew into a snarling rage. He blocked our path back to the cottage, so we fled south, and Pool chased us. Finally, we lost him in the woods here. We were coming back soon, according to plan, after we were sure we lost Pool."

Nash made a sound of disbelief, and his eyes roamed her body, making her empty stomach flip. "Is that so?"

"One hundred percent."

Nash pulled back the hammer on his pistol, and Becca stifled a frightened gasp. Her hands went up in surrender. "This isn't necessary. Johnny will be back any second now. Then we can reconvene at the cottage and plan the next steps in your brother's revenge."

Nash lifted a brow.

She didn't know if that was good or bad, but the delay kept her alive so far. "I'll get us some beer, my treat." She tried to smile, but her lips only flipped up and down. Her breath was shallow pulls.

"We have the best liquor in the area, stolen from that rich bastard Grignon. Why would we want plain ol' beer?"

"It's free?" Becca fought sobs of desperation.

"Everythin's free." His eyes roamed her body again, and Nash sucked in through his teeth, a slurping sound that made her want to crumble and sob.

"I have money. Lots of it." Becca dug for the coins Jonathan had told her to use just in a situation like this.

"I'll take it when I'm through with you."

Johnny, where are you? she silently begged.

Chapter 22

Jonathan slashed his way through the woods, carving a trail to the lumber camp not far upstream. Every few feet, he stopped and listened. The afternoon sun glittered through the canopy of trees overhead, lighting his path well, and a squirrel dashed for cover as he walked by. No voices. No human footsteps. He'd told Becca the bandits weren't hunters, just thieves and opportunists, but that wasn't entirely true. They didn't give chase for the average target, but if someone personally defied them, the bandits made it their life's mission to hunt down the perpetrator, stopping at nothing but food, drink, and sleep.

Jonathan was proud to be a third-generation corn farmer, but the patriarchs in the tri-village area considered him to be among the lowest of social standing. Because of that, his pickings had been slim, but once word spread about him leaving the bandits behind, his options would greatly improve. Assuming the women he chose would no longer reject him, who would he choose to be his equal, his partner?

Not Marisol, the couture clothier's daughter. The poor thing was forever black-marked being Jaime Perez's sister.

It wasn't Estelle, daughter of a lumberjack.

It wasn't Evelyn, daughter of a mason.

They were all once interested, but only one woman made him smile. She wasn't a farmer. She wasn't used to a life of little. She wasn't acquainted with his lifestyle. But still he wanted her.

Becca Wagner.

Something about her was maddening. Not in a Verity kind of way, but in a way he wasn't familiar with. Finding willing women wasn't ever the issue—before the townsfolk labeled him as one of the bandits—and finding the right one wasn't a priority. But then Becca fell into his life, and now, he felt lost but found at the same time. It didn't make any damned sense. One thing was certain, though—he never wanted to be without her. His cock stirred when she was around, but more than that, something about her woke him up, challenged him, and made him want to be better. He wanted her to be proud of him. He wanted to impress her.

Jonathan crunched his way through the thinning woods. Seeing as he wouldn't be needing the dagger before reaching the camp, he holstered the blade and swiped sweat from his forehead. He looked at the dirt, the callouses, and scars all over his hands. Remembering Mathew and his pretty city clothes, neat hair, and smooth hands, Jonathan wasn't built like the men of her time.

What if he went with her? Could he find happiness in her time—the world of scary things and horrible food? No, no he really couldn't. Jonathan wouldn't abandon the farm and leave the responsibility to Graham. His little brother had proven he wouldn't run off, but he wasn't ready to take over, to manage the employees and handle all the affairs of the operations.

Jonathan could never go with Becca.

At the edge of the clearing to the lumber camp, Jonathan watched from behind a tree. Men roasted food over fire pits. Others ate meals they had packed. Jonathan still had bandit money in his pocket, enough to buy plenty. He picked his target and strode over with his chin held high as if a shirtless man emerging from the woods was normal.

"You there," he said to his chosen man.

The filthy worker gave him a suspicious look over. "What?"

"I'd like to buy your lunch."

"No, thank you. I have a lunch."

"You don't understand. I'm going to pay you for your lunch. I want it," Jonathan said.

"Look, man—"

Jonathan tossed a dollar in coins into his lap, a weeks' wages, and the worker's eyes widened as he smiled. "Well, hell. Why didn't you just say so? Here." The man passed him a sandwich and an apple.

"Thank you." Jonathan tipped his head to the man and returned to the woods, ready to curl up with Becca for a long night's rest, but he didn't think much resting was going to happen...at first. Jonathan wanted to resume what the bandits had interrupted back at the farm. The memory of her lips on his and her hands exploring his chest, made heat rush to areas that only she could relieve.

Her flushed face came to mind. The sound of her voice was like music to his ears. The smell of her skin was an intoxicating drug, and the kindness she displayed—to his brother, and even in the face of danger—bowled him over. The sooner he returned to her, the more time they had. Jonathan picked up his pace until he heard talking.

Alarmed, he slowed his steps to imperceptible movements and shifted from tree trunk to tree trunk out of sight.

It was Nash, and he held Becca at gunpoint. Dammit. Jonathan set down her meal and retrieved his blade. He craned his neck for the remaining bandits but didn't see anyone else. Butch always had a tight strategy. This was unusual, and Jonathan didn't like when the bandits did new things.

He wagered how many rounds Nash had chambered against Jonathan's blade. He had one chance, and he had to make it count or someone—or both of them—were going to die here in the woods. The bandits didn't give burials to traitors. Not thoughts he wanted at the moment.

While in conversation, Nash tilted his head and shifted the gun just off to her side, approximately where Jonathan stood.

"Freeze or I'll shoot," Nash snarled.

He shouldn't have underestimated the man's skills. Jonathan displayed an open palm from behind a birch tree and stepped forward cautiously. The other palm rested around the handle of the blade hidden behind his thigh.

"Both hands where I can see 'em."

"No sudden movements," Jonathan said carefully. "We're all on the same team here." His empty hand made a placating gesture.

Becca swayed on her feet just slightly.

One chance. Just one chance. Jonathan calculated distance, trajectory, and most importantly—risk. His hidden hand moved forward, and with a sudden flick of the wrist, he sent the blade careening into Nash's gut. Not an instantly fatal hit, but it would take him eventually. For now, it bought them time.

With crushing fear on her face and something in her hand, Becca rushed at Jonathan.

Nash stared at his injury in disbelief, momentarily distracted.

Becca crashed into him and wrapped her arms around his neck, squeezing tightly. "Hold on and don't let go," she whispered into his ear. Her soft voice wavered as she fought back sobs.

She didn't need to say that twice. He'd planned to rush Nash and finish the job, but with her gripping his body like a lifeline, he changed plans. Jonathan bent, intending to lift her off her feet and run her back to the skiff.

A gunshot rang through the woods.

Becca squeezed around his neck tighter. Jonathan's vision rippled and darkened.

He'd failed.

He was going to die in moments, and everything he'd done to save the farm was for nothing. All the thievery, all the lives taken, all the sacrifices. For what end? To be left as a corpse rotting in the summer's woods.

And worse was going to be Becca's fate.

Because he'd failed.

Jonathan's stomach rolled, and his vision blanked to darkness. He thought being shot would hurt more.

In the end, he only wished he would've found himself a wife who loved him, and he wanted her to be Becca. That was all he really wanted. To hell with the rest.

Chapter 23

Present Day, Green Bay, Wisconsin

It worked! The transponder gizmo worked. Becca released Jonathan's neck, and he straightened. His alarmed gaze shifted from the half-filled parking lot with a restroom to a teenager drinking fresh water from a bubbler. Behind them more teenagers played soccer in a trimmed and painted field.

Becca knew that look. The same one appeared every time Becca had to give bad news to a family of a beloved pet not surviving surgery. Dr. McCall was talented, but he couldn't fix everything.

The man from 1854 was in shock, and stupidly, Becca wanted to laugh. See how well she adapted to the past? And the big tough guy couldn't handle a basic park. As she took in the amenities herself, Becca recognized where they were. The dense woods of the past became Cormier Park in the present. What a relief to be safely back home.

Jonathan's unfocused gaze swept the park and fixed back on the cars. He wobbled as if about to faint.

"Sit. It's okay. Just sit." Becca helped him down onto the grass. His eyes rolled back. Becca gripped his slick shoulders to stop his head from thumping the ground, but she only managed to lurch forward with his weight as he crashed backward. Becca did her best to cushion his fall, but she probably made it worse. She chuckled and blew stray hairs out of her face.

Suddenly Jonathan was peaceful. The lines of stress softened around his eyes. His bare chest gleamed with sweat, and she finally remembered Nash's gunshot. Becca's smile faded as she searched for a small caliber wound, fingertips tracing around his flesh. She didn't find any, so she turned him onto his side, which was much harder than she anticipated, and checked his back—nothing.

Laying him flat again, she palpated his thighs and flashes of heat rushed through her, but still she found no wounds. Her fingers brushed his floppy dark hair away from his forehead. She searched his face. Perfectly formed and handsome as ever. How could Nash miss at that distance?

Becca tapped his cheeks. "Johnny? Wake up. It's okay. We're safe. Johnny, c'mon, wake up."

His eyes fluttered open and slowly focused on her face. He brought a hand up to her cheek, and she nestled against it. "We're dead?"

Becca laughed. "You fainted. Welcome to my time."

His hand crashed down to the grass. "Are you sure? Because I feel like I must be dead."

"The ride through is rough. Come on up." She helped him to his feet.

Jonathan looked around again, less pale this time. He pointed to the parking lot. "What are those?"

She smiled. This was going to be fun. "Our version of horses. We'll be taking a ride soon, I hope. Let's go."

Becca led him over to the teenagers and waved her arms in the air. "Hey, I lost my phone. Can I borrow one of yours to call a ride?"

The boys stopped running, and one caught the ball. A lanky blond kid walked up to her and smiled. "Sure, lady."

He passed over his android, and while she called her friend Tess, the boy assessed Jonathan's scarred bare chest, trousers, and antique boots with a tilt of his head. Becca was not going to explain anything to the kid.

Tess didn't answer. It was a strange number, so that made sense. Next, she dialed Amanda. Same results. Shit. She called Kiko and still no answer.

"Thanks, anyway." She passed it back to him.

"No problem." The boy took his phone and tucked it into his pants and took off running back to the game. After a short whisper, all the boys' heads turned to them, but Becca paid them no mind.

A car honked behind her, and Becca turned to find Kiko in the driver's seat of her own Corolla. How the hell? It didn't matter. The woman wasn't human no matter what she claimed.

"That's for us," Becca said.

She grasped Jonathan's hand and jogged across the park to the waiting car. Kiko jumped out and came around to meet them. "Sorry I'm late. I don't know what's been going on lately." The small woman turned her hand over in front of her as if not seeing something she should. Since Becca believed Kiko wasn't human, Becca didn't know whether to be alarmed by that or not.

"Don't worry about it. We're alive, and we have a ride. I'm good. Johnny, you okay?" Becca asked.

He nodded and leaned in close to the paint, seeing his reflection. He kept his hands clear as if the car could bite. "How does this work?"

Becca opened the passenger side door for him. "Not even I could explain that. Get in."

Kiko slipped into the back seat, while Jonathan stared in awe.

"Butt goes there. Feet down there," Becca said, pointing.

Kiko chuckled.

After he got in, Becca closed the door after him and slipped behind the wheel. She leaned over the bewildered man from the past and buckled him in.

"What's this for?" he asked.

"To keep you alive in case of an accident."

"Is this safe?"

"Eh, safe as you can ask for."

She buckled herself and shifted into drive. The car moved out onto Broadway—the modern version, a four-laned road split with a grassy median. Becca navigated the city streets, and Jonathan's pale returned.

"Are you sure you didn't get hit?" she asked and glanced at his gleaming and sexy chest.

"I didn't." His whole body was taut with tension.

"You seem a little...lost?" Terrified was more like it, but she understood a man's pride.

"How fast are we going?" Jonathan asked.

Becca checked her speedometer. "About thirty-five miles per hour. Why?"

"Thirty-five miles...per...hour?" he repeated slowly with disbelief.

"Exactly as it sounds."

"It's an engineering marvel. I'm shocked at how this is possible without a horse pulling us," Jonathan said.

"Take a deep breath. This is only the beginning."

Jonathan's hands were curled into white-knuckled fists over his knees. She didn't enjoy his fear, but a little amusement at the turn of the table was harmless.

"Good timing, Kiko. None of my friends answered my call."

"With caller ID, I didn't think they would," Kiko said.

"You knew they wouldn't," Becca corrected.

"True."

"There's no way someone over a hundred years old is human. Sorry, I don't believe it." Becca searched Kiko's face in the rearview mirror. The quiet woman's lips lifted just slightly.

Jonathan broke from his enchantment. "A life span over hundred years is ludicrous."

"You're right. Kiko isn't human," Becca said.

"Yes, I am." Kiko crossed her arms over her chest and frowned, the most emotion Becca had ever seen on her. After all her years spent time traveling, not much must bother or surprise her anymore.

"Prove it."

Kiko smiled. "I'm not sure how."

"Who won the 1960 World Series?" Becca asked.

Kiko squinted. "I don't know."

"See? Only an alien, or a fossil"—she glanced at Jonathan with a smirk—"wouldn't know that. The Pirates toppled the Yankees, by the way."

"I only traveled to and from where my matches were. I didn't bet on sports...much, and I'm not a baseball fan."

"Pirates?" Jonathan's eyes were bug wide. "Did you say the pirates won? I thought there were only a few left on the Great Lakes. What happened since 1854?"

Becca laughed. "They're baseball teams. New York Yankees versus the Pittsburgh Pirates. Bottom of the ninth, all tied up. Bill Mazeroski hit a home run—the first home run to win a Series in baseball history." Every fan knew that game, even if Becca wasn't alive when it happened. Of course, Brad told her about it and made sure she remembered it. He talked about it as if he were there in person.

"You're speaking English, and yet, I don't understand anything you say." Jonathan stared at her in marvel.

"Welcome to my world." There was a nice double meaning she didn't intend. "I mean, that's how I felt when I was in your time."

Becca reached Kiko's house and pulled up to the curb. "Thanks for the help. I'll let you know if we need you, alien."

Kiko laughed. "I know." She winked and left the car, closing the door securely behind her. Becca waited until Kiko walked up the concrete steps to her house, half to make sure she got there safely and half to see if she'd vanish to another time.

"I didn't understand anything you two were saying. I feel like I'm completely lost—dropped into another civilization," Jonathan said.

Becca pulled away from the curb, disappointed when Kiko closed the front door behind her. "Don't worry. It'll get worse. There's so much that happened. We had people on the moon, robots on Mars. Oh, Pluto isn't a planet anymore—again. The Internet—that'll be mind-blowing, and cell phones. Oh, and I'm going to introduce you to fast food, because I'm starving. I just need to swing by my house and grab my purse."

"All I understood was food, and I agree. Your meal got left behind a tree."

"Oh, thank you, by the way. Where did you get food from?" She hoped he didn't hunt down a deer.

"I bought a lumberjack's lunch."

That was surprisingly sweet and honest. "Thank you, and I'm sorry about your knife." The one left behind in Nash's belly. Becca shivered at the image.

"Don't worry about it. I can get another from the Hartley's. Sam makes amazing blades."

"I'd like to see them." Becca smiled at Jonathan, whose knuckles and fists were still white with strain. She added, "You can relax. Nothing's going to happen right now."

"I don't think I can."

Becca parked in her driveway. The pile of Brad's things at the curb was heavily picked through. She forgot to tell him to get his stuff before posting it online. Oh, well. The prick deserved worse.

She leaned over and unbuckled Jonathan, and finally his knuckles loosened.

"Ride's done for the moment. Come inside." Becca opened his door for him and led the way up to the front door and unlocked it. Inside was a blast of horrible memories.

Where Brad watched baseball—if it wasn't at the bar.

Where Brad ate dinner—in front of the TV with a controller in his hand.

A blanket of misery wrapped tight around her body. This was a bad idea. Becca found her purse and snatched it up. When she wheeled around, Jonathan's head cocked in confusion.

"What is it?"

"After all the grand tales you told of the future, I was expecting something...I don't know. Less sparse?"

Becca chuckled. "This isn't how we normally live. I was literally searching for a new place to move to when Kiko showed up and sent me to you. You know, to save your life."

"I'm glad she did." Jonathan reached for her and embraced her body with a warmth that cast away her misery. For that moment, she was in the woods in his arms, safe—ish and...happy? Was she happy back then, even with the bandits hunting them down? That didn't make sense, but emotional situations could cause people to act or think irrationally. Was she irrational in her reaction to Jonathan's embrace? She didn't think so.

Becca's stomach growled. She reluctantly pulled out of his arms and said, "We really do need to get some food. Let's go for another ride."

Outside, Becca paused at her boxes of Brad's stuff and dug until she found her old favorite Hawaiian print T-shirt that would fit Jonathan. It sucked to see a reminder of her ex on him, but no shirt, no service was a common concern. Becca brought him to the drive thru first and inhaled a deep breath through her nose and smiled on the exhale. "Doesn't that smell great? Especially when you're starving."

"You were starving?"

"Figure of speech. Not literally."

"I don't know what I smell."

"Well, oil for sure, but underneath that noxious stench is the brilliant aroma of hamburger."

Becca placed a large order and checked the bags before passing them to Jonathan. She pulled over to eat since she just couldn't wait any longer.

She passed him a burger and unwrapped her own. He copied her. She bit off a mouthful and moaned. "Oh, man. Nothing tastes as great as steamy hot fast food when you haven't eaten for so long."

Jonathan's face twisted, something resembling what her face probably looked like when Viola passed her a hunk of Abner.

Becca chuckled. "It's cow, lettuce, tomato, mayonnaise, ketchup—"

"Ketchup?" He asked with a twist of his lips as if the red sauce was the most disgusting thing he'd ever eaten.

"Yeah. Number one favorite condiment in America. Try it."

"Ketchup in my day tastes like spoiled fish."

Becca cringed. "This stuff is nothing like fish. Trust me."

Jonathan bit off a chunk and chewed, nodding as he absorbed the flavors. "It's not bad."

"There's water. It's filtered." She nodded at the drink. "And fries, too."

He sipped the water and lifted his brows. "The water's pleasant."

Within moments, he drank all the water and ate all the fries.

"I'll loop around for more."

"Is it supposed to feel like this?" he asked, face twisted.

"Like what?"

"My stomach doesn't seem to enjoy this food as much as my tongue did."

"You get used to it." She shrugged. "Or you never eat it again."

She grabbed seconds through the drive thru, and this time, as she handed over her credit card, Jonathan asked, "How much did she say it cost?"

"Thirty-two fifty."

"Cents?"

"Dollars."

"Remarkable! Is this luxury dining for the elite? How can anyone afford this? That's more money than most people make in a month or three months. No wonder why life is so fast here. You have to work so hard just to survive the expense."

"You're not wrong," Becca said. She inhaled the next batch of food while parked in the lot, and this time Becca got some fries of her own.

"Is that...? Is..." Jonathan trailed off. "Is that...?"

Becca looked up to see a Ford F-350 Super Duty pulling a horse trailer.

He finally spit the words out, breathy as if blown away. "...a horse riding a chariot?"

"Yep." She chuckled.

"Oh." His palm went to his forehead.

She tapped his thigh with a smile and a chuckle. "Eat up. We have another stop to make."

Becca had to talk to Dr. McCall about fixing her life.

Chapter 24

When Jonathan had opened his eyes to a strange world, he was afraid. When he'd realized Becca had brought him to her home time, he was terrified. And the way Becca lit up at being home tore his heart out. Jonathan couldn't be here. He had to get back to his farm—to Graham.

But how?

Until then, Graham was going to have to take charge while Jonathan survived in a new world, starting with this itchy and unfortunate-patterned tunic she put on him. Jonathan would never again complain about his sticky sweaty linen shirts.

He wanted to be impressed with Becca's ease in handling such a terrifying monstrosity, but he couldn't understand it. The levers, the foot movements, it didn't make sense. The bandits he understood—their actions, their thought processes, their intentions—and Jonathan could plan accordingly. This weaving of speeding machines was too much for him. And as the car, as she called it, leaped forward through an intersection, Jonathan's body tensed, muscles trembling with the strain. He felt like a useless imbecile, a horrible foreign feeling.

Becca brought them to a place where the front yard was a hard material with yellow lines, and other cars rested quietly, but for once, Jonathan recognized the place. He leaned forward and relaxed his grip on the hand holds. This was—

"This is where I used to work," Becca said.

"Sam Hartley's blacksmith shop. What have they done to Sam's shop?"

"This place exists in your time?" Becca asked in amazement. "I wish I could've seen it. It's Animal Care of Wisconsin now. I guess Dr. McCall didn't change much when he remodeled it."

Becca put the machine to sleep, and Jonathan quickly climbed out and shivered, happy to have his feet on solid ground. He didn't want to do that again.

Becca led the way inside through glass doors, and when he spotted the woman sitting before him, Jonathan paused his steps and stared. His breath caught. Tears rushed his eyes. He couldn't believe what he was seeing, and he wouldn't blink, fearing she would disappear again.

"Verity?" Jonathan asked on a soft breath.

His spitfire of a sister was dwarfed behind a massive desk, staring at a box with light coming from it. Her wild hair was smooth and soft, and she was wearing the same strange clothing as Becca. Now he had someone to ask the question he needed answering, once he could loosen his tongue.

"Hi Verity," Becca said, capturing his sister's attention. "Does Dr. McCall have a free appointment slot?"

Verity lifted her head, and when her gaze found Jonathan, her lips parted and quirked into that smug smile Jonathan missed so much. Good thing he didn't bring her shotgun along.

"Sorry, Matt doesn't see filthy bears." She glanced at Jonathan's tunic and cringed. His cheeks heated at his sister's judgment. "But if you exchange this model for a smaller, cleaner, more dog-like one, I'm sure he could squeeze you in."

Jonathan leaned on the counter. "I can wash away what makes me a bear, Verity, but you can't wash away what makes you a noisy crow."

Verity grinned. "I see you haven't lost your touch, Johnny. Hold on a second." Verity stood, and Jonathan noticed the small swell of her belly. It was beautiful, and he was so happy for her. She was swallowed up by a door and came back out a moment later. "Matt will see you now."

"Thanks," Becca said and turned to Jonathan. She gave his forearm a squeeze. "Take a few minutes. I hope the walls are still standing when you're done." She winked at him, and he wanted to capture her sassy lips for gifting him time with his sister. The door swallowed her next, and Jonathan was alone with Verity.

"Didn't bring my shotgun, did you?" She leaned over the desk and checked his hands.

"Unfortunately, no." If he'd had it on him before fleeing the house, Becca would've never needed to sweep them to the future for safety. Nash would've been instant Swiss cheese. "Miss it?"

"I do miss having my life threatened every day." Verity's sarcasm, as healthy as ever.

"So you learned how to behave? I hardly believe that."

Her sassiness faded to a sharp tone. "My friends and family here don't keep me prisoner."

"I did what was necessary to keep you alive. I would've liked to see some appreciation, but it's nice to see you've grown up otherwise."

"And it looks like you haven't. Bathe much? Or do you need a woman in your life to keep you in line?"

"Keep me in line?" Jonathan wanted to confront her about what Butch had said about his sister, but Jonathan never imagined a chance to ask her. "Did you spend time with the bandits?"

"Very little. Why?" Verity asked, curiosity replacing the dry wit.

"Butch tells me he proposed to you."

Verity's brows lifted and terror filled her face. "You've been running with the bandits! You can't! Johnny, why would you?"

"Answer the question."

She dropped her eyes to the lit box and sucked in her lower lip. "He did, but I turned him down."

"Why did he propose?"

"Why? Are you saying that I wasn't worthy of a bandit's hand?" She narrowed her eyes at him.

"I'm asking what relations you had to cause him to propose."

"I gave him an onion...twice. I was nice when I passed by him...once." Verity fidgeted in her seat as if holding back information.

"Spit it out," Jonathan said, patience dwindling.

"Did anyone notice the condition at Grignon's estate?"

"The massacre is famous. I know Matt rescued you. What else happened?"

"Butch made a deal with Jaime Perez to kidnap me for the bounty. After the cash traded hands, Jaime offered the bandits more money to leave, so Jaime could get his revenge." Verity rubbed her hands on her face as if the memories still plagued her. "Butch agreed, but once the sack of coin appeared, Butch backstabbed him. The bandits slaughtered Jaime's men. I maimed Jaime again and if he survived, I made sure he'd never lay a finger on another woman again." She glanced toward the office door. "Sam killed him. Matt was there, too."

"That didn't answer my question." His tone was sharper than he'd planned. The further Verity's story progressed, the more Jonathan wished to be back home, armed, facing those bandits.

Verity sighed and her lips twisted. "Butch said he was impressed with my maiming, and he'd be proud to be my husband. Not exactly those words, but you understand. Matt was flaming mad." Her lips lifted back into a smile.

"That was it?"

"Of course, what else did you think…?" Verity trailed off, assessing him. "You think Butch and I…" Verity laughed. "No. Never."

That was a huge relief. "Joe Pool survived."

Her eyes widened in alarm. "He's not still searching for me, is he?"

"He's the deputy sheriff."

"What?" Verity's head tilted in disbelief. "If you're serious, you cannot trust him."

Jonathan feared his instincts were right on that man. "I don't."

"Now tell me why you've been running with the bandits."

He was ashamed to admit the truth to his sister, but he sighed. "The funds from my contract were almost gone, so when they tried to rob me—"

"You stopped them all by yourself?" Verity lifted a brow at him.

"Of course, I did."

Verity rolled her eyes, and Jonathan spoke a little louder for his pride's sake. "He was so impressed, he asked me to join. I couldn't turn down the money."

"What happened to the farm? To Graham?"

"The farm is still there, still ours. Graham's not happy about any of it."

Verity chuckled. "I imagine not. So, what brings you to the future? Or should I ask 'who'?"

Jonathan's head turned toward the door Becca had gone through. "Becca brought me."

"By choice?"

"Nash was about to shoot me when she did something, and next thing I knew, we were in a field with kids playing games."

"Kiko sent her to you," Verity said simply.

"That was the name of the woman."

"You know what that means, right?" Verity asked, a hint of excitement playing on her lips.

Jonathan shifted his weight and scratched at the ridiculous tunic. "I'm alive?"

"You are her true love. Kiko matches people through time. Matt explained it to me. He was the one sent to find me, just like Becca for you. Like April for Sam."

Then it wasn't a coincidence the perfect woman appeared in his backyard determined to save his life. All he wanted was Becca, and he wanted to tell her that, but how would they reconcile the differences in their worlds? She would have to choose. "I have a question to ask you."

"Go ahead."

Jonathan cleared his throat and shifted his weight again. He leaned against the desk and lowered his voice. "In the future, how long is appropriate to wait before proposing a hand in marriage?"

"Awe, Johnny. How sweet." Her lips curved into a genuine smile. "From what I've seen on TV, it's normal to wait months or years."

Jonathan straightened. "Years? That's an incredible waste of time."

"Here is very different from our day."

Jonathan shook his head. "Becca said everything in the future is fast. I guess not everything."

Verity laughed. "Just wait until you visit the DMV."

"What's that?"

"Department of Motor Vehicles, notoriously the slowest service in the country."

"Is that for the cars?" He sounded like an imbecile asking that, but he didn't know how to use 'cars' in the proper syntax.

"You got it. Buying, selling, updating licenses and registrations. Everything costs so much money."

"That explains your wages." Jonathan remembered how much Verity said she had made in one week, and he didn't believe it. He still couldn't believe Becca spent over fifty dollars for their two trips for food. Simply unfathomable.

"Doesn't go as far as you think."

Remembering the drive through, as Becca had called it, Jonathan leaned in. "Did you know horses ride chariots here?"

Verity laughed. "It takes a while to get used to."

"So how are you doing? Do you like it here?"

"I love it. I'll never go back. Come here. I'll show you some things."

Jonathan circled around the desk and stared at the lit box in front of Verity. A photograph...in color...was on it, of Verity and Mathew smiling together. Jonathan's brows furrowed at the familiar sight behind them, which he recognized from black and white newspaper images. Jonathan leaned forward to get a closer look. "How did you get to the California Gold Rush?"

"It's a museum for tourists now. Matt brought me for our honeymoon. We flew there, and you could never imagine what that's like. Have Becca take you flying. It's so worth it."

Jonathan laid a hand on her shoulder. "I'm glad you got your dream."

Verity glanced up at him with glistening eyes and nodded. A clicking sound came from her fingers, and bright colors flashed before his eyes. He didn't understand what he was seeing, but he noticed a hand touch her belly.

"I heard you have a family coming along. Congratulations."

"Thanks. Entirely an accident, but we're thrilled."

Two bright and shiny rings were on Verity's finger, and one of them bore a stone impossibly large. He could never give Becca something like that. The feeling of inadequacy, of their differences, crushed him again.

"Check this out," Verity said, pulling him from his thoughts. An image appeared of the earth. "Where do you want to go around the planet? I can use this mouse here and zoom to wherever you want to see. The Great Wall of China? Here we go." Verity moved the thing she called a mouse and sure enough, there was The Great Wall as he'd read about.

"Pyramids of Egypt? Big Ben in London? Or even the Grand Canyon. It's so amazing to travel the world while sitting in your chair," Verity said.

"Ha!" Jonathan exclaimed, excited to learn something outrageous wasn't true. "Becca said you could travel around the world in a day or two. I knew that was impossible. This isn't traveling."

"She's right. You can fly to these places if you want. I think it'll take two days to reach Australia. Everywhere else is closer. Oh, check this out."

Verity did more things with the mouse, and an image of a housecat popped up. A clicking noise came from the mouse and then the cat was in motion. Jonathan pressed a finger to it but only felt warm glass.

"Is it a real cat?"

"It was. This is a video. It captures things for you to watch later. Like this." Verity brought out a small black box with a glass cover and pressed on it until it lit up. She tapped a few things until Jonathan could see himself in the box, like a mirror. She pressed once more, and the box made a chime noise. "Say 'Hi, everyone'. It's recording a video of you."

Jonathan stared at it with a frown. He didn't understand any of this and had a sudden new respect for his sister mastering all this so quickly. "Hi, everyone?"

She touched the box a few more times and showed it to him.

Jonathan watched himself repeat what he just did. "That's unbelievable."

"This is just the surface. There's so much more than you can imagine."

Jonathan wasn't sure he wanted to.

The doorknob rattled as if it were opening.

"Johnny, stay away from the bandits." Verity sent one last warning. "They're bad news."

"Consider it done." It was the easiest promise he'd ever made her.

And likely the last.

Chapter 25

Stepping inside the clinic to request her job back after being in the past felt...surreal. She was still herself, but somehow she didn't recognize her life anymore. With Jonathan in 1854, she had been an undercover spy in the bandits and fleeing for their lives when discovered. Here she was what? A veterinary assistant, who now had to dodge her gloating ex. At any second she pictured him returning with that smug smile on his face, and she didn't honestly know if she could do that again.

Why did her present life feel so...meaningless? Empty? She needed time to adjust to the past, so now she needed time to adjust back. Was there such thing as time travel jet lag? Becca strolled up to Dr. McCall, who was busy at his computer. "Hi, doc."

"Becca!" Dr. McCall looked up with surprise. "What brings you here?"

"Can we talk?"

"Have a seat." Dr. McCall turned away from his computer and folded his hands together on top of his desk. There was an unusual sparkle in his eye.

Becca exhaled a deep breath, knowing what she was about to discuss would sound crazy. "Kiko tells me you time traveled and saved Verity."

His brows popped. "Uh, yes I did."

"I brought someone back with me, kind of on accident"—she knotted her fingers together—"and he's here visiting his sister."

"Johnny is here?" Dr. McCall stood.

"Just out there." Becca gestured over her shoulder. "I wanted to say that I'm sorry for my outburst the other day. Brad—"

"No apologies necessary." He stopped her with a raised palm. "I stand by my employees."

Becca had always known Dr. McCall was a good man. She didn't know he was that lenient. She'd always planned to ask for her job back—to resume her normal life—but being back here just didn't feel right, like she didn't belong.

"If you want your job back, it's yours." Dr. McCall sat back down.

Becca looked the kind man in the eyes. "I don't think I can."

"Are you going back?"

Becca's heartbeat skipped. "That's the thing. I think I want to, but I don't know if Johnny wants me, you know, in that way." Jonathan clearly wanted her in one way—his bed, but that feeling was mutual. The problem was, he'd clearly stated he wasn't interested in a relationship, and when he was—someday—he expected a big family to run the farm. In relationships, some differences were irreconcilable, and she didn't want to start something that was destined to end.

"If he can't see the amazing woman within you, then he doesn't deserve you. But I also trust Kiko. She told you her purpose?"

"She said my true love was back there, but I don't see how that can be."

"Well she told me she almost never gets the matches wrong. If she sent you to Johnny, I believe he's your true love." Dr. McCall sounded like a Disney movie.

"I'm not convinced," she said. She wanted to believe the doctor, and her eyes flicked to the door, where the better-than-Fabio waited. Heat rushed through her limbs. "I only just met him."

"If neither of you have those feelings yet, they will come in time."

"The farm—his livelihood, his everything—is struggling. He needs something from me that I don't think I can give him."

Dr. McCall held up a finger to interrupt her. "I have just the thing. I read diary pages and have drawings of the Hartley family, so I have an idea of how she's doing back then, which is very, very well. I forgot to tell her about a savings account I opened when I was there, but it turns out she doesn't need it. So here, take this, and use it however you need."

Becca accepted a dented card from Dr. McCall with numbers written on it and a bank's name from Bridgeport. The implications of the gift were simply too much, and not at all what she meant. "Oh, I can't take this. It's yours."

"Becca, take it and live the life you want. I don't need it. The Hartleys don't need it. The money was going to sit there until the bank closed and the funds transferred to the unclaimed assets division of the government. That was my fault, so I want you to take it instead of the government."

"That's more convincing." The corner of her lips lifted, and her eyes watered. Cash in hand would help Jonathan. Maybe they could compromise on the other problem.

Dr. McCall smiled. "Verity can handle the desk by herself. Whenever her morning sickness is too much for surgery, Kiko's been helping out. Go. Live your life. It's worth it." That sparkle returned to his eyes, and now Becca understood.

She tucked the card into her purse, intent on gifting it to a man in need of saving a farm, a family's life.

"Oh, and Becca?"

"Yeah?"

"Shower," he whispered.

She laughed and stood up. "It's on my to-do list."

Dr. McCall came around the desk and hugged her. "It's been good working with you all these years. If you ever need a reference, don't bother asking because I can't send messages back through time. Otherwise, I'd be thrilled to. Good luck to you."

Tears formed on her eyes again, blurring her vision, and she let them fall. A sad smile formed on her lips. "Thank you."

"And now I need to say hi to my brother-in-law. Is he still an intimidating scary guy?"

Becca laughed. "Intimidating, sure. Scary, not so much."

"Is he armed?" Dr. McCall asked, lifting his collar and tipping his head side to side as if loosening his neck muscles in preparation for a fight.

"He's seriously not that bad," she insisted with a chuckle. "And the only knife he had on him was left behind in a bandit's belly."

"Sounds like a fascinating story."

THE DOOR OPENED AND Verity stopped mid-sentence. Jonathan sucked in a breath anticipating Becca returning to him. She was the one—he was sure of it. There was no way he could wait months or years to make her his bride. He only hoped she'd accept him for the poor farmer he was.

But it wasn't Becca who greeted him. Jonathan hadn't thought his brother-in-law would be here, but of course, Mathew was Dr. McCall. "Hello, Matt. Long time, no see." Jonathan held out his palm in a friendly greeting.

"It's only been a couple weeks but feels like forever. How've you been?" Mathew accepted his hand, and the men clapped each other's backs.

"I have no complaints," Jonathan said. "I'm glad to see you two are happy. I wondered how things turned out for you all this time."

"Oh, that's right," Verity said. "How long have I been gone?"

"About seven months."

"Wow. It's weird to think about how time is so different," Verity said.

Becca approached, and Jonathan's breath caught. She was dirty—like him—but there was still something behind her eyes when she gazed at him.

"Can we just take a minute to realize," Mathew said, "the four of us are standing in the future? Two worlds blended together into one. Too bad Sam and April aren't here."

"Wait, where is April?" Becca asked.

Mathew smiled. "Eighteen fifty-two. Or at least, that's where she went. I visited her a year later. She married a good guy."

"Wow." Becca's eyes glazed over as Mathew's statement sunk in.

"Can concur," Jonathan said. "Sam Hartley is an upstanding man. Makes the best blades around."

"That's true," Verity said softly.

Silence fell upon the room and everyone glanced around, avoiding eye contact. There was an undertone of loss and sadness. Sam Hartley would never see his brother-in-law again. April would never see her brother. Jonathan had a feeling he wouldn't be seeing his sister again. But what of Becca? Would he be leaving her too? With the lump in his throat, Jonathan wasn't going to be first to speak.

Becca broke the tension, but her voice was thick. "We need to send Kiko a thank you card."

Mathew and Verity chuckled softly, but Jonathan didn't understand.

"The alien?" Jonathan asked.

Becca laughed. "She's not really... It was a joke."

Jonathan was still lost.

The bell above the door jingled with a customer, and Verity sniffed.

"I think we should be going," Becca said. "And I need a shower." She winked at Mathew, and the pretty city boy smiled.

Verity dashed around the desk and embraced Jonathan with a tight squeeze. "Good luck and behave," Verity said to him, her voice thick.

"Chin up, kid. I'll be fine." A lump squeezed his throat.

"I know. Just something I thought I should say." Verity turned. "Oh, good evening, Mr. Clark. Come on inside."

"Goodbye, sis." He kissed the top of her hair. "Mathew." Jonathan nodded his departure.

"'Bye, guys," Becca said casually.

Jonathan guided her out the door and walked her to the car. He trusted Verity was in good hands, and he'd sleep better at night holding onto these memories. But Becca's weak goodbye concerned him. Was she planning on returning to them later? After all, she'd wanted to go home, and for her, end goal reached.

Chapter 26

Becca drove them to a massive brick building with a smattering of cars filling its front. While they went inside, people pushed bright colored carts out. The doors to the brick building opened by themselves as if by magic, and Jonathan turned and waited to see how they closed behind him.

Becca grabbed him by the arm with a chuckle. "Carry this. Let's go." She pushed a bright colored basket into his hands. As they strolled along, Becca picked items and placed them in the basket. Jonathan stared at the endless options of fruits and vegetables. Glistening under lights, water misted on them while they waited to be purchased. He stepped closer to the humming. "It's cold."

"Refrigerator," Becca said simply.

"How does it work?" Jonathan asked, ducking to see below.

"Motors and coolant, but otherwise, I don't know. Keep moving."

It was incredible—nothing like the farmer's market or the general store back home. And that reminded him, Jonathan hadn't seen a single farm yet, so where had all this food come from?

Becca stopped in front of shelves filled with bright colored boxes and bags and bottles he didn't recognize. He couldn't believe most of it was food at all.

"See here?" Becca pointed. "Dozens of brands all making ketchup. If it was so gross, would they make so many?" She smiled and he wanted to kiss it away.

Jonathan shook his head at the wall of red sauces—just amazing.

"This is chocolate. I'm grabbing a few different kinds to see what you like. And down this aisle, I'll get you some Tums, just in case. I'm not sure if your stomach can handle modern food."

"I didn't realize food was something difficult to overcome. You must prepare yourself before you can eat? Is it dangerous?" Although, he wagered, her efforts to keep him safe in the future were less pressing than his efforts in the past, the basic function of eating being dangerous did disturb him.

"Depends on what you choose." Becca brushed his chest, and heat tore through him.

I choose you, Jonathan thought.

With the basket full, Becca led him near the front door to machines he couldn't describe. He waved his hands in front of the lit box, wondering if it was going to greet him.

An artificial voice said, "Good morning. Please scan your items and place them in a bag."

Jonathan leaned over her shoulder while Becca did whatever it asked for. "Uh, hi. I'm Johnny. How long have you been working here?"

Becca looked over her shoulder at him and laughed. "It's not alive."

"Seems alive to me."

"I never thought of it like that." A paper rolled out of the machine like a tongue, and Becca tore it off. "Let's go."

Jonathan waved goodbye to the nice machine. Fascination at everything around him while continuously searching for danger revved his body to the breaking point. He needed a place he could feel safe.

Becca drove them back to her house, and he carried the bags while she fumbled with keys.

"Is it necessary to lock the door?"

"People could break in and do all kinds of bad things. It's best to leave it locked, even though all that does is keep the honest people honest."

"Even now you have to arm yourself and protect what's yours?" Tension pulled at his chest, and the hours on end of strain were exhausting. Not even inside her home was safe.

"It's not that serious." Becca took the bags from him and set them on the counter. She rifled through the purchases and placed a few items inside a large glowing white thing.

Jonathan's eyes widened, and he stood off to the side. Becca didn't seem afraid.

"First thing's first," Becca said, turning around. "I need a shower. I stink. And you need a shower too." She paused and looked him over. "I didn't buy clothes for you. Hmmm. I could get another outfit from Brad's clothes out at the curb, if there's any left, or you can hang out in a towel while I run a load of laundry."

Hanging around, as she put it, while nearly naked sounded more fun than Brad's itchy clothes. "I'll take the load of laundry."

"Good choice." Becca strolled into a room and a single flick illuminated the space.

"Is this a bathroom?" He recognized a tub, a wash basin, and something he assumed people sat on—similar in shape to a latrine. The fixtures were a yellowish beige color.

"Everyday standard. This one was last updated in the 1980s—so, that explains the hideous shades of brown and yellow, but it's still so much better than a latrine."

The words stung. Another strike against her coming back with him. He plastered a smile on his face. "I'll take your word for it."

"Oh, if you need to use the toilet, you can wipe with the paper there, and flush when you're done. Verity didn't understand that. The lever"—she pointed—"cleans it all away."

Jonathan hadn't thought of it, but his sister would've learned all this before him. If she could do it, then so could he.

Becca leaned over and turned a knob. Water flowed like rain above his head. "How does that work?"

"That's one I can answer, a little. Water pressure from the city's water supply brings it into the house. It fills the water heater, and when I turn the knob, the pressure forces it out up here. The knob dictates the amount of cold or hot mixed to the desired temperature. Or at least, that's how I understand it."

"It's marvelous."

"After a day like today, it certainly is." Becca gripped the hem of her blouse. "Would you like to share the shower with me?"

Heat rushed through his body, cumulating where he needed it most. "I would be delighted. Let me help you with that."

Jonathan grazed her skin while he slipped the blouse up over her head. Becca's arms wrapped around her middle. He'd seen the scars as she'd scooped water out of the sinking skiff. He didn't mind them then, and he certainly didn't mind them now. "There's no need to hide. You're beautiful just the way you are."

Becca's arms loosened, and she moved to him. "That's the sexiest thing anyone's ever said to me."

Jonathan's lips found hers, and his hands pulled her close. She slipped her hands between them, eagerly unbuttoning his itchy tunic, and his lips trailed down her throat.

Becca's head fell back with a moan.

When the fabric loosened, he flung the material away.

Becca caressed his bare flesh, and Jonathan held her gaze as nerves all over his skin sprung to life, awakening his body in a roar of lust. She drank in his shape shamelessly, and the intensity on her face twitched and lifted his cock.

Her shallow breaths lifted her breasts in her skimpy undergarment, and while he admired her shape, Becca untied his trousers. The soiled fabric fell to the floor, and his fingers worked at her skirt, but he couldn't find the ties. "Pardon me, but I'll need assistance with your dress."

"Skirt pants," Becca corrected with a smile. "I don't blame you." She reached for her hip and unhooked the material. A strange noise followed and the fabric split.

The skirt pants, as she called them, fell to the floor.

Modern women didn't wear many layers.

Jonathan approved.

In mere moments he would finally be with the one woman he wanted above all others. The one who stood by his side whether in the thickest of danger or in the softest of sheets. Becca was strong, quick-witted, and impossibly kind. She was perfect. Warm steam billowed around them like a cozy blanket.

Jonathan pulled her close, and with a moment's assessment, he figured out how to unclasp her breast undergarment, and he watched her breasts spring free. Not too much, not too little, like he'd judged.

Becca's arms shifted to cover herself again, but Jonathan stopped her. "Don't be ashamed of your body. I will show you how to enjoy it."

"On the contrary, Johnny. This roadmap on my body means I know how to enjoy it. Let me show you." Becca used her toes to tug her socks off, and Jonathan took the moment to remove his, loving this challenge of hers.

Only one piece of fabric stood in the way. Becca gazed at his drawers and the changing shape beneath them. "May I?"

Jonathan smiled. "This is your game."

She unbuttoned the baggy fabric and tugged them down. They dropped to his feet, revealing all of him, and she stared.

"Everything all right?" Jonathan asked, not at all fishing for compliments.

A smile played at her lips. "Everything is definitely okay, but the water's running. I'm going to toss in the laundry real quick." Becca scooped up their clothes and vanished naked out the door. He heard clicking and a rumbling of another machine.

She returned in a flash. "Good to see I haven't missed anything. Let's get cleaned up quick because we have more important things to do." She prowled over to him and grabbed his hand.

Jonathan followed her into the steamy stream of water, trying not to get distracted by the hot rain inside the building.

Becca pulled her hair forward, revealing her back. Jonathan made quick work of the soap bar, and his slick hands caressed every morsel of her skin. She murmured under his touch, eyes closing under the sensations. The fresh scent of a spring forest filled his nose, and he set the bar down. With rinsed hands, he swiped the soap off her skin. Every inch of her was wet and slippery, including her breasts and the creases down below. His cock throbbed and bounced in anticipation.

Into his palm, Becca poured out a different soap from a bottle and said, "Shampoo for the hair."

Jonathan massaged it into her scalp, and the strands of wet hair clung to his arms. His heart thundered in his chest. When he finished with her scalp, she rinsed, and rinsed, and rinsed, until Jonathan wondered if she were delaying his washing to torture him. It was, indeed, torture to wait, but he loved the view.

Jonathan's lips found her throat again and trailed light kisses along her shoulder. She turned around with the soap in her grip. "Your turn."

Jonathan spread his arms in surrender. With lathered hands, Becca rubbed his body, alighting nerves with her enthusiastic touch. Every single piece of his flesh learned the pleasure of her touch, places no one else had ever touched, except the one area begging for her attention. Becca lathered again, smiling slyly.

He tensed with anticipation, desire, and need. His breathing quickened, and he braced himself for the ultimate touch. Becca gripped his length and stroked the skin clean and rubbed his balls until he wasn't sure he could hold himself back. Becca had controlled herself under his touch; Jonathan could do the same. He held back a cry of pleasure.

Becca released him.

"Now your hair," she said. A devious smile crooked her luscious lips, and Jonathan growled with lust. She lathered his hair—he had to bend down for her to reach his whole head—and he rinsed quickly.

They were finally clean.

Jonathan gripped her tight, and with all the build up of desire unleashing, he kissed her hard. His tongue explored her mouth, and the water shut off, but he paid it no mind. His hand found her delicate, sensitive area and began exploring, rubbing and pressing against her. Becca's legs trembled, and she panted. She had never been sexier than at this moment, under his touch. His fingers, his tongue, pulled the pleasure from her. Jonathan's mouth found her breast and licked, but his fingers kept moving.

Becca tensed. Her hands pawed at him for purchase and fastened onto him like a vice. Her breath hitched and at once, her body tightened, and she cried out his name. Becca turned her drowsy smiling face toward him. "Thank you."

"You're welcome?" He'd never been thanked, and it felt unusual, but if anytime she'd ask, he'd oblige. His cock throbbed with a need for release.

"Your turn," she said.

"I like this turns game you're playing."

"I think you'll like this more." She dropped to her knees on the shower floor.

Jonathan was horrified. He bent and lifted her. "What are you doing?" he asked.

"I'm showing you what I can do."

"On the floor?" So disgraceful.

"There's always the bed, if you prefer."

Jonathan scooped her up in his arms and strode down the hall.

"You passed it." She chuckled. "Back one room."

"Too many rooms. It's like trying to find the cheese in a maze."

He carried her to a bed, a massive bed, and set her down gently. He climbed over her, using his knee to push apart her legs, and he nestled himself at her junction while his lips recaptured hers.

His cock rubbed against her thigh and feminine opening as they shifted together. He trailed kisses down her throat to her breast and back up. Pressure built inside him, and he couldn't wait any longer. "May I?" His voice was huskier than he'd expected.

"Yes. Yes, please," Becca begged.

Jonathan positioned himself and slowly thrust his way inside with small movements. She moaned and arched her back. He was a charged horse ready to race. He pulled back again, and with a swift movement, seated himself fully, and she cried out again.

"Faster. Go faster," she begged.

"As the lady wishes."

A smile played at her lips for only a moment, and Jonathan gave her what she asked for. Rapid banging thrusts sent her breasts bouncing and the walls rattling. Jonathan watched her face as it shifted. Her mouth gaped open, and her eyes squeezed shut as the throes of passion took her to her place of happiness again. He took her there, and he wanted to take her there every day.

Lust ripped through him, sending heat surging through his veins, and at once, his release was met, and he stilled as the waves of his pleasure filled her up. Panting, Jonathan lowered himself just above her chest, so he didn't crush her. He kissed spots he felt needed attention on her shoulder and throat.

"I didn't know men knew about the female anatomy in your time. I figured you all just assumed everything was hysteria."

Jonathan's cheeks burned. "Some of us are just better at knowing women."

The smile on her face was worth more than every moment of his life up until now. No matter what Verity had told him about modern women wanting to wait for months or years, Jonathan had to ask Becca for her hand.

Becca groggily rolled over. "I'm exhausted."

After their long day running from the bandits, he didn't blame her. Becca curled up next to him, and they drifted off to sleep.

Chapter 27

Becca hopped out of bed and slipped into a fresh T-shirt and underwear, feeling sore but clean and refreshed for the first time in days. She padded to the laundry room and sniffed the clothes that had been sitting, shrugged, and switched them to the dryer. She headed to the kitchen and put on a pot of coffee. Then she dug into the good stuff.

"Ah, here we go." She lined up all the chocolates and placed the bottle of Tums next to them.

Jonathan strode out of her bedroom with a towel around his waist. Cleaned, sexed, hair tousled, rested—he was too handsome to be real. "You have quite the collection of reading material in here."

Becca cringed. Only Dr. McCall and April knew of her choice in books, since she'd brought one to work with her every day. "You checked out my romance novels?"

"They all seem to have this same man on them. Who is he?" Jonathan held up a copy.

Becca buried her face in her hands for a second and said with a big smile, "He's a very handsome model. A favorite of publishers a few decades ago."

"Is he real?" Jonathan studied the image.

"A real man who was paid to have his photograph taken."

"That's a job?"

Becca smiled and crossed to him. She retrieved the book from his hand. "My mom was a fan of the bodice rippers when I was little. As a teen, I used to steal them here and there. A couple years ago she moved, and when I was helping her, she intended to throw out the whole collection. I couldn't let that happen, so, now they're mine."

A fiery lust tore through her as he stood in only her towel. "I...I just tossed the laundry in the drier. So...in a half hour you'll be back to your old self." Becca returned the book to her end table and headed back to the next pile she wanted Jonathan to experience.

Jonathan strolled out after her. "I'm curious about this machine that washes laundry without any human assistance."

"It involves more water lines, and I add soap. After that, can't help you."

A light humming noise came from the floor as Becca's floor cleaner undocked itself and began its programed path through the house.

Jonathan shifted his feet as if it were a mouse. "You have a varmint in here!"

Before he could stomp or kick it, Becca grabbed him. "It's a robot sweeper."

"What's a robot?" Jonathan watched its calculated moves with curiosity.

"It's a machine that's a little more independent than most."

"The talking machine at the market, that was a robot?"

"Maybe." Becca lifted a bright colored chocolate candy to his lips. "This isn't the most nutritious breakfast, but I insist you try this."

Jonathan stared at it accusingly. "This is food?"

She chuckled. "So they say."

Jonathan frowned.

"It's good. Just try it," she insisted.

He parted his lips, and Becca slid the candy into his mouth. His lips captured her fingers on the retreat, and heat flushed through her again. Everything he did was sexy.

Jonathan chewed, and his face twisted with disgust.

Becca cringed on his behalf. "That bad?"

He swallowed. "That tasted like something I couldn't describe, but it's not good."

"Okay, try this one."

She slipped a chocolate covered peanut butter candy into his mouth. "Oh, you don't have a peanut allergy, do you?"

"I don't know."

"Well, I have antihistamine medicine on hand just in case. Let me know if you feel any tingling or swelling."

Jonathan chewed, fiery gaze trained on her. "This one is better. Still not what I'd call food, but there is definitely tingling and swelling."

"Oh!" Becca rushed across the kitchen and frantically shuffled meds around looking for the right bottle when a hand stopped her.

"Not that kind."

Becca's face heated. Unsurprisingly, Jonathan wanted a repeat of last night. She did too, but she couldn't. What had she done? The more time they spent together was only going to lead to more disappointment and heartache. As soon as his clothes were dry, they needed to talk. "I'm going to get dressed."

Becca ducked under his arm and went to her bedroom. She put on a new bra, a clean blouse, and chose a pair of shorts. She moved Kiko's transponder gizmo into her clean pocket. A knock on the door frame turned her head. Oh, but he was something beautiful to look at. Sculpted in all the right places, tanned from outdoor labor, and piercing green eyes. And that towel hung precariously low on his defined hips. A ripple of need tore through her.

"Everything all right?" he asked.

"Yeah, no. Uh, yeah. I'm fine. Why?" Becca babbled.

"You're avoiding me." Jonathan strolled across her room and touched her forearm.

Becca buttoned her shorts, tension making her movements stiff. As the word popped into her head, her eyes moved to Jonathan's lower half, but she forced her gaze away.

"Talk to me," he added.

Becca didn't want to tell him anything while he wore only a towel. She sat on the bed, right on the pile of sheets they had just had glorious sex and spent the night cuddling.

Jonathan sat next to her and let the towel split open over his thick thigh.

She turned her eyes away.

"What's bothering you?"

"I think, you know, we avoided—" The drier beeped. Thank god. Becca sprung off the bed. "Clothes are done. Two outfits don't take long to dry." Becca rushed to the laundry room and bunched his toasty clothes in her arms. She set the disheveled pile next to his lap.

Jonathan touched his clothes, inspected the machine's work. "They're so soft."

"It's the fabric softener."

"It's nice."

"Yeah."

As Jonathan smoothed the material of his trousers, he seemed genuinely impressed with what the future offered. Sure, a little fear was normal, but since Verity handled it, could Jonathan? Did she really think he'd leave behind his farm and brother? No, he wouldn't, and she couldn't ask that of him. The compromises he'd have to make were just too much.

Before she could resume the painful conversation, the doorbell rang.

Becca frowned. "I'll get that," she said.

Jonathan shoved his feet into his trousers while Becca answered the door.

Swinging it wide, she instantly tensed and scowled. "What are you doing here?"

Without answering, Brad barreled his way into their marital home and looked around like a real estate investor. "Quick to move on, I see."

"Divorce papers tend to do that to a person." Becca folded her arms across her chest.

Brad gestured his head at the front window. "My stuff looks trashed. You could've told me."

"Banging Chastity. You could've told me." Blood boiled under her skin. "What are you doing here?"

"You're right. I screwed up. You look good, Bex."

"Don't call me that."

"You're my wife. I always call you that."

"The moment the judge rubber stamps the paperwork, we aren't married. There's nothing between us."

"Are you sure?" Brad closed the distance and placed his hands on her upper arms. She wished it was Jonathan's sweet face towering over her, not prick Brad.

Becca shrugged out of his touch. "While I was here, pregnant, trying to learn as much as possible for our daughter's health, you were sleeping with another woman. What makes you think I want to see you?"

"C'mon Bex, we all make mistakes. I miss us. I miss you. I miss the baby."

A spear of pain lanced through her chest, while an army of tears marched across her lids.

Chapter 28

Brad's apologetic words surprised her. Even if Becca believed his love for her was still there—he had a proven track record for lying—she didn't feel the same way about him any longer. She'd meant what she said—there was nothing between them.

"We can try again." Brad smiled at her. "Your body's not broken until the doctor confirms her suspicion. You just have to let them run the tests."

She swiped the tears aside. "You said too much. You did too much. There's no coming back from that. Go to Chastity."

"I can't."

And there it was. "So that's the real reason you're here?"

"She just realized I wasn't over you yet." Brad gripped her arms again.

Anger burned. "Oh, bullshit. You were over me while we were still married. I never want to see you again, except in front of the judge. Get out of my house."

"My name's on the lease."

"Get your hands off her," Jonathan's deep voice commanded, and Brad's head spun in surprise, but he released her.

Jonathan, bare-chested with clean trousers and old-fashioned boots, uprighted himself from a comfortable lean against the door frame and approached with calm authority.

Becca's heart fluttered with pride and fear.

Brad's face curled into a sneer. "I see. You've moved on yourself. You're no better than I was, princess. All your self-righteous shit talk. Who's this guy?"

The robot floor sweeper made a sharp turn and headed straight for Brad's feet. He kicked it away, and it tumbled onto its back, wheels spinning fruitlessly in the air.

"I am the man who's telling you to leave." Jonathan stood nose to nose with her ex. Jonathan was a little shorter but built like a wrestler. Brad was softer from watching baseball and playing video games, but he was still strong as a brick wall, and he had reach, too.

"You're going to kick me out of my own house?"

"You don't live here, Brad," Becca reminded him.

"This is my place just as much as yours," Brad said to her while staring down Jonathan.

"I gave the landlord my notice. Get out."

Brad turned to her with more surprise on his brow. "You're moving, and you didn't intend to tell me?"

Becca's arms waved over the boxes. "Did you think I was just holding a garage sale? Leave, Brad. We're done. I owe you nothing."

Brad took a step toward the front door and paused. With a quick flash, he spun and clocked Jonathan in the jaw.

Becca gasped and covered her mouth with her hands. "Brad!"

Jonathan recovered from the sucker punch, snorting and rubbing his jaw. "I'm not going to warn you again, Brad." He spat out her ex's name. "Get out, like the lady said."

Brad craned his neck and gave her a sneer. That look was unlike any she'd ever seen on him before. Brad's arm flashed through the air for another sucker punch, but Jonathan stopped the fist with his open palm.

Brad backed up a step with lifted brows.

Finally it was over. Brad had met a man who could best him. Becca truthfully never saw a man catch another's fist. It was quite impressive.

Brad swung again.

Just like the warnings Jonathan had given Perez's men before he shot and killed one, eventually his patience wore out. Fists hammered against eyes, jaws, kidneys, and bellies. It wasn't long until Brad realized he was completely outclassed, and like a coward, he darted to her utensil drawer and slid a butcher knife out. The stainless steel glinted under the kitchen lights, and Becca's heart pounded in her ears while her feet remained frozen. She'd never seen this side of Brad. She didn't know if she was grateful to see it now, while Jonathan was here to help her, or if she regretted antagonizing him.

Her ex-husband slashed the air, trying to be intimidating, and Jonathan backed up, but he didn't appear afraid at all. Brad approached and struck Jonathan. Red lines dripped from Jonathan's bare chest, including one angry diagonal split.

Becca gasped in fear. "Stop, Brad. Just stop!"

He ignored her. Both men panted and grunted with the strikes and parries.

What could she do? She had to do something. Boxes. There were boxes of her stuff everywhere, but nothing useful. Brad's picked-through boxes were outside. She'd already rummaged through them to retrieve Brad's Hawaiian-print shirt, and...the baseball bat. Becca rushed to the bat resting in the corner and held it over her shoulder. "Brad, stop."

Her ex still ignored her. Jonathan was unarmed and unprotected. He parried many strikes, but Brad had the advantage. If she didn't stop this, one of them would end up dead. As much as she hated her ex now, he didn't deserve to die. The police would be too late.

Becca swung the bat down on Brad's knife arm. He shouted in pain and dropped the blade. He cradled his injured arm.

Jonathan struck out an arm to block Becca from Brad's strike zone, and his bare foot kicked the knife away.

Both men were panting. Becca repositioned the bat, ready for another strike. Jonathan took it from her and pointed the blunt end at Brad's head. "Get out and don't return. I won't tell you again."

Brad scurried to the door. "Crazy bitch." One last insult before he ran off.

Becca trembled and tears returned to her eyes. It was over. Jonathan panted next to her, blood smearing his chest, and guilt weighed her down.

"Are you okay?" she asked with a shaky voice.

"I'm fine. Looks worse than it is."

"Sit, and I'll get you cleaned up." It was the least she could do. Becca retrieved her first aid kit and an armful of towels. Returning to his side in the kitchen, she pressed against the active bleeders, swiping away the excess blood to see the real damage. "You were holding back."

Jonathan smiled. "Had to, but it felt good to get the blood pumping again for a good cause."

Becca smiled back. "You didn't need me to disable him."

"Not at all, but I took pleasure in watching."

She'd never felt safer. Her hand shook as she inspected the largest bleeder. It was pretty gnarly. "This one needs stitches, but you don't have health insurance. If I take you to the emergency room, they're going to ask questions. I can take you to Dr. McCall's clinic and see if he'd do it."

"Can you do it?" Jonathan asked.

"Yeah," she answered on a breath. Her shaking hands threaded a needle with nylon from the kit.

Jonathan clasped his hands over hers and said, "I never would've let him harm you."

"I know." She poured rubbing alcohol onto a cloth and said, "This is going to hurt. You should probably lay down."

"I'll be fine, City."

Becca blushed with his nickname for her. "Then hold on to the countertop, if you need to."

Jonathan just gave her a reassuring smile.

"Okay, tough guy. Don't say I didn't warn you."

The cloth pressed against the torn flesh, and Jonathan's teeth clenched. The knuckles of his fists turned white, but otherwise, she couldn't tell he was in pain at all—he looked like his usual self if slightly irritated. She shook her head in disbelief and gave him pain medicine. He didn't fight it. After a short while, she finished stitching him up.

"Doing okay?" she asked, hands more stable now.

"Just fine." His jaw was relaxed, his hands too. How the hell?

"Are you numbed from all the ways you almost die on the farm at any given moment?" Becca recalled his casual brush-off.

Jonathan laughed. "You're amusing. It simply doesn't hurt that much."

Becca sterilized the smaller cuts and bandaged the sutures. She returned her supplies to the cabinet and tossed the soiled towels in the wash machine. She returned to him and the sight of all those stitches hurt her. They were her fault.

Jonathan was flexing his hands and inspecting the smaller cuts. "You were going to tell me something before we were unceremoniously interrupted."

Becca leaned against the counter next to him. She wanted him so much, but it wasn't fair to him to give up his dreams. The pain lashed through her. "I think"—she paused to speak without a break in her voice—"you should go home."

Jonathan stilled. "Is that what you want?"

She sucked in her lower lip, fighting her chin from trembling.

Jonathan swiped away limp locks from her face. "I believe your silence speaks volumes. I don't understand why you're asking me to leave, because I was going to ask you something very different."

Becca stared at the bloody linoleum, and a lump formed in her gut. "Like what?"

Jonathan reached for her chin and tilted her face up to meet his. "I want your honest answer."

"Okay." Becca looked at the floor. She didn't think she could give it.

"Look at me."

Becca shifted her eyes to meet his. Lust was no longer there. She saw—affection? Respect. Appreciation. Her heart rattled in its cage, and she fought her eyes to stay on his.

"Becca Wagner, I've learned women of your time expect a longer courtship, but I don't want to waste another minute. You're perfect to me, the one. Will you marry me?"

Her breath caught in her throat. She didn't know if she loved him—it was far too soon to know, but he wanted to marry her. Tears barreled right through her defenses.

"That isn't typically met with tears of sadness," he added.

"I can't," Becca whispered. Her arms covered her belly, and she fought a sob.

Jonathan blinked. He searched her face as if he didn't understand. Then he inspected her furniture and her belongings. The rejection appeared on his face, and he stepped back. "Are you sure?"

She nodded, and a small sob escaped her tight lips. The pain squeezed her chest so hard words couldn't form.

"I understand. I see. Well"—Jonathan cleared his throat as if the emotion threatened to break it—"if that's your decision, good day." Jonathan blew past her toward the front door.

She followed in a hurry. "Where are you going?"

His hand landed on the knob, but he wouldn't look back at her. "Away." He swiftly closed the door behind him before Becca could stop him.

Her feet were frozen—lead weights trapped in concrete. Her chest squeezed, and her lungs screamed for air. Her face pounded with pressure, and her vision was wavy with tears. Becca's knees gave out, and she sunk to the floor. Sobs wracked her, leaving her face a glistening sloppy mess, and her feet tingled with lack of blood flow. She wished a pit would open beneath her and a truckload of bricks would drop on her undeserving broken body.

Kiko would scoop him up and bring him home where he belonged. That was the way it had to be. Didn't mean it hurt any less.

Becca's luscious pile of chocolates called to her. She stood on wobbly knees and sleeping feet and crossed to the counter. She collected the lot and brought them over to the couch. If only her body were functional, she'd give Jonathan a whole houseful of babies. As it was, he deserved someone who could give him what he wanted. Becca began a feast of despair.

Chapter 29
1854, Astor, Wisconsin

THE WRETCHED NOON SUN beamed upon his shoulders, and his feet were weary with the long walk over dust and dirt, passing by farm fields. No one had bothered him on his miserable journey home. Perhaps the pain, frustration, and anger were too apparent on his features, or maybe the blood-soaked white bandage secured across his bare chest warned them away.

From the moment he'd laid eyes on Becca Wagner, he'd known she was from the future, and therefore untouchable, but his heart couldn't resist her. He'd meant every word of the song he'd sung to her on the river. It worked on his mom, but not on Becca. What did it matter now? He knew all along he wasn't good enough for her. All his aching pain was his own stupid fault, and he hoped to suffer a long time for it.

'Will you marry me?' Jonathan had asked.

'I can't,' she'd said.

From the discourse and fight, Jonathan understood Brad was an adulterer who hurt her. Jonathan remembered the dents on her ring finger and her tearing up at what she'd left behind in her own time. She wasn't ready to forgive Brad, and in the end, it was none of Jonathan's business. Jonathan was a fool to propose to a taken woman, a fool for thinking she wanted him, and a fool in hoping she'd be willing to live in his primitive robot-free world.

So when a petite woman had intercepted him on the sidewalk and asked if he wanted to go home, he'd said yes.

Jonathan stared at his front door while his tongue was dry with dust. If the bandits were dead, he'd be homeless soon. If the bandits were alive, he'd be dead soon.

But he was where he needed to be. It may not be fancy with robots and machines, but Jonathan could do all the same with two capable hands. He wasn't impressed with those marvels—curious, yes, but he wished Becca didn't need them. Since she'd claimed to be an outdoor girl, he'd hoped she'd choose him and his basic farming life over the fancy things the city offered. His hopes were too high, and they crashed down hard. Wallowing in agony over a woman he could never have was pointless, but logic had no place in love.

Yes, he loved her, and he couldn't do anything about it.

Jonathan stepped into his house with dead weight squeezing him.

"Graham?" he asked, cupping his hand alongside his mouth for projection. "Graham, are you in here?"

No answer. No thundering footsteps. How long had he been gone?

Jonathan checked the stack of newspapers by the fireplace and found the most recent sitting on the top. He'd been gone almost two weeks! His brain felt like scrambled eggs. Jonathan dropped the paper back onto the stack and left through the back door. No workers in sight.

"Where is everyone?"

Jonathan crossed the yard to the barn and checked inside—no one. He skimmed the fields. The corn was only about thigh high. No one was standing or bent over. He walked around the pig pens, and fresh corn had been thrown for them. On the backside of the barn, Jonathan opened the wooden door for the smokehouse, and still no one.

He scratched his head and frowned. He went back inside, and on a whim, strode into his bedroom and pulled aside the hidden cubbyhole cover.

"Stop, please don't. I don't know where he is." A boy's terrified voice.

"Graham?"

"Johnny? Johnny!" Graham rushed out of the small hole and crashed against his chest.

Jonathan grunted from the patched wound.

"Where've you been?" Graham caught sight of his bandages. "What happened to you?"

"You wouldn't believe me, but I'm here now and I'm going nowhere."

"That's a relief."

"Where is everyone? The fields are empty."

"Good," Graham said.

Jonathan's temper surged and pounded in his skull. He better not have sent everyone home to shirk his responsibilities. "Why is that good?"

"It means the bandits didn't kill everyone."

And the temper washed away just that quickly. "When were they here? What happened?"

"I told the workers if they spotted the bandits to flee, and they showed up today. I didn't know what to do, so I borrowed Verity's hiding hole and hoped the workers made it away safely."

"So the sheriff didn't get them yet," Jonathan said, disappointed. "What's going on with Sheriff and Pool?"

"Don't know; don't care. Where have you been?"

Jonathan sighed. His brother wouldn't give up the questions, so there was no point dragging it out further and wasting time. "After the bandits broke in the last time, Becca and I fled through the woods and took a skiff upriver. I'd planned to return to the farm in a few days, but Nash found us. I would've taken a bullet to the chest if Becca hadn't brought me to the future. Oh, I also got to see Verity."

Graham knocked on Jonathan's head. "Are you feeling all right?"

Jonathan swatted his hand away. "I'm serious. Verity is in the future with Matt McCall. They're married with a baby on the way."

"That is some masterful creativity. I didn't peg you for it." Graham crossed his arms over his chest.

"Fine. Anyway, I ended up losing my eight-inch to Nash's soft belly. Care to ride with me to Hartley's?"

"There's no way you're leaving this farm without me."

The ride over was quiet. They passed very few people on the roads traveling to work or market. Jonathan kept his eyes peeled for any sign of the bandits, Sheriff, or Pool, but they made it across the bridge and to the blacksmith's shop unmolested.

Jonathan entered the front door of the office with Graham on his heels. A toddler sat on the floor playing with a small toy wagon, and Jonathan smiled at him and sunk back on his haunches. "Hey there, little man. How are you doing?"

"Good."

"Keep fighting the good fight."

The child was completely engrossed in his toy.

Jonathan messed his hair and stood. A grin pulled at his face while a pang of envy curled in his gut. "Good evening, April. Is Sam around?"

"Of course." April turned her head and said, "Audrey, can you bring Sam out here?"

From the side door, a young woman emerged. Her eyes darted straight to Graham and flicked away, then returned again as she moved to a door behind April. Graham's face colored red, and his lips parted ever so slightly. Jonathan smiled at his brother's infatuation.

The girl disappeared through the door, and Jonathan jabbed Graham with his elbow. "She caught your eye?"

"No," Graham mumbled and stared at his toes.

"Audrey's a good girl," April said with encouragement. "Sam and I adopted her after the massacre at Grignon's estate. She was the scullery maid."

"What she must've witnessed. Poor thing," Jonathan said.

"It's taken her some time to relax. She no longer wakes with frightful nightmares. She's okay now."

Sam pushed through the door. "Good day, Johnny. What do you need today?"

"A new dagger. Lost the last one."

"Oh, who's the new owner?"

"Nash. He didn't see it coming." Jonathan smiled.

Sam grinned, understanding what Jonathan had meant. "Don't worry none. If you retrieve it, the mess cleans off, and the blade will be good as new. In the meantime, come see the selection." Sam jerked his head for Jonathan to follow him into the shop.

On the other side of the door, Audrey waited for the men to pass. As she slipped back through to the reception area, she gazed at Graham. Seemed like the feeling was mutual.

"Here are the options. Take your pick," Sam said.

The daggers hung on the wall in an organized row by size. Jonathan selected the one best resembling the blade he'd lost. Perhaps in a few weeks' time he would seek out Nash's body and retrieve his favorite. In the meantime, a man couldn't venture around these parts unarmed. "This will do."

"Excellent choice."

"Say, Sam? Is Audrey available for affections? I think Graham has his eye on her," Jonathan said.

"Ah. Well, that's up to the little lady. We don't force contracts around here, ever since the last one didn't turn out so well." Sam winked. "If she's willing, I'll encourage it."

Jonathan gave him a knowing smile. "Thank you."

Sam followed him back out to the front, where Graham and Audrey were sharing pleasant discourse. A sweet shyness came from her, and Graham was being kind and courteous. Jonathan always knew the boy had it in him.

April held the toddler in her lap, bouncing and making silly faces.

"I'll take this one today." Jonathan placed the dagger on the counter.

April paused from her entertainment and smiled. "Great. I'll get you settled up then."

Jonathan paid for his replacement and tucked it into his ankle holster. Now he felt whole again—an unstoppable, complete, real man. Except something—someone—was still missing.

Had he tried hard enough? He didn't have months or a year to wait for her to change her mind. The farm couldn't wait that long.

"Graham, coming home?"

"I'll catch up with you later."

Jonathan nodded with a smile and rode his horse in a leisurely pace back home. There was hope yet for the boy. He wished there was hope for himself.

Chapter 30
Present Day, Green Bay, Wisconsin

AFTER DROWNING HER SORROWS in too many calories and falling asleep with Fabio on her chest, Becca freshened up and stared at her boxes with her hands on her hips. She'd already given notice. She had to leave, but she didn't have a job to know what suburb to choose. After smashing Brad's forearm with a baseball bat, it was extremely unlikely he would ever return to the veterinary clinic. Besides, he didn't have Chastity to flaunt in her face anymore.

Dr. McCall had already offered Becca her job back. What better way to slip back into her old life than to grasp it by the horns and take charge? Then she'd just move nearby—a change in scenery would do her good. That was the plan.

Becca hopped in her Corolla and drove straight to the clinic before realizing it didn't open for a few more minutes.

She couldn't use the employee door—that would make her feel icky. Becca waited in her car staring off at the eye-piercing reflections on cars in the neighboring lot. Tree leaves swayed lazily on a light summer breeze. A cyclist rode by with competitive tight clothing and a football-shaped helmet.

Images of Brad and Jonathan's fight filled her head again. She forced them away with a useless wave of her hand. Jonathan had proposed to her. She would've given anything to say yes, but she couldn't. The pain and rejection on his face was her fault, her decision, but it was the right thing to do. Still hurt terribly.

She still wished it could've gone differently.

The clock on her dashboard switched over, and Becca left the car. The front door was still locked. She sent Verity an apologetic smile through the glass doors.

Verity came around the desk and unlocked it for her. "Hi, Becca. How are you?"

What a loaded question. "Okay, I think. Is Dr. McCall in?"

"Come on in, and I'll get him. Is Johnny still around?"

Becca followed her inside. "He went home."

"Oh." Verity was clearly disappointed. "I figured that was goodbye. Just wish it hadn't been so."

"I know what you mean." Becca sat in the waiting room as if she were a customer. It felt foreign, and she didn't like it, but soon, that would be fixed.

"You aren't going after him?" Verity asked.

"It's not that easy," Becca said, putting her best smile on display, but she didn't feel it.

"It never is." Verity returned to her seat behind the desk.

Dr. McCall approached with a big friendly smile. "Hey, Becca. Back already?"

Becca stood and gave her old boss the same fake smile. "In the flesh."

"What can I do for you?"

Becca fidgeted with her purse strap. "You'd offered my old job back, and I'd like to take you up on it, doc. I'll even play your favorite Springsteen in surgery."

Dr. McCall said, "Sit down."

Becca sunk back into the plush waiting room chair.

Dr. McCall took the seat next to her. "I don't believe in fate. People are free to make their own choices and live with the consequences. But I do believe in destiny, and I believe you're destined for greater than this clinic where you're not meeting your potential, that empty house of yours, and asshat Brad. He disappointed you in more ways that I could even count. You've been a great employee, Becca, but you got your calling card from Kiko. She's granting you a new life; your own true happiness. Whatever the reason you're here, it's not for a job.

Trust your instincts, and go to Johnny. You won't regret it." Dr. McCall craned his neck to address his wife. "Right, dear?"

Verity nodded with a smile.

Dr. McCall didn't know her whole story, and she wasn't about to make excuses for her decisions to him. There was a line with her boss she wasn't willing to cross. Becca held her composure through his rejection and useless pleading. She stood, determined to solve this on her own. "Thanks for the advice, doc."

Dr. McCall stood and smiled. "Don't worry. Everything will work out in the end."

Becca swallowed back the emotion threatening to spill over into her voice. "Goodbye, doc. 'Bye, Verity."

"Goodbye!" They both chimed together.

"And good luck," Dr. McCall added.

She was going to need so much more than luck.

Becca drove back home feeling lower than low. She dropped her purse on the kitchen table and parked her rear end on a chair with her shrinking pile of treats. She flipped open her laptop and ate three candies before doing anything else. Becca balled up the tiny wrappers and opened a tab on her Internet browser. She searched listing after listing for a veterinary assistant position. She found a match to her skillset at a bigger emergency clinic open 24 hours on the other side of town. Becca preferred smaller work environments, but when she needed to be paid, she wasn't so picky.

She jumped up from her chair too quickly and smarted her thigh against the edge of the table. She rubbed the irritating streak of pain away, and her hand rolled over a shape in her pocket.

The transponder gizmo. She turned it over in her hands, studying it. The powers it gave were unbelievable. She didn't see a way to choose a time or place. It was simply a little round box with a lid, and beneath the lid was a red circular button. So simple, yet so insanely complex. Maybe she could sell it to NASA.

Nah, she didn't need the government getting their hands on this kind of tech. There was a reason the public didn't know about it, and Becca was going to keep it that way—not that anyone would believe her anyway.

A sudden thought made her gasp. The bank account card! She had left it in her skirt pants. Becca dashed through the house and found the pants in the laundry basket. She dug in the pocket and breathed a sigh of relief when she found the card intact and legible.

She set the two items on the table and crossed the kitchen for paper and a pen. From the listings, Becca wrote all the potential employers. She sat at the table and stared—the transponder gizmo and bank card versus the paper and pen.

Which future did she choose?

How ridiculous! She couldn't choose Jonathan, because she couldn't give him what he wanted, as she'd reminded herself dozens of times already. But Kiko had said she was granted three trips there and back. She used one and failed right away. The second one she brought Jonathan back here. So she had one remaining trip. That meant she had a chance to give him the bank card, apologize, and leave him be.

But she was curious if the article she'd read had changed any. Becca keyed an Internet search for Jonathan Arris to find out his new fate, since he'd accepted the sheriff's deal, preventing his arrest and subsequent murder. Jonathan should've lived a long happy life with a wife and many surviving children.

Becca clicked the link and read aloud, her eyes disbelieving the very different obituary.

Jonathan Eugene Arris, 32, died unexpectedly in his home August 4, 1854. Johnny was the brave, headstrong owner of Arris Farms. He always made sure everything was kept in working order, and food was on the table, even if he cooked it himself. Johnny was a great role model, but sometimes role models made mistakes. Even if some people didn't agree with everything he did, those people now realize Johnny was right. He had reasons for his decisions, but it shouldn't have ended like this. I miss you, brother.

He is preceded in death by his mother, Yvette C. (Colson) Arris, his father, Franklin B. Arris, and his sister, Verity M. Arris. Jonathan is survived by his brother, Graham.

Services will not be held publicly.

It never mattered that Becca had made Jonathan accept the sheriff's deal. He was still murdered. Becca stared at the pixelated black and white photograph uploaded from an ancient newspaper clipping. The words blurred together, as if her laptop had dropped under the sea and the ripples interfered with her focus. She'd failed him, the one man who treated her like an equal and respected her, who cooked for her and saved her life—the best person she'd ever met.

It didn't even matter if she could give him children or not, because he wouldn't live long enough to have any.

Becca could do something to get him what he wanted—the chance for a family. She needed to go back, prevent whatever happened in his home on that date, and give him the money he needed to run the farm without the bandits. Becca grabbed the bank card, slapped her laptop shut, and went to her bedroom closet for a suitcase. This time she'd go prepared.

Becca rolled several outfits and filled the suitcase. She brought her purse to the kitchen cabinet and threw all the medications and bandages she had in there, filling that too. Not enough room for everything she wanted to bring. From one of her packed boxes, she dug out a pair of backpacks and filled one with her romance novels, just in case. Now she felt better. The second one she loaded with toiletries. The hairdryer and curling iron were useless with no electricity. Oh, she packed her menstrual cup.

Wait.

She was coming back. Why was she taking her whole life with her?

August fourth. Becca had no idea when that was. She might be there a while, so she'd need all her necessities. Then she'd return home to Fabio, chocolates, and a new job across town. It was a plan.

Becca slung her purse across her chest, slipped her backpacks onto her shoulders and gripped her suitcase. She pulled the transponder gizmo out of her pocket and lifted the lid.

A knock at the door surprised her. Becca dropped her suitcase and fisted the baseball bat before answering it.

Kiko, the short, calm woman—alien—with long black hair stood before her, panting.

"Kiko, hi!" Becca swung the bat casually down to her knees. "Come on in. Is everything okay?"

"I need to stop you," Kiko said, completely ignoring the bat.

"What?"

"You can't use that button. It will take you back to when the sheriff was making the deal with Johnny. It only creates a tunnel there and back—static, unalterable until it's reset for the next couple. If you use that button, Johnny won't remember you, because he wouldn't have met you."

Becca would have to gain his trust all over again and convince him to take money from a stranger. She'd first found him half naked with water pails over his shoulders, and a suspicious, calculated gaze. Becca couldn't handle seeing that again, not after all they'd been through. That would be awful. "How do I go back without him forgetting me?" Becca tucked the gizmo safely back into her pocket.

Kiko smiled and lifted her palm. "I can send you to the right time. Assuming I don't glitch again…"

"What?" Becca's heart pounded in her ears.

"I've been having trouble with my abilities for a couple weeks now. I don't know what's going on, but I'll get you there in one piece."

"One piece?" Becca repeated. "As opposed to how many?"

Kiko grimaced and placed a hand on her forehead.

"Are you okay?" Becca reached out and touched Kiko's shoulder. That was the second time Kiko had a headache while helping Becca. Considering what Kiko was responsible for, Becca was alarmed.

"Just a headache. It'll pass in a moment."

"Do you want some ibuprofen?"

"No. It's going away, just one more moment." Kiko exhaled a deep breath and reached out an arm toward Becca. She closed her eyes in concentration. "Ready?"

"Kiko?"

The woman opened her eyes.

"Thank you."

Kiko's friendly smile relaxed her. "It's the ends that make my job amazing. Ready?"

Becca centered herself. "Let's do this, alien."

Kiko chuckled, and her palm pointed toward Becca as if working a summoning spell. Becca's vision blurred and her stomach flipped around once again. She hated this part, but she had to save Jonathan's life.

Still.

Then maybe he'd choose her.

Chapter 31

1854, Astor, Wisconsin

JONATHAN FRIED A SLAB of pork fresh from the smokehouse. Steam billowed from the cast iron pan, and he flipped the sizzling meat to a fresh hiss of grease. That hamburger, as Becca had called it, was nothing compared to this. Sure, what the bandits fed them was less than savory, but that hamburger in a bag was not much better. Nothing good made a person sick after eating it.

Oh how he missed her.

Becca had rejected his proposal, and he'd respected her decision. Should he have fought harder for an explanation?

He didn't need one.

Becca was a complex woman, capable of crying hysterically at nothing, consoling his little brother in grief, making Jonathan laugh, fibbing her way into the bandits, joining them on a robbery, and beating her husband with a baseball bat. She was from a foreign world of robots and machines. She would never have been satisfied with his failing farm, a lack of flushing toilet, and having to manually sweep the floors and process laundry. It was a lowly, ordinary life, but at least it was honest now.

Jonathan brought down a small pan off the wall hook, and his sweat-soaked shirt snagged on his stitches, tugging them uncomfortably. He grimaced. Jonathan had removed the bandages, but it was too soon to cut off Becca's handiwork. He didn't want to either. The regular stabs of pain were good reminders of the woman he fell for when he shouldn't have.

Jonathan dropped a scoop of lard into the pan and melted it over the flames. Despite all that, what he wouldn't give to be serving up three plates instead of one. After the way Graham and Audrey had been getting along, Jonathan didn't think the boy would be returning home today either. Good for him.

Maybe Graham would make a life for himself with Audrey over in Bridgeport. Graham hated farming. Maybe he'd choose blacksmithing instead—an honorable path. Then, with no responsibilities left, Jonathan would walk away. He'd leave behind the bandits still in the wind, the bastard sheriff and his useless deals, the failing farm. The workers could find jobs elsewhere, and Jonathan would sell the animals and leave.

The summer's humid breeze drifted through the kitchen window, fluttering his flame. Jonathan wiped his sweaty brow. After Graham had told the workers to flee the bandits, they hadn't returned. They could use a week or two off anyway, and Jonathan could use less wages to pay. If only it would rain, some of their lost labor would be hedged. So after lunch, he'd return to the fields, single-handedly, and do his best to keep the farm functioning. Alone.

With a tip of the basket's lip, Jonathan confirmed Mrs. Cottlewood still hadn't been by today. After he was done watering the animals, he'd take care of the trip to the market. Jonathan served himself a single plate and sat down at the table. Alone. He unfolded a napkin in his lap and lifted his fork and knife. He paused and set them back down. This was nothing like Becca feeding him chocolates, or her enthusiastically having him try the fries and hamburger she loved. His growling stomach was silent. He swiped away tears from the agony of missing her. He'd proposed empty-handed, but he didn't believe that to be the reason she'd rejected him. He wasn't empty-handed here. Jonathan had stashed away Mother's jewels for a rainy—or in his case, a not-rainy—day, the only things of value still left. He considered digging them out, but what was the point?

Still, Jonathan stood up, his chair scraping against the hardwood floor, his meal left untouched, and he tossed the cloth napkin on the table. He crawled into Verity's cubbyhole and opened a deeper side panel that no one knew about but him. Jonathan had stashed the family valuables in case of a repeated robbery attempt. He hadn't thought of it before, since Becca had spun his brain in a flurry, and at the time, this wouldn't have been useful anyway.

Jonathan slid out a box filled with glittering jewelry. He picked the biggest, brightest, shiniest bauble, and put the rest back. It wasn't as fancy as what Verity wore in the future, but it was the best he had, and only the best would do for the woman he loved. Jonathan smiled and brought the round emerald and inlaid gold ring out to the kitchen. He spit-shined it until it sparkled like new.

For now, he'd carry it around as a beacon of hope for Becca, or a bribe if caught by the bandits.

A knock at his front door tensed all the muscles in his body.

Graham wouldn't knock, but the bandits wouldn't either, unless they were trying to catch him off-guard.

Jonathan slipped the jewel into his pocket, double checked the new blade at his calf, and butted Verity's shotgun against his shoulder. If just one bandit arrived, he'd plug them dead, assuming the weapon was loaded. He didn't know if Graham had used it in the past week or so. If two, he'd catch one with a bullet and the other Nash-style. If more than that had come, he'd improvise. Seeing as how all that remained in his life was an empty husk, he didn't fear his dismal odds.

"It's unlocked," Jonathan said, aiming and waiting for it to open.

The door swung open, and Jonathan blinked. "City?"

Becca, hair smoothed, legs bare, and weighed down with several bags, stood on his doorstep. She gasped at the sight of the barrel pointed at her chest.

Jonathan tossed the shotgun onto the kitchen counter. He should've fought for her. He should've done anything more than take 'I can't' as a definitive answer. "I'm so sorry," Jonathan said.

"You have a right to be defensive. No apologies necessary."

The gun wasn't why he apologized. Since Becca was here, he didn't want to screw up again. He needed to do this right. "Please come in."

Becca stepped inside, and a wave of heat, gratitude, and relief washed through him. Tears pricked behind his eyes at the miraculous second chance he'd been gifted. With a racing heart, he took the suitcase from her hand and checked the front yard for threats before closing the door behind her.

"Are you hungry? I have fresh pork ready for you."

"Did Kiko tell you I was coming?"

"I haven't seen the alien. The extra's for Graham, but he hasn't returned after laying eyes on Audrey Hartley."

Becca dropped her bags near the couch, and Jonathan noticed the baseball bat dangling from her fingers. "You brought that?"

Becca chuckled and offered it to him, but he didn't take it. He said, "Keep it. It's better if you have a weapon you're comfortable with."

"Am I supposed to strap it around my waist? Take it. Put it somewhere useful." She pressed the bat into his hand, and he set it next to the shotgun. Becca added, "As much as I loved your breakfast, I am curious about how dinners taste around here. I can't imagine anything's as feral as Viola's meal."

"Certainly not. Please sit." Jonathan served her a steaming plate while Becca unfolded a napkin and placed it in her lap. Jonathan joined her at the table, his plate still warm.

Becca cut off a bite and groaned as she chewed, just like she had with the modern hamburger. The sound from her throat swirled the heat low in his groin, reawakening that deep desire. He watched luscious lips open and close, and a different kind of appetite roared.

"This is amazing. So much better than anything I could make. You're not eating?" Becca asked.

"There's something else I have a hunger for."

Becca set down her fork and knife, seemingly unaffected by his attempt at charming her into his bed. "There's something we need to talk about. The reason I returned."

"What's that?" Jonathan wasn't in the mood to talk any longer, but when a woman from the future was serious, he'd learned to listen. He feared she wasn't here to be his wife.

A knock at the door turned both their heads. Once again, Graham wouldn't knock.

"Oh, no! What day is it?" Becca asked. Worry creased her brow and her chest rose and fell with shallow breaths.

Jonathan rushed to the shotgun. There wasn't anything special about the day he could recall. "The fourth, why?"

"She didn't give me enough time again! They're here!" Becca jumped out of her seat.

Jonathan picked up the shotgun and held it up against his shoulder, aimed at the door. He didn't take chances anymore. "It's probably Mrs. Cottlewood, and I'm going to scare the soul right out of her old body. She's due any..." he trailed off as the front door swung open, creaking on its hinges.

Too late.

And it wasn't Mrs. Cottlewood.

Chapter 32

Jonathan didn't remove his finger from the trigger.

Becca rushed to his side—admirable, but she should've headed to the cubbyhole instead. She couldn't escape now, but Jonathan had no intentions of letting this visit go that far sideways.

The sheriff casually strolled in. "Johnny, drop the muzzle or I'm gonna think you have ill intentions against me."

Reluctantly, Jonathan lowered the gun. "Sorry, Sheriff. Can't be too careful these days."

"Indeed."

Sheriff Clint Nelson stopped inside the kitchen with his hands on his hips. His posture wasn't relaxed, social, or friendly, and before another word was spoken, a second man entered his house. Jonathan stiffened at the sight of Joe Pool, the smarmy deputy sheriff.

"Howdy," Joe Pool said, hands not far from his pistol holsters.

"Tell me you have good news," Jonathan said warily.

"You tangoed with the bandits an' survived. Congratulations," Sheriff said.

"You found them?" Jonathan asked.

"Oh, ya. We found 'em," Sheriff said dismissively, as if they'd been hunting for a child's missing shoe.

"So, the deal's completed," Jonathan stated, but he had a feeling something lurked beneath the surface of Sheriff's words. Jonathan squeezed the shotgun in his hand, wishing he could keep it aimed.

"Not quite," Sheriff said.

"What happened to our manners?" Becca said with a bright smile, and Jonathan shot her a look. "Surely you two would like a glass of water. It's roasting hot outside." Becca crossed to the kitchen, heading straight toward the bat. Wise woman.

"Hold on there, Miss Becca." Sheriff's palms lifted to stop her, and Becca obliged. "We're fine, but thank ya for the offer."

Becca returned to Jonathan. If she weren't here, he would've taken Pool and the sheriff out already, using his gun and dagger. But now that Becca admirably stood by his side, he needed to be more careful. Jonathan gestured discreetly, urging Becca toward his bedroom and to the cubbyhole. She understood his silent message, and she moved a few imperceptible steps. Wise woman. "We shook on it, Sheriff. Location for freedom. Deal's a deal."

Pool's hands twitched, and with that flick of distraction on Jonathan's part, Sheriff pulled both pistols with years of practiced speed—one pointed at Jonathan and the other at Becca. She gasped and froze in place. Nothing about their visit gave him a warm and friendly feeling.

Sheriff said, "Drop the gun, kid. We don't want things messy."

Anger surged through Jonathan's veins at being threatened in his own house. Bending and setting the shotgun on the floor, he demanded, "What's this about?"

"It's just business. Now you two stay put." Sheriff addressed his once-criminal-now-law-enforcing partner, "Pool, I've got these two. You're clear to go get 'em."

"Let Becca go free," Jonathan pleaded. "She's not part of this." He closed his hands into fists, preparing to fight Pool's attempt to cuff him.

Becca gripped his upper arm as if to stop him from doing something stupid. Jonathan planned to do whatever necessary to keep Becca safe from Sheriff's irons. Erratic thumps from his chest echoed in his ears. Verity had called him a bear, and now Becca was about to see it.

"On the contrary, kid, she said it herself. You're both bandits, and you'll get your just rewards." Sheriff glanced at his deputy again and with a stern warning tone, reminded him of his duty, "Pool, now!"

Becca gasped again. The hand on his arm trembled. Jonathan threaded his fingers through hers, a small comfort.

"Yes, sir." Joe Pool saluted with the wrong hand and rushed out the front door.

Becca snuggled up against his side, and Jonathan pulled her close. He didn't like the unexpected, and something wrong was happening here. "What 'just rewards' are you talking about?" Jonathan asked.

The sheriff grinned. "I'm proposing a new deal for you."

Jonathan's blood chilled. All this problems began with a deal, and he wanted nothing more than to untangle the mess he'd already made. "Like what?"

"You'll see."

Becca's bat, his new blade in his ankle holster, and the shotgun on the floor were all too far away. The sheriff might be old, but his trigger finger worked sufficiently. "You don't have to do any of this, Sheriff."

"Oh, but I do."

"Why?"

The sheriff laughed. "Why? The oldest damned reason in the book, kid. Why does anyone do anythin'? Money."

Jonathan grew more tense by the moment. If Pool wasn't going to arrest them, what had he scurried off to? "What exactly are you doing?"

"Securing my retirement."

Jonathan held Becca tight, teeth clenched in so much irritation he didn't think he'd eat for a week.

Pool returned and let himself inside the gaping front door, a smug smile on his traitorous face. He unhooked his holsters and trained his pair of revolvers on him and Becca, too. The odds were dismal and growing worse by the moment. "Boss, they's right behind me."

"Perfect."

They?

A group of three filthy, barbaric men climbed his porch steps with creaking thumps. Jonathan's brow furrowed, and his heart leaped into his throat. The last time he saw this exact image in his home, he'd been robbed, and he nearly killed the leader of the bandits. Instead, his life had been turned upside down when he'd joined them. Sheriff's new deal had nothing to do with keeping Jonathan and Becca safe from jail.

"Well, hello there, men," Sheriff greeted the remaining bandits.

Fingers led the way inside. His size made him a good shield. Butch entered behind him, and Ruddy took up the rear. The redhead's usual pleasant demeanor was gone. His best friend, Nash, was noticeably missing and likely dead in the woods.

Sheriff and Pool holstered their weapons, and Butch and Sheriff shook hands.

"Fine work, Sheriff. Although I thought the job would've required more effort than just walkin' in the front door. Still, a deal's a deal," Butch said and turned to his second-in-command with a nod. "Fingers."

As Fat Fingers passed a sack of jingling coins to the sheriff, Pool rubbed his hands together like a small mutt about to be tossed scraps. Sheriff checked the contents with a childhood glow in his eyes. Crooked bastard. Jonathan should've always expected as much, but he still wanted to vomit.

"Nice doing business with you." Sheriff tipped his hat and turned to leave.

"Ruddy, Fingers," Butch commanded in that calm warning tone of his.

The couch was too far away to hide behind. The bedroom and the backdoor were too far to run toward. If Jonathan made a move for the gun at his feet and the knife at his ankle, he'd still only succeed in disabling two of the three bandits, leaving Becca vulnerable to unacceptable risk.

The pair of bandits unholstered their own pistols, but they weren't aimed at Jonathan or Becca. Brows lifted, Jonathan watched as a pair of bangs dropped Pool and the sheriff to the floor.

Becca yelped and startled next to him. Jonathan squeezed her tighter, uncertain what the hell was happening right now.

Joe Pool and the sheriff curled on the floor, groaning in pain, clutching different areas of their torsos since they couldn't reach the holes in their backs.

Butch bent over and collected the jingling sack Sheriff had dropped. He checked the contents and tossed it back to Fingers. To the sheriff he said, "And there's the deal. Pleasure doing business with you."

Jonathan's gazed flicked to Ruddy and Fingers, standing by the door, and Pool and the sheriff, squirming on the floor. He was so damned confused who, if anyone, was on his side.

The leader straightened and strode toward him and Becca, an unreadable calm on his features. "Now, we have one last piece to play," Butch said, tipping his chin up.

"Is this some kind of game to you?" Jonathan asked.

Butch grinned. "Boy, life is a game. You either play to win or find yourself discarded like the day's trash. I'm the master of the win, but when someone makes a move I don't appreciate, I have to teach that player a lesson. Think of it as a generosity of my time. You and the woman disappointed me, and someone here has to pay for it."

Butch hated weakness. Jonathan had to lean into that. "I'm no traitor, so whatever it is you think I've done, you can forget it and get out of my house. We wouldn't want a repeat of last time, would we?" Jonathan asked.

"Oh, you mean givin' up our location to the sheriff, fleeing the stakeout, and killin' Nash weren't traitorous decisions?" Butch asked.

"I didn't know what the sheriff wanted with your location, and I didn't know it was a trade secret. Becca wasn't feeling well. We left quietly so we wouldn't disturb you, and we haven't seen Nash." Jonathan was full of shit, but he was willing to do whatever it took for Becca's sake.

"And you consider that the truth?"

"That's what happened."

Butch reached around his back and revealed Jonathan's old eight-inch friend smeared with dried streaks of blood. "Then whose is this, I wonder?"

Jonathan was going to reclaim that knife. It was his favorite.

Two more bangs echoed through the small room.

Chapter 33

Butch shifted his attention to Ruddy dropping to the floor and Fingers holding his injured belly with surprise.

Now was Jonathan's chance. Verity had called him a bear, and now Becca was going to see what she truly meant. Jonathan collected his new dagger and gripped the shotgun.

Butch went for the revolver in his holster as he turned to face Jonathan again.

Seizing the opportunity, Jonathan plunged his blade straight into Butch's throat. "I do whatever I must to protect mine. I warned Perez. I warned the sheriff, and I warned you. Doesn't anyone listen anymore?"

Butch's eyes widened, and his mouth silently opened and closed.

With a glare of hatred and a not-so-gentle pull, Jonathan freed his blade. Blood poured down Butch's neck, tunic, and vest like a waterfall of death. When Butch dropped to his knees, Jonathan flipped the blade around in his hand and whipped it across the room at Fingers.

Fingers only had time to open his mouth in surprise before the blade sliced at his throat. It wasn't a direct hit.

"Hide," Jonathan commanded Becca.

She wisely rushed off toward his bedroom.

Butch was done for. No threat. Fingers and Ruddy, however, were still capable of destruction. And Pool and the sheriff were down but not out. Jonathan lifted the barrel at Fat Fingers and squeezed the trigger. It didn't fire. Dammit, Graham! Jonathan dropped the gun and dashed for Becca's bat. He gripped it in his fist and ducked below his table just as a gunshot rang out. Fingers had fired at him. Before he could try that stupid move again, Jonathan reeled back and with all the strength in his muscular body, he swung the solid wood against Fingers's head. The man tipped against the wall and slid down, smearing blood on his way.

Jonathan wound up once more for Ruddy.

"You killed ma best friend," Ruddy said.

A loud gunshot shook the room.

Jonathan didn't dignify Ruddy's claim with a response. With Ruddy's head turned at the distraction, Jonathan slammed the bandit's head with the bat, and the redhead was lights-out permanently. Jonathan wheeled around for his next target, and Joe Pool, still lying on the floor, had a pistol aimed at him, but after a beat, the revolver fell out of his grasp, and Pool's head dropped to the floor.

Becca held a rifle still aimed at the deputy. "Joe was going to shoot you in the back," she said. "So I found this one hanging in your room."

Jonathan held up a finger, silently asking her to wait. He checked the sheriff, but the bastard was already gone. All the threats had been eliminated.

Jonathan dropped the bat and approached Becca, blood still surging. Breaths pulled from his lungs, but he gently removed the gun from her hands. "I think your mission is finally accomplished. No sheriff means no arrest. No arrest means no murder. If it weren't for you, I wouldn't have made it, so thank you."

"Just doing my job," Becca said softly.

"Is that all this is?" Jonathan asked, trying to hold back the sting of her statement.

Yet another knock at the door had Jonathan tensing, and he almost shouted in frustration. This time Becca ducked behind the couch.

A gray-haired lady walked in and stepped over the bodies and puddles of blood. "Oh, dear. Looks like I missed a party." Mrs. Cottlewood carried a basket of fruits and vegetables in the crook of her left arm.

Jonathan crossed the room and eased her burden. "You're late."

"Barry had a fit, but if he hadn't, I would've missed all this. You've got the sheriff, some bandits, and one of Jaime's men splayed on your kitchen floor looking like the aftermath of a battle. Now that's something special."

Mrs. Cottlewood was always so great. His lips lifted in a smile. "The crooked sheriff, the weasel Pool, and the bandits are all over. No one has to live in fear around here, and we can all start over."

"Where's the rest of the bandits?" she asked.

"Nash is rotting in the woods. Brawley's taking a drink down the Fox River."

Mrs. Cottlewood's smile creased her eyes. "I always knew you could do it, son." She patted his arm, and her eyes teared up. Her gaze shifted. "Oh, hello there, dear."

Becca stood by the couch and waved to his house assistant. Jonathan introduced them.

"What wonderful timing," Mrs. Cottlewood said. "I'm glad you found yourself a wife, because today is my last day, and what a glorious one it is."

"I'm not—" Becca started.

Jonathan cut her off, not wanting her to even think such negative thoughts. "I'm saddened to hear it, but I wish you and Barry well."

"Barry will be thrilled to hear of this story, and so will the whole tri-village area. You're a hero, son. Don't forget it."

Jonathan swatted the air. "I only protected what's mine, and Becca saved me right back."

Becca smiled shyly.

"Don't be so modest," Mrs. Cottlewood said. "You're my hero and Barry's. Many years ago, our grandson was tortured by little Eddie Butcher."

"Theo wasn't the bully?" He'd heard the boy harassed Butch, and Butch had only retaliated, thus beginning his nickname and terror-filled reputation.

"Oh, heavens, no. Butch here was torturing many kids. He maimed Theo, and when we demanded the sheriff do something about it, Sheriff refused, saying he wasn't going to punish his kin."

Jonathan's brows rose in surprise. Sheriff and Butch were related?

"Ultimately, our daughter and son-in-law moved away for Theo's sake, and the stress on Barry was going to put him in an early grave. Now our daughter, son-in-law, and grandson can move back home. Theo even has kids of his own I'd only heard of in letters. Don't you worry, Barry will make sure the whole area sings your praises."

"That's not necessary," Jonathan said. "But thank you, Mrs. C. Thank you for your years of help, and good luck with your retirement."

Mrs. Cottlewood winked and strolled out with her empty basket.

Jonathan and Becca stared after her.

"Wow," Becca finally said.

Jonathan sank onto the couch and put his trembling hands over his face. "Justice for Theo, wherever he is, has been finally served."

Jonathan's house was full of bodies, but there was no one to arrest him for it since the mayor was missing and their entire police force was dead.

Becca sat next to him.

Now wasn't the time for him to worry about himself. Jonathan straightened. "I'm sorry you had to see all this. You're a great shot by the way. Not many people have what it takes to shoot a man."

"Can we not talk about it? I'm holding on okay, as long as..." she trailed off, pressed a fist against her mouth, and shifted her eyes away from the carnage.

"How about you give me a hand, and we'll never speak of it again?" Jonathan said.

"A hand how?"

"The pigs gotta eat."

Becca cringed, and said reluctantly, "Deal."

"Do you keep your deals?" Jonathan asked with a sly smile.

"Maybe." Her teasing tone sent blood rushing through his body. The sooner they finished this unsightly task, the sooner Jonathan could ask her the most important question of his life—again.

Becca followed him to the kitchen. Jonathan's stomach flip-flopped over what had just happened, but he didn't have time to process right now.

Jonathan relieved Pool of his weapons and picked up the deputy by the underarms. Becca hoisted Pool's ankles. They carried him out the back door to the pig pen. Next to the gate, Becca dropped Pool's ankles and pushed it wide. Jonathan dragged the body inside the pen and left him in the mud. Butch was next, and while digging through the scoundrel's pockets, Jonathan found a pocket watch. It was Tim Van Cook's from the fish market. He transferred that to his own pocket. Ruddy and Sheriff were next, and finally, Fingers—who was much harder. Jonathan dug in Fingers' pockets for the sack of coins. He opened it. It wasn't much, and he really needed it for himself, but it wasn't his. More weapons were added to Jonathan's personal stash, however, including his old and his new eight-inch blade.

Sweat poured down his chest and face trying to heave that massive flesh mountain in the scorching August heat. With a final grunt, the worst was finished.

Jonathan guided Becca back into the house, and they both worked on their hands and knees to clean the blood off the floors and walls.

"I think I'm going to throw up," Becca said.

"It's almost over. Take a minute and catch your breath." Jonathan rung out the red-stained rag.

Becca tossed her filthy rag into the basin and sat back, breathing rapidly with the effort.

"Thank you for everything," Jonathan said. "I couldn't have done it without you."

Her eyes misted.

Jonathan added his soiled rag to the basin and sat next to her.

Becca swiped at her face with her shoulders, and she smiled with a sadness pulling at her beautiful face. "I couldn't let you die."

"Not even Graham was going to help me?" Jonathan asked.

"He found you afterward and wrote your obituary."

Her past tense was unsettling. "Thank you for sparing him that."

"It wasn't just for his sake that I returned." Becca's nose scrunched. "It smells terribly in here. You need bleach."

Jonathan opened all the window sashes to sweep away the coppery stench. Since the hardwood floors were dark, the house appeared untainted, just like it had been. Jonathan washed his hands clear of the filth and returned to the couch. Becca washed her hands and sat next to him, silently.

Her mission was complete, the danger eradicated, and now Jonathan feared she would leave. It was now or never. "City, I need to ask you something."

"We weren't going to speak of Bandit-gate again. That was the deal."

Jonathan chuckled. "It's not about that."

"Okay." Becca looked at him, brows tilted in worry.

Jonathan inhaled a deep breath, preparing himself for the most important moment of his life. Her answer determined whether the future she'd granted him would be a life worth living. Foreign butterflies danced in his gut. "There's never been anyone as perfect for me as you, and I promise I'll do anything in my power to keep you safe and loved."

Becca blushed bright red, and her eyes glistened.

Jonathan kept going. She needed to hear it all. "My feelings for you haven't changed; they've only grown, and I love you, Becca. I love everything about you, from the line in your hair, to the marks on your belly, to the comfort you give my undeserving brother, and the way you saved my life. I love that you can drive amazing machines fearlessly, that you can disarm a man with a bat, and that you're willing to use a gun to save me, which I hear isn't so common in your time."

Becca's eyes glistened, and her lips lifted into a tiny smile for a fraction of a second.

Jonathan reached into his pocket and brought out his mother's emerald ring. "You're extraordinarily beautiful and strong, stronger than anyone I've ever known. Becca Wagner, will you do me the honor of marrying me?"

Becca's tears spilled, and Jonathan's heart leaped into his throat.

"I"—her voice broke—"I can't give you what you want."

Feeling like his lungs were squeezed, he managed to say, "What's that?"

"I can't give you children." Becca's lower lip trembled, and the tears flowed over her cheeks.

Jonathan smiled reassuringly. "It's you I want to marry. Anything else is just good fortune, but I would be the happiest man on earth to have your heart in return."

"You're okay with just me?"

Jonathan grinned and swiped away the tears on her cheeks with his thumbs. "Just you is perfect."

Becca sniffled and shifted her posture on the couch. "Ask me again."

"Becca Wagner, will you do me the honor of marrying me?"

Becca's smile gleamed, brightening Jonathan's heart and lighting a fire in his chest.

"Yes. Absolutely yes, Johnny. I love you."

Jonathan slipped the ring on her finger. His lips pressed against hers, gently at first and slowly growing with the love that filled him and the desire that controlled him.

"Johnny," Becca said, pulling back.

"What is it?"

"Where—or when—are we going to live?"

Jonathan grinned. "I said I would do anything in my power to keep you safe and loved, so it's your choice."

Becca smiled, and her lips found his again.

Chapter 34
One week later…

THE DAY AFTER THE slaughter in the farmhouse, Jonathan had brought her to the courthouse in Navarino. They'd wed at once, and Becca couldn't have been more thrilled. The workers were back in the fields, singing as they carried pails of water and feed. Much needed storm clouds rolled in, but so far no rain had followed.

Every time someone knocked on the door, Becca had tensed and fought the urge to run for Verity's panic room, even though most visitors were townspeople coming to personally praise Jonathan for dispatching the bandits and the crooked sheriff.

Jonathan was a hero to everyone.

Especially Becca.

And Becca reacted no differently to this unannounced knocker. She dried her hands on a towel and picked up the revolver she and Jonathan kept near the door—Ruddy's, if she remembered right. Becca held it steady as she answered the door.

Becca's brows rose. Graham was finally home, and he brought a girl. "Becca! It's great seeing you again."

"Graham, this is your house. You don't need to knock." Becca waved them inside.

The boy walked in, hand in hand with a pretty young lady with long blond hair and bright brown eyes. She wore a demure plain dress and a shy expression, and Becca didn't want to scare the girl, so she discreetly set the pistol down.

Graham was bubbling with excitement. "I heard about the bandits, the sheriff, and his deputy. Everyone did. It was in the newspaper. Did you see?"

"I saw it." The article was amazing. It boasted Jonathan's brave undercover pursuits in bringing justice to Theodore Cottlewood and peace to the tri-village area for the first time in decades. Jonathan had blushed bright red while she'd read the article aloud, and ever since, Becca had received praise for Jonathan everywhere she went. She was proud of her husband, even if everyone gave him all the credit.

"I figured my brother was still quick with the trigger and didn't want my head blown off," Graham said.

"We've been a little on edge since it happened," Becca admitted.

"Becca, this is Audrey. Audrey this is...my stepmom?" Graham asked, confused.

Becca didn't take offense. She thought it was hilarious. "How old do you think I am? Don't answer that. I'm your sister-in-law." The kid was young enough that he felt like a child to her. Becca turned to the girl and held out her hand to shake. "Nice to meet you, Audrey. How are you?"

The girl glanced at Becca's hand and then the floor. She curtsied and bowed instead. "I'm rather well, thank you, ma'am."

"It's Becca. We aren't that formal here," Becca said to set the girl at ease.

"Audrey is going to marry me, so she's staying with us now." Graham wore the biggest grin on his face.

"Oh," Becca said in surprise. She was so happy for him, but they were teenagers, and she'd forgotten how quickly men proposed in this time—within days of meeting. Come to think of it, she'd agreed to marry Jonathan after only a few days as well. Becca would've thought it was crazy before, but after their wild adventure together, testing them under the happiest of times and the worst of duress, Jonathan was nothing but loving, respectful, and protective. He was perfect, and it had nothing to do with Dr. McCall's insistence they were each other's true love, or that Kiko never made a mistake in the matchmaking department.

Or that he was absolutely sexy and handsome as hell.

"Welcome to the family," Becca added and crushed the girl against her. "We're huggers. You're going to have to get used to that."

Audrey smiled shyly, and the screen door slapped shut. Becca was used to it now, but Audrey startled, and everyone turned to see Jonathan enter. He was a fine sight—bare chested, broad shouldered, and tanned. Becca's eyes roamed his body in a flash of lust.

"Good to see you, kid." Jonathan held out his hand, and when Graham took it, Jonathan pulled him into a hug.

Graham cringed at the face full of sweat.

"And good to see you again, Audrey," Jonathan said, releasing his little brother. "How are you?"

She curtsied again and watched Graham swipe his face clean. "I'm well, thank you. No offense, sir, but you're not going to hug me too, are you?"

Jonathan laughed. "Call me Johnny, and I'll spare you."

"Thank you, Johnny," she said.

"You didn't spare me," Graham complained, now wiping his hands on his pants.

"You're my brother. I don't spare you anything."

"Audrey and I are getting married," Graham repeated for his brother.

Jonathan smiled, warm and kind. "Welcome to the family and welcome to the farm."

"Thanks, Johnny," Graham said, beaming again. "So, I'm going to spend time with my future bride."

Audrey's cheeks burned bright pink, and he ushered her upstairs.

With the pair of them out of sight, Jonathan swooped down and kissed Becca with fiery lust, sending her heart thumping and heat curling down low.

When he released her, he asked, "Can you grant me a favor?"

"Anything," she answered a little drowsily.

"Make sure that girl doesn't slave away in here. She was the scullery maid at Grignon's estate. Matt, Verity, and Sam rescued her during the now-famous massacre, and I don't want her to think she's back in that role again."

"She looks like she needs to loosen up. I'll make sure she gets some good girl time and fun leisure activities."

"Thank you." He kissed her forehead and said, "Want to go for a ride?"

"What kind?" Becca made a point to stare down below and imagine what she knew was there.

"I have an errand to run. Join me."

Becca and Jonathan saddled up a pair of horses and mounted for a ride to the neighboring village of Navarino. Jonathan stopped them outside Tim's Fish Market.

"But you don't like fish," she said, confused.

"We're not here for food." Jonathan took her hand and brought her inside. At the counter was the lanky Tim Van Cook, who'd been a blubbering mess when Becca caught the tail end of his robbery.

"Tim," Jonathan greeted stiffly.

Tim jolted in his pants and scrambled for something under the counter. He paused. "Oh, it's you. I heard about the take down of the bandits. It was true, right? And you aren't here to rob me?"

Jonathan dropped the sack of coins he'd taken from Fingers on the counter and added the pocket watch on top. "These are yours."

Tim's eyes widened in surprise. "But...but why?"

"I'm not a thief."

Tim's face spread with pure joy. "Oh, thank you. Thank you so much. Ten percent lifetime discount for the Arrises!"

Jonathan chuckled. "Not necessary, but Tim?"

"Yes?"

"Being prepared in case of a robbery means having your weapon ready and available." Jonathan plunked down a pistol, closer to Tim's size. "This was Butch's. I'm sure he'd hate that you have it."

"Uh, thank you," Tim said, marveling at the gift.

Jonathan and Tim exchanged nods of understanding, and Jonathan guided Becca out of the store.

"That was very kind of you."

"None of that was mine to keep."

Becca bit her lip. He'd given away a lot of money, even if it was dirty money. "I know how much the farm needed that. Can we make a stop in Bridgeport?"

"What's over there?"

"Something we need." Something Becca needed to see if it was real before she got his hopes up.

"All right then."

Becca and Jonathan rode their horses back toward Astor and swung east over the bridge into Bridgeport. She so wanted a shower, and her legs ached from a few hours of leisurely riding. How long until her legs adjusted to the pounding of the saddle?

"Where's this place we're going to?" Jonathan asked.

"The bank, but I don't know where it is."

"It's just over here." Jonathan led them down what appeared to be a few blocks' distance, and sure enough, the giant letters of 'bank' were painted on the front.

"I'll be right back." Becca dismounted and slipped inside the building. Jonathan watched her, but she hid her smile of excitement. He wasn't the kind of guy to accept money freely. Becca figured this was one of those occasions where it was better to ask forgiveness rather than permission.

She went to the teller and passed him the card. "Withdrawal please."

The slender man in a fancy brown suit opened a logbook and slid his finger until he reached the right number. "How much?"

"All of it," Becca said, excited there was something to offer.

"Are you sure you want to withdraw all of it?" The teller's brows lifted.

"How much is in the account?"

"Four thousand dollars."

Becca blinked, and blinked some more. That was a big chunk of change to her. She couldn't imagine how much that was to Jonathan. She needed his input. "I'll be right back. Hold on."

He passed the card back to her, and Becca returned to Jonathan, who'd stayed mounted.

"All set?" he asked.

"Not quite."

Jonathan hopped down, concern knitting his brow. "What's wrong?"

"Nothing. Dr. McCall gave me an account for us, and I was going to cash it out as a surprise, but the amount is much more than I expected, and I don't know if it's wise to have that much lying around."

"How much?" Jonathan asked.

"Four thousand dollars."

"What?" Jonathan barked his reply, and his hand went to his temple.

Becca smiled at his reaction and nodded to confirm.

Jonathan paced a few steps back and forth and raked his hair. "That would cover the farm workers for many years. Shit, that's a lot of money. From Matt?"

"He said his sister doesn't need it, so he wanted to pass it to his brother-in-law instead. As a final thank you."

"That's too much. It's just way too much. Dammit, I wish I could buy him a beer."

"You're not turning it down, are you? Matt told me the government will confiscate it after it goes to an unclaimed asset division or some such gobbledygook."

Jonathan shook his head and smiled. "I have pride, but I'm not about to look a gift horse in the mouth. Take out a hundred. That'll float us for a couple months."

Becca did as he asked, and they rode back home. In the kitchen, Jonathan gave her a kiss, and the lines of stress around his eyes eased, reminding her of something she'd forgotten. "I need to check your stitches."

"You just want me naked."

Becca laughed. "True, but I really do need to remove them if they're healed now."

Jonathan flipped off his shirt, and the sutures were clean. The skin was knitted together. She found a pair of scissors from her first aid kit and removed each one.

"Almost like new," she said. Her fingers ran along the rough texture—all because Brad was a possessive psycho and couldn't take 'no' for an answer. Jonathan paid the price to protect her.

"Better than new." Jonathan leaned over and captured her lips briefly before heading toward the back door. He called after, "I have work to do. I'll be back for you, my love. If you need anything, I hung a bell out the back door here." He pointed. "Give it a ring, and I'll be here."

"I love you! Stay safe. I don't want to find out how many ways there are to almost die on the farm."

Jonathan laughed and got to work.

Chapter 35

THE NEXT DAY, BECCA was just finishing up the dishes from breakfast, while Audrey was working on making a wedding dress for herself in a side room. A knock on the front door chilled Becca. She grabbed the revolver and repeated her cautious steps, but when she opened the door, she stood back with wide eyes. "Kiko?"

"Congratulations. I heard about the nuptials, or saw, anyway."

"You knew everything that was going to happen." Becca stepped aside.

Kiko entered. "I did."

"Is it a blessing or a curse?"

"Most of the time, a blessing, but a vacation sure would be nice." Kiko's face pinched in pain.

"The headaches are back?" Becca asked with concern.

"They never went away, and truthfully, they're getting worse. The reason I dropped by is I need to retrieve the emergency responder. I presume you're planning to stay?"

"Oh! Of course I am, but you knew that. One second." Becca dashed off to her and Jonathan's bedroom and collected it from the dresser drawer. "Here it is."

Kiko held out her hand to take it, but she buckled over with her hands fastened to the sides of her head.

Becca snapped alert and bent down to her. "What's wrong?"

"My head feels like it's splitting in two." Kiko grunted and tumbled over. Her face was pinched in pain. Becca thought through all the things she'd brought from the future for a solution, but before she could do anything, Kiko relaxed and climbed up on shaky legs, breathing deeply.

"That didn't look normal."

"I'll have a chat with my boss." Kiko shook her head and rubbed her eyes. There was fear, confusion, anxiety—all things that alien Kiko had never shown before. "It's gone."

"What's gone?" Becca asked.

"My visions are flickering like an old drive-in movie." She lifted her hand and inspected it as if wondering why it was attached to her. "Creating the tunnels is sparking, fading." Her terrified eyes bore into Becca's. "Something is very wrong. I don't know what I'm supposed to do." Her breathing quickened, and her eyes searched the floor. The calm and collected Kiko suddenly seemed more—human? Her hands went to her scalp, burying themselves under her dark curtain of hair.

"It'll be okay," Becca said, hopeful. "Take the gizmo and go back home."

A sudden sense, making Becca want to escape, urged her toward the door, like a cloud of dread permeating the air inside the house. How strange. Becca didn't move, but it felt...uncomfortable?

"You feel that?" Kiko asked.

"I do, and it's not awesome."

"I gotta go." Kiko opened the transponder gizmo's lid.

"Wait! Are you going to be okay, for real?"

"Of course. Everyone gets their happily ever after. Don't worry about me."

Becca nodded, not entirely believing her, and Kiko vanished with the press of a button. Becca still worried. Kiko never needed the transponder gizmo before.

BECCA HAD PULLED HER straight, limp hair back into a ponytail, slightly missing her curling iron but grateful for all the hair thingies she'd packed, and she'd filled a basket with some fruits to share. Becca stopped at the Hartley's blacksmith shop over the river and looped the reins over a post. She stared in amazement at the cabin where she'd worked. It was breathtaking—so similar, yet so much newer. Becca squared her shoulders and pushed through the door, preparing herself for who she was going to see.

A toddler stacked hunks of wood on the floor. The once modern reception desk was now rustic and handmade. And the woman behind the desk was none other than her dear friend and co-worker April McCall.

Becca walked up to the desk and said, "Hi, loser."

April's big blue eyes rounded and watered, and a grin split her face. "Did you want to get the mail this time? It's more work having to pick it up at the post office."

"I didn't come here to win again, but I brought a snack." Becca lifted the basket.

April chose a piece of fruit. "Thanks. What are you doing here? I mean, what happened with Brad? Where's your...?" April trailed off, pain pinching her features.

"Brad and I divorced. He was cheating, and the baby...she didn't make it."

"I'm so, so sorry. I had no idea. Matty never said anything." April moved around the desk and embraced her.

Becca was so grateful to have her friend back, someone who truly understood everything she went through. "I suppose Dr. McCall was shielding you from terrible news, and besides, who thought we'd see each other again?"

"I get it." They pulled apart, tears glistening in both their faces. "Can you believe what just happened to us?" April asked.

"No. I really still can't." Becca sniffled. "Did you bring your art stuff along?"

April nodded. "Did you bring your book collection?"

Becca chuckled. "Of course."

"I missed you," April said.

"I missed you more. Stop by for a barbeque this weekend. You and Sam. Audrey is settling in well. And who's this?"

The toddler ran over to April and bear hugged her leg. April picked him up. "This is little Mathew. Matty, say 'Hi' to your Auntie Becca."

"Hi, Auntie. Momma, I'm hungry."

April passed the toddler to Becca's arms, and she used every ounce of strength in her body to keep standing. Functional body or not, she would be auntie and stepmom or sister-in-law and she'd be damned proud of it.

Her family just kept growing.

"Here you go." Becca offered little Matty a bite of her apple, and the little squirt mowed down on it and smiled with a mouthful. She feather touched his face and palmed his chubby cheeks before setting him down. He was so precious.

Little Matty returned to his blocks, chowing down on his apple, spittle and drool rolling down his chin. Becca smiled through watery vision.

She was auntie.

She was sister-in-law or stepmom, whichever they preferred.

She was wife.

She was whole.

One year later...

Becca washed the dishes from breakfast, and Jonathan sneaked up behind her, wrapping his strong arms around her growing belly. She'd been shocked to find out she was pregnant, but every day was filled with cautious optimism and feeling for kicks.

"How's my favorite girl?" Jonathan whispered and kissed her jaw.

"Baby is still kicking, and my feet are swelling."

"Wonderful."

Becca frowned.

"I mean, wonderful the baby is kicking. I'll give you a foot massage tonight."

She set the plate down and turned in his arms.

"You're beautiful." He winked. Jonathan's hands slipped from her belly to her back and pressed her against him.

"Ugh. Come on, Johnny. We don't want to see that," Graham said while slipping a shirt over his head.

"Good thing you're going outside then," Jonathan said.

"You should be joining me," Graham countered.

"Five minutes."

Graham rolled his eyes and left.

Jonathan took her lips, savory with breakfast bacon, and showed her the bond between them had only grown.

Quiet footsteps coming down the stairs pulled them apart. Jonathan leaned in close. "I'm going to work. If I don't go now, I won't, and Graham will be something to deal with."

Becca chuckled. "Just go. We can handle this."

He gave her a quick peck on the cheek and rushed out the door.

Audrey came down the stairs carrying a load of laundry.

"How are you today?" Becca asked.

Audrey, newly pregnant, had been cursed with a nasty case of morning sickness. Becca was seven months along now, and she'd been lucky to avoid it.

"Same as yesterday."

"Did you flush this time?" Becca had Jonathan install a hand pump inside the now-bathroom. It wasn't the same as indoor plumbing, but several hand-pumps brought a load of fresh water to rinse the toilet away. Piping was installed through the house and routed to the latrine out back. They'd worked on it together, and Becca was satisfied.

Graham was marveled by it, and a newfound respect grew for his older brother. It only lasted a few days though.

Audrey wasn't as surprised. Apparently the Grignon estate had something resembling rudimentary plumbing, so she was able to figure out how it worked with minimal excitement.

Sweet girl. It was nice to have a sister-in-law, even if she was much younger. They couldn't chat about regular stuff from the future, but Audrey was still great. A warmth of family spread through her.

Very soon both of them would be bringing in new members of the household, and although Becca was excited beyond belief, she was still cautious.

"I did flush." She carried the load of laundry out to the clothesline.

Becca filled a basket with fruit. She brought it outside and passed it out to all the workers, so they could take a break. "It's starting to rain, come inside until it passes."

The workers laughed and wrapped arms around each other's shoulders. One bit an apple, another sucked down grapes, and the rest carried their treats inside.

This July, the corn was over knee high with the regular rains, and with Dr. McCall's help, they had plenty to keep the farm producing, and even earning a small profit. Turned out the workers were more productive when given breaks and rewards. The Arris family would be just fine until she and Audrey could fill the farm with children, and Becca would be proud to do it, knowing this was the only home for her.

Jonathan and Graham rushed inside with the sudden downpour, and everyone perched around the living room and kitchen.

"George, your turn," Jonathan announced.

"All right, all right. So, one day a lady walked into a fish market…"

The crowd erupted in laughter, and Becca blinked away her tears of happiness.

Jonathan wasn't Fabio. He was better. Thank you, Kiko. Wherever you are, may beautiful things befall on you, Becca wished.

Epilogue
Present Day, Green Bay, Wisconsin, One year earlier...

Intense pain split her head in two again. Kiko Takai's weakened legs buckled underneath her, and she crashed to her knees on the carpeted floor of her own living room. The emergency responder tumbled from her grasp. Her jaws stretched wide like a hungry whale's maw, hands pressing her temples as if the counterpressure could alleviate the agony. Something was wrong, and she was alone.

Kiko tipped over, laying on her side, curled into a ball, while the pounding and stabbing in her skull continued. Kiko's breaths jerked in and out of her chest. Her pulse roared behind her ears. Words—screams—couldn't come out. Her body was paralyzed in a state of indescribable pain.

And then it stopped.

Just as fast as it started, it ended.

Kiko uncurled and winced as she sat up. Her body felt like pulverized steak. She panted while standing on shaky knees.

Kiko's mouth dropped open as it dawned on her—no more flickers of matches to be made. "My visions."

She lifted her hand and inspected it. "The tingles are gone, too." She flexed her fingers in relief, finally an end to the centuries-long tingle of a hand that fell asleep and was slowly waking up. Nothing short of torture. Her lips spread into a cautious smile.

They were gone. Her abilities had faded away.

A hundred years had passed since Kiko Takai last experienced the emptiness of only seeing through her own eyes. Then the implications dawned on her. What was she supposed to do now?

Her breathing quickened in panic, and she searched the floor as if the answer were in front of her. Her hands returned to her scalp.

The mystic cloud had followed her back from 1854, descending, causing a sudden sense of urgent escape meant to shoo mortals away. Kiko stood firm even with the need to run screaming in her head. Just the fact that she sensed it meant something was wrong—plus the whole head splitting thing—and she needed to speak with her boss.

Kiko was mortal again.

And Chaos was coming.

DEAR READER,

Becca had the five healthy children she always wanted. Find out Roger's fate in Kiko Takai and Eric Woodson's story **Years to Savor (Matchmaker in Time Book 4).**

As an indie author, I'm thrilled you decided to share your time with me, exploring the crazy worlds residing in my head and keeping me up at night. Your reviews are very important to me, so if you enjoyed this book, please consider leaving some stars for Jonathan and Becca's story, **Days to Hide (Matchmaker in Time Book 3).**

Don't forget Kiko's backstory, which is now highly recommended before reading book 4, in **Minutes to Live (Matchmaker in Time Book 0.5).**

If you found any typos or errors, I blame my cat. Rat her out at: support@stephanieflynn.com.

Thank you for your support!

Also By Stephanie Flynn

Find my catalog at StephanieFlynn.com

Immortal Protector series

0.5 Vampire's Distraction

1 Vampire's Deception

2 Vampire's Secret

3 Vampire's Promise

3.5 Elf Bound

4 Vampire's Demand

Immortal Protector Side Tales

Deer Holiday

Love Claws

Depths of the Heart

Matchmaker in Time series

0.5 Minutes to Live

1 Seconds to Act

2 Hours to Arrive

3 Days to Hide

4 Years to Savor

Pirates in Time series

1 Pirate's Prize

2 Pirate's Treasure

3 Pirate's Plunder

Time Travel Romance Shorts

Fateful Time

One Crazy Time

If you like your urban fantasy without the romance, too, check out Stephanie Flynn's other name, Marie Flynn!

About Stephanie Flynn

Stephanie Flynn writes action-packed paranormal romance filled with adventure, suspense, and danger. She lives in Michigan, USA, with her husband and kids, and she spends her writing time surrounded by a herd of normal cats who bat everything off her desk, including her coffee. Check out her website for more books: StephanieFlynn.com

www.ingramcontent.com/pod-product-compliance
Lightning Source LLC
Chambersburg PA
CBHW080851190726
48292CB00011B/2949